MIRAMAR
BAY

MIRAMAR BAY

DAVIS BUNN

KENSINGTON BOOKS
http://www.kensingtonbooks.com

KENSINGTON BOOKS are published by

Kensington Publishing Corp.
119 West 40th Street
New York, NY 10018

All Kensington titles, imprints, and distributed lines are available at special quantity discounts for bulk purchases for sales promotion, premiums, fund-raising, educational, or institutional use.

Special book excerpts or customized printings can also be created to fit specific needs. For details, write or phone the office of the Kensington Sales Manager: Attn. Sales Department. Kensington Publishing Corp, 119 West 40th Street, New York, NY 10018. Phone: 1-800-221-2647.

Kensington and the K logo Reg. U.S. Pat. & TM Off.

First Kensington Hardcover Edition: April 2017

ISBN-13: 978-1-4967-0830-4
ISBN-10: 1-4967-0830-X
First Kensington Trade Paperback Edition: September 2017

eISBN-13: 978-1-4967-0831-1
eISBN-10: 1-4967-0831-8
Kensington Electronic Edition: April 2017

10 9 8 7 6 5 4

Printed in the United States of America

This book is dedicated to

Chip MacGregor

For the friendship
The guidance
And the challenge

CHAPTER 1

Connor Larkin stood with the other passengers waiting to enter the Greyhound bus. The nighttime travelers were exactly as he remembered from his early journeys. They were silent and they were weary, and many of them treated the bus as their bed for the night. As Connor climbed on board, he knew he was doing the right thing. He intended to make a complete break. Nothing could be further from his current existence than this.

He took the first window seat where the one next to him was still empty. Connor was six-three and linebacker lean, and he didn't want to crowd somebody who was already settled in for the night run. Three minutes later, a woman who almost matched his size stopped and asked, "You mind?"

"Not a bit," he replied. She must have seen he meant it, for she offered up the best smile she could manage.

Night busses held to an established cadence. Soon as the doors sighed shut, the chatter faded. People settled in as best they could and went quiet. Those who didn't care to sleep talked in respectful murmurs. Even the fretting baby was soon silenced. The bus rumbled its way out of the downtown Los Angeles terminal, stopped twice for additional travelers, then joined the freeway and headed north.

There had once been a time when Connor had loved nothing more than a long bus ride. He had just turned sixteen and was trapped in an imploding family. Connor had not just been escaping. He was building his dreams. He was traveling toward a tomorrow all his very own. He had not thought of those trips in years.

The tires hummed and the night comforted. Connor reveled in being anonymous, at least for a few hours. He had no idea what he would find at the end of this journey. Nor, just then, did he much care. He stared at his reflection in the dark glass to his right, and decided that running away was the first thing that had felt good in far too long.

The woman leaned over and jammed Connor hard against the armrest. She knew what she'd done and grimaced an apology. Connor shrugged in reply. She set a tablet in her lap, plugged in earbuds, and said, "This is the only chance I get to watch my shows."

Connor watched her connect to the bus Wi-Fi and then dial into the number one LA entertainment cable show. That meant everything he was running from flashed up in brilliant color.

The program's anchor was a cable lollipop named Peyton Stein. LA was full of Peytons. Her program and *Hello* magazine had been granted exclusive coverage of Connor's main event, in return for the agency's publicist having the right to edit everything prior to release.

The image shifted from Peyton's report to a clip of Connor's most recent appearance in a US drama. He played the bad guy, as usual. The thirty-second spot showed him being caught by the hero, who launched into a furious assault that ended with Connor being thrown off a bridge. The camera followed his free fall into the torrent below, then cut back to Peyton's brilliant smile.

Connor should have been accustomed to seeing himself on-screen. His acting coach forced Connor to watch and learn and critique and grow. However, the required detachment was lost to him now.

The next clip came from earlier that same day. Connor watched as he and his fiancée emerged from the intimate engagement party attended by seven hundred of their closest friends. They had rehearsed this next act five times, until the lights and expressions and cadence were camera-perfect. Connor saw his eyes go round as two tuxedo-clad waiters pulled the quilted covering off his engagement present, then shout with delight as his fiancée offered him the gold-plated key to his very own Maserati Ghibli.

Then the woman on the bus noticed Connor watching and pulled the bud from one ear.

Connor's dread rose with the bile in his throat. He knew what was going to happen next, clear as if it was scripted in the slightly stale air. She would cry out his name. She would wake up the entire bus. Then his one chance of escape would be stripped away.

Instead, she turned in her seat, looked straight at him, and said, "You think this is for real?"

"Excuse me?"

"A guy this good-looking marries an heiress, she gives him a Ferrari, and they live happily ever after?"

"Maserati," Connor corrected.

"What?"

"The car. It's a Maserati."

She waved that aside. "Whoever heard of such a thing? I mean, that's not real life, is it? It has to be something they cooked up inside their executive suites. Like, hey, let's find this perfect guy and this superrich girl and we'll have this bash at the Hilton—"

"Beverly Hills Hotel."

"—And we'll invite all the beautiful people, then we'll put it on the TV. And next week we'll show the wedding."

"The wedding is in five days," Connor said.

"See, that's just it. I don't think there is going to be any wedding."

Connor was an actor. He was paid to pretend at emotions. So right now, he nodded slowly, like he was giving the woman's comments a lot of serious thought. He said, "You may be right about that."

"You like, I could turn on the sound and we could watch this together."

"Thanks," Connor said. "That's really kind, but I've seen it already."

Every time Connor glanced over, there he was on the woman's tablet. She kept scrolling back and forth between the various episodes, living the impossible dream. Closing his eyes no longer blocked out the memories. Peyton, the cable lollipop, had a breathless way of speaking as long as the camera was rolling. However, in the seven sessions they'd had together, she had not spoken once with Connor after the lights went off. Not even a hello. Her attitude had said it all. Connor was just another momentary episode, there to suck dry and discard. His fiancée was amazingly adept at handling the LA publicity machine. As a result, people like Peyton treated her as a keeper.

Then he corrected himself. His ex-fiancée.

They had not officially broken up yet. When Connor would fail to show for the rehearsal dinner in four days' time, he assumed the lady would bid him a tearful farewell. In front of the global press. No doubt it would be her finest hour.

Connor's stop was the juncture where the 101 joined with the Pacific Coast Highway. Steep hills cut jagged slices from the night sky. From here to the ocean was fourteen and a half miles of a single snaking road. Miramar, his destination, occupied a bowl where the cliffs eased back from the sea.

Between Miramar and where Connor stood were two valleys given over to vineyards and avocadoes and rich verdant farmland. He was standing in a parking lot shared by a 7-Eleven, a diner, and a Motel 6. Connor waved to the woman watching him from the window, and waited while the bus pulled away. Now that he had arrived, he had no idea what to do next.

His satchel felt like it weighed two hundred pounds. The night air seemed impossibly heavy. Connor had done nothing for five days except prepare for the next shoot with his beautiful bride-to-be. But he had also not slept. Exhaustion threatened to smother him. He was tempted to take a room for the night, but highway motel chains tended to want troublesome items like IDs. Plus Connor knew he ran the risk of getting stuck there. Just lay on the bed for days, trapped by the vise of so many wrong moves. Connor hefted his satchel and crossed the lot and entered the diner.

The little restaurant had a slow end-of-watch feel. Connor sat at the counter and ate a moderately good meat loaf. But the green beans had been cooked to limp submission and the potatoes were barely okay. Connor had worked in his family's restaurant until he was old enough to escape their constant bickering. He had learned early and well the artwork involved in making a fine meal. The food had been very good and the patrons had remained loyal, at least for a while. In the end, the screeches emerging every time the kitchen doors swung open had driven the patrons away. It felt comforting in a strange and disembodied way to mull over his past while eating. Normally, Connor kept such ruminations buried deep.

Connor was so engrossed in the lost years that he did not notice the cop until he heard someone ask, "You coming or going?"

The counter curved slightly, and the cop had taken a stool three away from Connor, granting him a position where he could study Connor's face. The police officer was ugly as a bull elephant, lumpish and big-boned, with features creased by childhood scars. Connor replied, "Coming, I hope."

The policeman lifted his coffee cup at the waitress' approach, nodded his thanks for the refill, and slurped noisily. All without taking his eyes off Connor. "You got friends around here?"

"Not yet."

He squinted, a sudden tightening of his features. Connor realized he had just seen the guy smile. "What brings you here?"

Such conversations had been a fairly constant part of his early years. A good-looking kid on the road, traveling by overnight bus, cops were always on the lookout for runaways. Connor had learned that honesty was the safest move. He said, "I came for a weekend on one of the ranches up in the hills. The place didn't suit me, so I spent all my free time in town. I didn't want to leave." Connor shrugged. "Now I'm back."

"Which ranch?"

"Hearst Highlands."

The cop whistled. "That place runs, what, a couple of thousand a night?"

"Something like that."

The cop took in Connor's faded T-shirt, worn jeans, woven rope belt, hiking boots. "You were working up there?"

Connor made do with a nod.

The cop picked up his bill, swung his stool around, and stood. "What say we settle up, I'll give you a lift into town."

CHAPTER 2

"Miramar was originally named Castaway Cove, but I guess you already knew that."

"I told you, I've been here just once," Connor replied. "For a weekend. That's it."

"See, the thing is, I'm pretty sure I know you."

The police car was old and smelled of industrial-strength disinfectant. It took dips in the road like a boat in heavy seas. Connor's head bumped against the wire-mesh barrier separating them from the rear seat. His left knee was jammed against the computer station. A shotgun and bully stick were slotted into position between him and the cop. The radio hissed words Connor could not understand.

The policeman went on, "You get in trouble while you were here for that weekend?"

"No, Officer."

"Chief," the big man corrected. "Name's Porter Wright."

Connor did not speak.

"I'm good with faces. I need to be in this job." He stopped at a traffic light and glanced over. His lumpish features were hard as stone. "It'll come to me."

Wright turned off the town's main avenue onto a narrow side street, drove two blocks, then entered a restricted parking area surrounded by hurricane fencing. He pulled into the first slot by the entrance to a nondescript single-story building of painted cinder blocks. He cut the motor, tapped the wheel with his trigger finger, and said, "Guy in my line of work learns to trust his instincts. Mine are telling me I know you. Which usually means I've either locked you up or run across an alert with your photograph. So you can tell me who you are, or we can head on back out to where I picked you up. And I'll let you go, but only if you promise never to show your face—"

"My name is Connor Larkin."

The sheriff twisted his bulk around so as to face Connor. "I know that name. . . ."

"I'm an actor."

Chief Wright grunted. "Sure, now I know. You're the bad guy."

That was good for a chuckle. A lot of people were soon going to be thinking just that.

The cop continued speaking. "This past week, it seems like every time I go home, my wife and daughter are watching some show about your wedding thing."

Connor nodded. "'Wedding thing' pretty much sums it up."

"Is it true what they say, you've died on-screen almost a hundred times?"

"Ninety-seven and counting."

The silence was punctuated by the radio's soft drone. Finally Wright asked, "What on earth are you doing here, son?"

Connor suspected the policeman was very adept at extracting confessions. The soft-spoken question punched him in the heart. He said the only thing that came to mind. "I was hoping maybe I could find a little of what I've lost."

* * *

Porter phoned a guesthouse two blocks farther into town, woke up the proprietor, and said he had a fellow wanting to hang his hat for a few days. The chief hesitated at something the other person said, his gaze tight on Connor. "Hang on a second there." He covered the phone. "You got one of them fake IDs?"

"No."

"If you use your real name, somebody is bound to blow your cover."

Connor's weary brain ran through the myriad names his more recent roles had saddled him with—all of whom, of course, had kicked the bucket. Not a promising start to his visit.

Porter said, "How about we keep things simple. Connor Smith sound okay?"

Connor found the act of being renamed by a cop somehow comforting. "Works for me."

Porter finished the call, then walked him down silent streets. "The owner of a local guesthouse is an old friend. Back in the fifties, the place was used by abalone fishermen operating the big trawlers. I confirmed you've misplaced your ID and will be paying cash."

"Thank you. A lot."

The key was waiting for Connor in the front mailbox. The current owner had torn out walls and turned fourteen cramped motel rooms into seven bright and spacious studio apartments. Connor tried to put some heartfelt thanks into his farewell, but the chief just smiled and said, "Do one thing for me."

"Sure."

"When this all comes out, and you know it's bound to, stop by and let me introduce you to my wife and daughter. You'll make their day."

Connor said he would, then carried the cop's gently stated warning into the shower. He washed off the journey and fell into bed. The sea breeze filtered in through his open window. Everything should have been perfect, but Chief Wright's final words resonated through the dark room. His secret was bound to come out. Connor resigned himself to another night of tossing and turning and a few frantic dreams.

The next thing he knew, it was two o'clock in the afternoon. Connor was well accustomed to sleeping whenever the hours were available. For everyone but stars, acting meant fourteen hour days or longer. Most actors didn't object because they had so much downtime between shoots. Every good gig was followed by weeks of auditions, meetings, story conferences, classes, and more auditions. But for the past three and a half years, Connor had been working pretty much nonstop. And then came, as the cop put it, the wedding thing.

The studio apartment had a well-appointed kitchenette, with a basket that contained filters and two packets of ground coffee. Connor was too much of a stickler about what he ate and drank to use either sweetener or powdered milk, but many location shoots offered their lesser actors nothing else, so he had grown accustomed to taking his coffee black. He dressed and extracted the wad of cash from his valise. He had stopped by two ATM machines and withdrawn the maximum before running. He entered the motel's office, paid for a week's stay, then asked the manager where he could find an all-day breakfast.

The diner was right where the manager said, on the corner of a street that meandered down the gentle slope and ended at the beachfront. Up here, a dozen or so blocks off the water, the town had an air of genteel seediness. The shops were done up nicely, but without the chichi atmosphere of wealthier towns around LA and San Francisco. Many of the structures dated back to the time when Miramar was home to the world's largest abalone fleet. Few buildings sported more than three stories, and most had a slightly faded, sea-worn air. Connor feasted on a three-egg omelet with spinach and avocado, hash browns, and fresh biscuits with honey. Then he sat in the booth, pretended to study the street beyond his window, and wondered how on earth he was going to fill his days.

He had never been good at doing nothing. Sitting around and studying his navel was definitely out. Connor had worked his entire life. At twelve, he had started as weekend kitchen help in his parents' restaurant. He had loved the work as much as he had hated his parents' constant bickering. Connor had done well enough in his classes to stay under the family radar, and spent every free moment striving to follow his own dream.

It was the dream that had brought him to LA. The dream he had managed to destroy.

That was enough to draw him from the booth. Connor had always been most comfortable when moving at full speed. Pushing ahead meant less time to look back. Looking back only brought regret. Connor paid his bill and left the diner and headed down toward the sea.

There was a great deal to like about Miramar, starting with its location. California's central coast was a rare haven, isolated by distance and winding hilly roads from the frenetic tension that dominated the urban centers. Miramar was almost exactly midway between LA and San Francisco. Both cities had seaside resorts that were closer and filled with people who valued all the things that Connor was fleeing. The result for Miramar was a seaside sanctuary whose residents were quietly satisfied to leave well enough alone.

Connor walked and breathed the salt-laced air. Gulls mewed overhead, and somewhere in the distance a buoy's bell clanged as it rocked with the waves. He was glad to find the place was as nice as he remembered. His unsettled restlessness pressed him on, down the slope, toward the sea.

CHAPTER 3

It took the worst day of her recent life for Sylvie Cassick to realize just how many friends she had.

She stood in the restaurant's kitchen, watching as her assistant chef gutted the day's fish. Porter Wright, Miramar's police chief, stood beside her. On the counter's other side was a narcotics detective from the county sheriff's department. One by one the fish were slit open, carefully inspected, then returned to the cooler.

Did people ever actually have an easy life? Was it like the magazines for some people, where they could design their goals and then watch everything slide into perfect order? Sylvie often wondered about this. She thought it might be nice at some point to meet someone like that. Then again, perhaps she might grab a kitchen cleaver and give in to a case of lethal envy.

There was no room for such thoughts, but here she was anyway, crowded into the corner of her own kitchen. As she watched the detective inspect each fish in turn, she wished she could have everything go her way, just this once.

The restaurant kitchen had once been a second dining room, and the three cooks had worked in a lean-to, where the alley now ran. The former owners had built a state-of-the-art facility, one of the few things they had done right in Sylvie's opinion. The very same owners had turned the upstairs into an illegal casino. Between hands of Texas hold 'em, they had also sealed any number of drug deals. Sylvie had known all this for years, but the detective repeated the stories as he worked. The detective's tone suggested he thought Sylvie should be down in Lompoc, doing five to ten with the former owners.

A steel counter ran the length of the kitchen, dividing the cooking area from the smaller space used by the waiters. Front and center on the shiny steel workstation was the reason behind this morning's ruckus. The eleven bags of white powder glistened in the bright overhead lights, mocking Sylvie's attempts to hold herself together.

People often said she was remarkably calm, the sort of woman who could weather any storm with a smile. Sylvie had heard the words since her teenage years, when she had been hired at age sixteen to serve as the hostess in a fine restaurant. The manager had even thought enough of her appeal to help her obtain a fake ID. These same people also liked to say that despite her magnetic beauty, Sylvie Cassick, at age thirty, possessed an ancient's eyes. Sylvie was amazed at some of the secrets people divulged to her. Making the rounds of her restaurant often drew forth some hair-raising sagas. Recently she asked a couple she had never met before why they felt they could trust her with their darkest secrets. The pair replied that something about Sylvie left them certain she had heard far worse.

Every time Sylvie looked at the eleven kilos of cocaine, she wanted to shriek, pull her hair out by the roots, and prove every single one of those people wrong.

The detective's name was Walker, and they had disliked each

other on sight. Walker stood on the counter's opposite side and watched as Bruno, her assistant chef, gutted the last three fish. "Who was it that found the drugs?"

"Asked and answered," Porter Wright replied. Miramar's chief of police was ugly in every way, except the one that counted most. His face was scarred by acne or bad diet or too many hard days. His eyes were piggish and his voice was gravelly. But for some reason, Porter Wright had appointed himself Sylvie's guardian. As a result, Sylvie considered Porter one of the finest men on earth. Porter said, "The fellow gutting the fish found the dope. The restaurant's proprietor made the call."

"Why don't you take a hike, Chief. Let me speak with the lady here without you getting in the way."

"Happy to." Clearly, Porter did not think any more of the detective than Sylvie. "Soon as she either asks me to leave, or she lawyers up."

Walker was compact and tight and viewed everything with a suspicious squint. "You seem very intent on helping her hide something."

Porter shifted his bulk. "You don't want to take me on, son. Not in my town. You really don't."

Sylvie knew Porter had been a cop in San Diego. He had pulled the plug after twenty years, moved north, and taken over a department that some had called lazy and others downright crooked. A bust of this size required Porter to call in the specialists at county level. Porter had sounded like he was apologizing when he told her. Now Sylvie understood why.

Walker demanded, "Who brought you the fish?"

"Now you're getting somewhere." Porter straightened. "Why don't you and I head on down to the suppliers, and let Ms. Cassick get ready to open up."

Walker looked like he wanted to argue, but pulled a card from his pocket and set it on the counter next to the fish. "If you happen to think of anything more—"

"I'll call the chief," Sylvie replied. "Just like today."

Walker cut a dark look at Bruno, and said, "I'll be in touch."

"Long as you contact me first, you're welcome in Miramar anytime." Porter remained where he was as the detective left by the back door. "I heard about that fellow."

"He scares me."

"If Walker comes sniffing around you or any of your staff, you call me before you even tell that guy hello." Porter lifted his gaze. "Bruno, you hear what I'm saying?"

"I ain't saying another word to that guy."

"You'll have to go in and make a statement. Just make sure you don't do it alone. Now tell me about your buddy."

Bruno was from an old-time central coast family, small-boned and narrow featured. For generations, his family had run a boat hunting the abalone; but when that industry faded, Bruno's parents had migrated north to Santa Cruz in search of work. He had gotten involved with drugs as a teen, did a stint in juvie, got out, went back to the dark side, and wound up in Lompoc doing three to five. He had been out and clean for six years. "Carlos and I were best friends as kids. I can't believe he'd do that to me."

Porter asked, "He still ganged up?"

"He swore he was done with all that. But I hadn't seen him in, like, forever."

"His family still live over on Randolf?"

"That's what he said, but who knows if it's true?" Bruno looked like he was about ready to cry. "I'm so sorry, Ms. Sylvie."

Porter answered for her. "You did right, start to finish. Sylvie, walk me out."

She followed Porter through the restaurant and out to where his car was parked. From the neighboring slot, the detective impatiently beeped his horn. Porter turned his back to the man. "Santino supplies your fish, right?"

"Ever since I first opened."

"My guess is, they got a boat that slipped out of port about the same time your Bruno slit open that fish. Anything else you can tell me about Carlos?"

She had been through it all before, but talking helped. "He had an attitude. And the tats. But he worked hard."

"Always first to show up," Porter said. "Helped unload the produce, clean the fish, all that."

Sylvie put her hands to her face. She could feel a headache coming on, the sort of migraine attack that painted her entire world a grim, thunderous gray. "I've been such a total idiot."

"No, you haven't. Straighten up now, folks are watching."

"What am I going to do?"

"Same as always. Open on time. Be the gracious hostess. Make sure your guests have a good meal and take home some happy memories."

"You know people are going to hear about this. What do I tell them?"

"That you're trusting me to handle it."

"I am, you know."

"See?" He gestured her back inside. "Now go talk to your staff. Tell them I said everything's good."

"You don't want to do that yourself?"

"They need to hear it from you."

Sylvie stood there on the sidewalk, watching the man amble over and settle behind the wheel. She waved him off, just another grateful citizen showing respect to the local force. It all could have been so much worse. If Porter was not chief, if he'd had the day off, if a thousand things. Sylvie tried to remind herself of that as she passed back through her dining room and kitchen, and let herself out the rear door. The day could easily have been a total disaster.

The alley had once been a wretched place, especially on a hot afternoon like this one, when the six wheelie-bins were never really cleaned and the tight little lane stank with the residue of a thousand fish dinners. Then Rick, her senior waiter, had come up with the idea of turning a patch of crumbling concrete into an off-duty alcove. The boys had equipped it with cast-off garden furniture, a canvas overhang, and an old wagon-wheel table. They drilled holes in paint buckets and planted a variety of flowers. Now the bins were pressure-washed three times a week, and the alley remained spotless.

Rick was there now, along with Marcela and Bruno and Sandy and Carl, her chef. Sandy, her pastry cook, saw himself as the spokesman whenever the group needed to have a word. Like a lot of locals, Sandy had been born elsewhere, but was now determined to claim Miramar as his own. In Sandy's case, the elsewhere happened to be Swindon, which he assured Sylvie was a British city so ugly it won prizes on four continents. Sandy gestured to where Bruno sat, staring at the concrete by his feet, and said, "Tell the lad he did good."

"Sandy's right," Sylvie said. "I'm proud of you. And grateful."

"See there, lad? There's no way you could have known your mate was bent."

"We all make mistakes," Sylvie went on. "We've all trusted the wrong man at some point."

Sylvie stayed out there long enough for them to know the assurance was genuine. She deeply cared for them, her pack of misfits. Two had done time at Lompoc. Sandy had some past he never talked about. Marcela, the number two waiter, carried her own measure of bad memories. The five bore stains of a very hard road. But they were clean, they were good at their jobs, and they were *her* misfits.

Rick, Bruno, Marcela, Sandy, and Carl: Five lives brought together by careless fate. Now their afternoon delight was this tight corner of broken concrete and cast-off furniture. Sylvie wanted to tell them what it meant to be trusted with their last fragile threads of hope. But they were not the type of people who put a great deal of store in such words. Sandy would make a joke, Carl would shrug it off. The emotions would be lost. So she remained silent. When Sylvie thought it was okay, she returned inside to face the challenge of pretending this was just a normal day.

CHAPTER 4

Estelle watched Connor Larkin cross the forecourt and enter the office. She had recognized him instantly, and wondered what he was doing here. There had been too many lonely nights where the mindless infotainment shows had brought her both comfort and escape. She followed him into the lobby and stood back, pretending to read a magazine. Under other circumstances, she might have spoken to him. Just then, however, Estelle was too frightened by what she intended to do next. She heard him confirm that his name was Connor Smith and watched him pay cash for a week's stay. All this was curious indeed, since she knew for a fact that his wedding was in four days.

When he had received directions to a local diner, Estelle approached the manager and said, "I'd like to extend my stay, please."

"Let me check." The owner was Mrs. Ware, who possessed an innkeeper's firm no-nonsense attitude. "Yes, we can certainly make that happen. And I'll offer you the long-stay discount."

"Thank you."

"How much longer will you be with us?"

"Two more days, I think. I'm not sure."

"Well, let me know as soon as you can. We can get very full over the weekends." She accepted the credit card, ran it through the machine, and smiled at the otherwise-empty lobby. "That was quite the handsome young man who just left. Wonder whose heart he's going to break next."

Estelle knew the owner was only making polite conversation. At another time, she might have been tempted to reveal what she knew about the man who just paid cash for a week. However, her nerves formed a great lump in her gut, making the simple act of drawing breath an effort. She accepted her card and headed for the exit.

She stepped into the afternoon sunlight, slipped on her sunglasses, and forced herself to cross the lot and head down the sidewalk, just like a normal person out for a normal walk. She had left the room determined that today would be the day. Three times she had started out. This was the farthest she had made it. She had faced many hard events in her life. None of them seemed quite so difficult as this.

Estelle knew where she was going, since the private detective had included photographs with his report. She had gone online and mapped out her directions. She had selected that particular motel because it was within walking distance of her destination. She had everything planned, right down to the moment when she arrived. At that point, her mind simply froze. She had no idea what to say, how to act, whether she should start with an apology—nothing.

She continued slowly down the broad avenue toward the sea. Her legs felt like water. She realized she was not going to make it, so she stepped into a coffeehouse and ordered a latte. She sat in the sun, pretending to watch the street and the pedestrians. Her mind was a complete jumble, but the coffee did its work. Eventually she felt able to rise and continue on.

Estelle spotted the young actor again, seated in a diner across the street. She saw him rise to his feet and leave the restaurant and start down the other sidewalk. She found it remarkable how no one else seemed to recognize him. Maybe people here ignored the latest Hollywood gossip. Or perhaps Miramar was the sort of place where people had the decency to let even actors go about their business in peace.

The man who called himself Connor Smith meandered down the gentle slope, almost directly across the street from Estelle. He showed none of the delight or excitement she had seen recently on the cable show covering his wedding. Connor moved with the slow cadence of having nowhere to go. If he noticed the older woman watching him from the other sidewalk, he gave no sign.

Estelle thought Connor Larkin was right to run away, if that was actually what he was doing. She had seen him on any number of shows and had been drawn to Connor Larkin's characters because she was convinced he was different. He was a man who cared. He was, at heart, a good man. Estelle was certain Connor's fiancée was anything but those things. Kali Lyndon was a vapid woman, a celebrity queen who financed her passion for the spotlight with an inherited fortune. She had never done anything productive in her entire life, as far as Estelle knew. Kali was beautiful in a Photoshopped sort of way, and no doubt she would do wonders for Connor's career. Kali Lyndon, however, was wrong for him.

Estelle halted the mental prattle because she had arrived. She had been so involved in her internal dialogue she had not even noticed where she was. All the fears rushed back in a tsunami that locked her up tight. She could not breathe, much less force herself to cross the street. She steadied herself with one hand on the nearest parking meter and tried to tell herself that this was why she had come. This was why she had hired the detective and gone through nights of soul-searching and flown across the country and . . .

Then she saw Connor Larkin step through the entrance.

From across the street, Estelle heard strands of music from her past. Frank Sinatra sang "Fly Me to the Moon," a melody that pierced her as sharply as a blade through her heart.

Estelle had no choice but to admit defeat and turn away.

She was wrong to have come. She should have left the past buried and at least half-forgotten.

CHAPTER 5

Connor drifted down the sidewalk, still locked in memories about his early days. His mother had returned to her place by the cash register while Connor was in his bassinet. The restaurant's staff had all known Connor's real age when he started working alongside his father in the kitchen. Connor had learned early and well the lessons of haute cuisine. But beneath the restaurant's polish and the money, the family business had radiated a bitter unhappiness. Finally the year he had turned nineteen, it all fell apart. By then, Connor was already traveling the roads, chasing his own dreams.

Then an all-too familiar melody drifted through an open doorway, halting Connor in his tracks.

The restaurant he faced was called Castaways. The building itself appeared to be the oldest structure on the block, a two-story affair with the tall false front of bygone eras. Cast-iron tables and chairs flanked its broad front entrance. The long windows were embellished with flower boxes. The wood was varnished; the glass was polished; the brass handles to the open

French doors gleamed. Connor thought the understated elegance suggested a woman's hand at the tiller.

Connor stepped through the open doorway, and fell in love.

Sylvie walked to the bar and opened the cabinet that held the restaurant's sound system. She put one of her father's favorite albums on the turntable, and stood there listening with her eyes shut. She had often done this in the restaurant's early days, when it was all too much and she thought she would never learn everything required to keep the place up and running.

Her father had been a gentle dreamer. The fact that so few of his dreams ever came true had only deepened his joy when one was realized. He had always called Sylvie the marvel that made every day complete. Even when she was bad, Gareth Cassick insisted that he was blind to all but the delight his daughter brought him. There had been some hard years for them both, for Sylvie was her mother's child as well. That woman had left them when Sylvie was twelve. Sylvie's clearest memories of her mother were mostly strident demands for her father to grow up, support the family, make something of himself, and do a job that mattered. Then her mother was gone, and for a time, everything was good. If not good, at least life had been a great deal quieter. Sylvie's teenage years had brought out a bitter edge to Sylvie's character. She had never been a screamer. Her early years had seen too much of that. Instead, she had developed an acrid sharpness. She could wound with a single word. Her father had simply accepted her tart rage as his due, and loved her through those years.

Gareth would have adored this place, she knew. The light fell through the west-facing windows, painting the old wood with a honeyed gleam. The sea peeked between the roofs like a scattering of blue gemstones. Sandy was in back, doing his magic with pastry and spices. The air carried the gentle incense of promise and good times for all.

Her father had loved the crooners of the fifties and sixties.

When she pounded the walls of their home with arena rock, he listened politely. When she condemned his own music, he simply said it was an acquired taste. And acquire it she had, especially on days like this, when she would have given anything to hear his gentle optimism, and have him assure Sylvie that better times were just around the bend. Not yet within sight, but coming to them both . . . and very soon indeed.

She whispered to the empty room, "Pop, I could sure use one of your hugs just now."

The man who entered her restaurant was too handsome for his own good. Sylvie started to say they weren't open yet and could he return in a couple of hours. Something held her back, though. He fumbled the sunglasses from his face, like his fingers weren't working well. He stood just inside the entrance, where the sun struck him fully, and gave her place a very slow sweep. The light played through his shoulder-length hair, not blond and not brown, but a mixture of both. His face was lean and strong without being cavernous. His hands were what her father would have called cowhand big; they fit well to strong arms and broad shoulders, atop a waist that was almost too narrow. He wore a simple T-shirt and stonewashed jeans and canvas boots. He was, in a word, gorgeous.

Then she saw the tears. His gaze was so clouded she wasn't even certain he could see her approach. Sylvie saw no need to ask if he was all right. Clearly, he was far from okay. In fact, what she actually thought was, this guy's day might have been as bad as her own.

Sylvie asked, "What is it?"

Of all the ways he might have replied, all the words to emerge from that stylish two-day growth, Sylvie would have never expected to hear what he said. Not in a hundred billion years.

The guy's voice was deep and resonant and downright beautiful. He said, "Bart Howard wrote that song in 1954. He was interviewed after it hit number one for six different artists. He said he had trained for twenty years so he could write it in twenty minutes."

Sylvie said weakly, "Excuse me?"

"Originally Howard titled it, 'In Other Words,' " the guy said. "The singer who had been buying Howard's work considered it too cabaret in style and refused to use it. Then Kaye Ballard recorded it."

"On Decca," Sylvie said. "As the flipside to 'Lazy Afternoon.' "

"Right. Decca wanted Howard to change the lyrics. He fought them, Kaye backed him up, and the song went out like he wanted."

Sylvie said, "Then Peggy Lee recorded it. Nat King Cole. Sarah Vaughan. Brenda Lee. Connie Francis."

The guy said, "Then came 1964 and the Apollo moon program, and Frank Sinatra put it on the album . . ."

"*It Might as Well Be Swing,*" Sylvie said. "What we're hearing."

"Quincy Jones did the arrangement," the guy said. "Count Basie's orchestra backed him."

Sylvie asked, "Why does that make you sad?"

He almost managed a smile. "All that stuff, it used to be really important."

"It still is," Sylvie said.

He looked at her. Really looked. "Can I please have a job?"

CHAPTER 6

When Connor left the restaurant, he headed downhill. He felt impacted at gut level by the woman he had just left. Her image was so clear, she might as well have walked alongside him. Sylvie Cassick held herself with the grace of a former ballerina, slender and balanced and impossibly erect. Her hair was a honey-eyed trace off pure black, like smoke blowing through a night-clad sky. Her eyes were the gray of morning mist, light and soft and brilliant. Connor put her age at somewhere around thirty, the same as himself or perhaps a year or so younger. Still, there was a timeless quality to the woman, as though she had managed to compress centuries of life into months. She held none of the electric beauty that defined the current Hollywood fashion. Her cheekbones were too pronounced, her gaze too direct, her lips too full. Connor thought she was the loveliest woman he had ever seen.

Not that it should have mattered. At least, not to him.

Miramar's finest shops were clustered along an avenue two blocks off the seafront. The pedestrian area had tiled avenues with elevated concrete basins holding flowers and blooming trees. There were benches for the elderly and a woman in a tuxedo making balloon animals for the children. There was a cupcake factory and an upscale café and shops touting local vineyards. The streetlights were modeled after Parisian gaslights. The entire area covered three blocks, and then Connor was back into the world of well-tended houses on small lots. The sea's presence was strong here, a brisk mingling of salt and seaweed and biting wind. Connor stopped by a tree-lined park and watched the children play. He was falling for the idea that a place like Miramar might truly exist. And even if it didn't, even if his first impressions were nothing more than whispers of dreams long buried, Connor could think of nothing he would like more than to spend his life living the myth.

He had a purpose now, and he was on the clock. He would enter into this new role by using the talents he had developed in Los Angeles. There was no alternative, not if he wanted to blend in and remain unidentified. Which he did. Desperately.

Connor's first big break had come on *CSI*. They had liked his work so much the producers had offered him roles in the two spin-offs—but only if he could change his appearance so that viewers who had seen him get shot on the first show wouldn't realize he was back from the dead. Connor had worked with a professional stylist who had been in film and television for years. She had taught him a lesson that defined the very best character actors, the people who shifted not just roles, but personalities. She had shown him how no amount of face paint or costumes or cosmetic alterations would help most actors because they were too rigidly defined within themselves. If a performer could learn flexibility at the deepest level of his personality, then the exterior changes merely amplified this shift.

By the time Connor found the shop he was looking for, he had defined his new role.

He wanted a new beginning. What was more, he wanted to *deserve* it.

* * *

Connor entered the men's store and bought two pairs of black gabardine slacks, a white knit shirt, two long-sleeve white-on-white dress shirts, a mock alligator belt, and black loafers. He paid central coast prices, not Beverly Hills, but the purchases still put a sizeable dent in his cash.

He asked the saleslady for the best hairstylist in Miramar, and she directed him to the corner where the shopping lane met the main road. He entered and asked for whichever stylist could cut him without delay. A young woman with flashing dark eyes and an overtight skirt introduced herself as Lucia and led him back. "What are we after today?"

Connor held his thumb and forefinger about an inch apart. "Trim it down to this length, and part on the left side."

"All this lovely hair." She took a fistful and lifted it away from his neck. "You sure you want me to cut if all off?"

"I have to look respectable," he explained.

"Good luck with that." Lucia smirked at his reflection. "You got 'bad boy' written all over you."

"I'm starting a new job." He checked his watch. "In less than two hours."

"Guess we better get started, then." Lucia led him to the basin. As she shampooed his hair, she said, "Bet it was a woman, she hired you."

Connor smiled. "Guilty."

"You see? That lady, she's not out to *respect* you. She wants you to walk in, raise the temperature in her office."

"Restaurant," Connor corrected.

"Yeah? Which one?"

"Castaways."

"Oh, that's good. Sylvie is one smart lady."

"You know her?"

"Everybody knows Sylvie. She took a bad place and turned it right around." Lucia toweled him off and led him back to the chair. "Last chance."

"Do it." His hair was darker when wet, the color of sour-wood honey in sunlight. He watched her snip away, and hoped it would prove this easy to make the internal shift. "What can you tell me about my new boss?"

"She's got a past. I'm not saying I know what it is—and even if I did, I probably wouldn't tell. But the lady, she's what, thirty? Thirty-one?"

"Something like that, I guess."

"She's old for her age. My grandmother would say her soul's been around for a long time."

Connor thought back to the conversation about music, and the way she had watched him struggle for control. "Have you ever eaten there?"

"Oh, sure. Last time, let's see, it was for my birthday, not the last one, the one before. The food's really good. Like, French."

As Connor watched his new persona take shape in the mirror, his mind returned to that first moment in the restaurant. He shivered.

Lucia noticed and said, "I know, they keep it like an icebox in here. You want, I could ask them to turn the temperature up a notch."

"Thanks, I'm good." He had left LA driven by restless long-ings for some small fragment of his old passions. That first mo-ment in Castaways had crystalized everything. It was far more than a wonderful conversation with a lovely woman. It opened a door he had thought locked and barred forever.

Connor Larkin had been born to sing, or so he had thought growing up. But obviously he had been mistaken. Nowadays a growing tsunami of fans insisted his real purpose in life was to die.

During his teens, Connor had learned to play piano because he couldn't find anyone to accompany him. All his friends had thought the crooners of the fifties and sixties should be left in the grave. Connor, however, loved the soft melodies and the big bands and the polished sound. Dean Martin was his favorite, but he had learned to sing them all. Frank, Sammy, Tony, the Elvis ballads—an entire lost generation of silky-smooth voices. By age sixteen, Connor had felt destined to join their ranks. Two months before his twentieth birthday, his ambitions took him to LA.

Connor soon had all the gigs he could handle, so long as he played to rooms of drunks and clinking glasses and brassy laughter and fat guys shouting at waiters. Connor had wanted more, though. He wanted the lights. He wanted . . .

Connor had been singing at the silver wedding anniversary of a Hollywood producer, when an agent approached and introduced herself as Ami Chen. She was with CPP, one of the three agencies that had a dead-solid lock on the Hollywood A-list. Only Ami Chen did not work with singers. She handled stars.

Ami liked his voice, but she loved his looks. Connor was rugged and handsome and rakish. According to Ami, the cameras would eat him alive.

Ami arranged for him to take acting lessons between his singing gigs. When she deemed him ready, Ami sent him out to casting calls. By this point, the acting was far more than some sideline activity. Connor had already endured four and a half bruising years making the rounds of music producers and getting squeezed from all sides. LA was filled with wannabees who shone in momentary spotlights, but dwelled in the city's bitter shadows. His gigs paid the rent and bought him a secondhand car, but he basically lived hand to mouth. His four flatmates were all one bad week away from the bus ride back to Iowa or Nebraska or wherever they shipped their broken dreams. The back roads of Hollywood were packed with brittle laughter and tense desperation. Connor was far from the only handsome young face who forgot why he had made the trip west.

Then to his astonishment, Connor was offered an acting gig.

At first, Connor played the guy in the soaps who got it in episode three, after trying to take off with the money and the hero's sweetheart. Even such a small advancement drew bitter envy from his flatmates. Connor had leapt from nowhere straight into speaking roles. When he was hired for a third gig, Connor had no choice but to move out.

Then the medical shows started offering him regular work. As the casting directors put it, Connor made croaking look good.

Then he did a Syfy drama playing a thief of technical secrets who deserved to get it in the end, and did. These were followed by the three *CSI* shows. That was when the online cult thing started.

When his agent first got wind of his following, neither of them believed it was real. Then Ami started fielding calls from abroad.

Connor did his death-throes in six Mexican telenovelas. He became the most popular American bad guy on Japanese television. He was devoured by wild beasts in India. Twice. He was attacked by a killer scorpion in Australia. He got bitten by a viper in Brazil. When he came back to the States, it was to play the evil genius in that year's e-game smash hit. By that point, Connor Larkin was dying as often as once a week.

Connor was still growing accustomed to the idea that people actually *liked* watching him get eaten by fickle fate, when he was invited to appear at the Las Vegas Comic Con. The convention organizers informed Ami that Connor's online following fit their demographics. They flew him out first class. He was met at the airport by a limo, given the penthouse suite at Caesars, and paid ten thousand dollars for a two-day gig.

When Connor showed up, he was *mobbed.*

Three days after he returned to LA, Connor bought a home in the Beverly Flats. He finally accepted what his agent had been saying for almost a year. This was no longer a string of gigs. Connor Larkin had a new career.

*   *   *

Lucia worked swiftly. She finished by trimming his neck; then she blew his hair dry. Her inspection grew increasingly serious as she gave his length a final check. "You want something in there?"

"Wax, please."

She opened the vial, rubbed it over both palms, her black eyes flashing a warning now. She worked it into his hair, then combed it into place. "I guess you clean up pretty good."

"You're an artist."

Lucia trimmed a final wayward strand; then she waved the scissors in his face. "Don't you go breaking Sylvie's heart, you hear what I'm saying? Else there's gonna be a lot of folks around here, looking to trim more than your hair."

Connor did not say what he thought, which was that the last thing he wanted from this time and place was a woman. Not a casual fling, which was clearly what they were all concerned about, and especially not a serious romance. The very idea filled him with grim humor. Connor thought of all the reasons he had to remain single as he climbed the road back to his little apartment. All the tales he could tell Lucia of other flashing dark eyes.

The problem with bad romance was that Connor's story had not started with Kali Lyndon. She was merely the outcome. Connor had become very adept at clamping down on the hollow ache that such thoughts brought forth. However, no matter how fast he walked the broad avenue, he could not escape the sense of being convicted. Lucia's warning had hit home as fast as a punch on an open wound.

When he passed through the parking area adjoining the studio apartments, Connor spotted the woman he had seen earlier in the office. She was seated in a little fenced area he had not noticed until then, a miniature garden with a couple of shade trees and a Jacuzzi and a small kiddie pool. Connor thought the woman held herself oddly, as though some severe pain kept her slightly hunched to her left.

He started to let himself into his room, but instead he un-locked the door and set down his shopping bags and turned back. The LA habits were part of what had to go. They didn't fit this new role. Connor walked back over and asked, "Excuse me, ma'am. Is everything okay?"

Large sunglasses covered a considerable portion of her face, but Connor had the impression that she came slowly back to reality. She said weakly, "I saw you."

"Excuse me?"

"On the street. You walked into that restaurant."

"Castaways. Right." He pointed back to his open door. "I'm due to start work there in about twenty minutes."

The news twisted up her face momentarily. All she said, though, was "That's nice."

"Ma'am, can I get you anything?"

"I'm . . ." She flicked the fingers of one hand, shooing him away. "I'm right where I deserve to be."

Connor had the distinct impression she had dismissed him. "Well, I'm over there if you need anything."

He crossed the lot, picked up his bags, and entered his room. He showered and shaved, then dressed carefully and returned to the bathroom's full-length mirror. He held himself there, practicing the same technique that had taken him through so many other roles. Clamping down on all the regrets and all thoughts of who he was and who he was not. There was no to-morrow, not for Connor Larkin. Right now there was only this new role. It grew from the tight clump of pain and tension and everything else he would not let himself feel, because just then it belonged to another person. He grew the role from within, by reshaping these emotions and the life energy they repre-sented.

When he was ready, Connor said to his reflection, "This is important. Make it count."

Then he turned to the door, like he had a thousand times before. On set after set, an usher hovered just outside his dressing room door, the director waited with the final words of guidance, then he stepped to where the lights gleamed and the cameras aimed and the people watched.

The big difference this time was that Connor only had one take to get it right.

CHAPTER 7

Sylvie continued with her preparations for what needed to appear as just another ordinary day. Being here in her restaurant, among the people she cared for most in the world, certainly helped. She patrolled all twenty-three tables, adjusting a fork here and a goblet there. She spoke with Gustavo, the new busboy. She phoned Porter Wright, whom Connor had said might be willing to vouch for him. She entered the kitchen and checked the vegetables. She even managed a joke over how the fish did not need any further scrutiny. She discussed the night's specials with Carl, her chef.

The kitchen staff loved these moments, for Carl was the most taciturn man she had ever met. He could go through the most frantic nights, when everyone else was shouting and rushing about, and not speak anything other than "pickup." Plus he would only say that if the ringing of his bell did not bring the waiter running. The kitchen crew loved speaking for Carl, making suggestions about possible concoctions, trying to come up with something outrageous enough to make him object. Her worries diminished in volume. Sylvie was ready to do what she was best at: giving her friends and patrons a memorable evening out.

When she returned to the dining room, Rick was stationed behind the bar, serving their first three customers. Sylvie waited down by the waiters' station. When he joined her, she asked, "Where's Aubrey?"

"On her way. Her mother's had a bad day."

Aubrey was the best bartender Sylvie had ever employed. Her mother, however, was quietly slipping into a fog denser than anything that had come rolling off the Pacific. Aubrey refused to even discuss putting her mother into a home. She had arranged for neighbors to serve as caregivers. Aubrey's system worked fairly well, unless there was a bad day. Such bad days happened with increasing frequency. Sylvie said, "Join us in the kitchen for a second."

When they were all together, she announced a new waiter was starting that night. His name was Connor Smith, and he had come recommended by Porter Wright.

Rick was the one to ask the inevitable. "Is he a con?"

"Porter did not think so."

"He doesn't *think*?"

"That's what he said." Sylvie pointed to where Carl was filling bowls with his all-day stew. "Go have your dinners. I'll handle the bar. When you're done, somebody bring me a sandwich."

The bar was one of the aspects she most loved about her place. Castaways had originally been built as a saloon and rooming house. The owner had been a retired ship's captain, and had positioned the establishment so he could have an uninterrupted view of the sea. Now, even with so many irregular rooftops segmenting the horizon, it was still a lovely place from which to watch the sunset. The captain had ordered a set of great bay windows to be built facing west, like a landlocked version of the stern windows that would have adorned his private cabin. About half of the original panes were intact. The handblown glass threw wavy patterns of light over the varnished floor and the walnut wainscoting.

The bar ran down the front half of the north wall, curving out slightly like a ship's bow. The waiters' station was a broad space by the eastern corner, separated from the rest of the bar by brass rails. Two paces farther east opened the double doors leading to and from the kitchen. The bar was original, as was the brass footrail. Sylvie had found the four spittoons in a local garage sale.

Half an hour later, Marcela returned and brought Rick with her. The restaurant's headwaiter was tall, lean, and carried himself with a deceptive calm. Sylvie was one of the few people on earth who knew of Rick's carefully hidden past. Most people saw what Rick wanted them to see, a man who walked through life with bulletproof ease, utterly content to be both alone and untouched by the trauma of close relationships.

Marcela set the plate with Sylvie's sandwich on the counter and asked, "This is really all you want?"

On days when he came in early, Carl put a beef-bone stew on low heat and let it simmer for hours. The result was a concoction that had carried Sylvie through many a long night. "Have him put a bowl to one side. Right now, this is fine." She could feel the headache building, still far enough away that there was no actual pain, but her stomach rebelled against the very thought of food. Sylvie ran through what she knew about their new waiter, which was almost nothing.

Rick and Marcela gathered by the bar's serving station, leaning in close enough for their conversation not to be overheard by the growing number of early customers. Marcela said, "That's not much to go on."

"I know. But there was something about him. . . ." Sylvie tried to stow away a sudden smile, and failed. "He likes Sinatra."

"And you like him," Rick said.

"I did. Yes. Why exactly, I can't say."

Rick asked, "He said he was raised in a restaurant?"

"His earliest memories are of his family's place," Sylvie confirmed.

Marcela asked, "And Porter vouched for him?"

"Sort of." Sylvie related her rather curious conversation with the police chief. "He hesitated at first. Then he said that he thought it would make for a good fit. At least for a while."

"Meaning the guy isn't a keeper," Marcela said.

"To tell the truth, I have no idea what Porter meant."

Rick said, "We need another set of hands. Desperately."

"He can't be much worse than Carlos," Marcela said.

"Carlos was hidden away in the kitchen," Rick pointed out. "We're talking about putting Connor Smith on public display."

Sylvie was about to respond when she spotted a sharp-looking guy heading down the opposite sidewalk. The change from the man she had met earlier was so drastic that for an instant she thought she might have it wrong. Connor now wore a proper waiter's white-on-black outfit, except that his shirt had an extra button undone, something she would never have permitted on anyone else. On him, the opening formed a V that accented the triangular shape of his upper body. "Wait. Here he comes now."

Marcela watched him cross the street. "That's him?"

"Yes. Connor Smith."

"You didn't say nothing about him being so hot."

"I didn't notice."

"Then you are one sick lady," Marcela declared.

Sylvie noticed Rick's studied frown, but there wasn't time to ask what troubled him, because two customers were trying to get her attention from farther down the bar. "In that case, you can show him the ropes. Rick, you'll need to seat any early diners. Call Aubrey and tell her we need her on deck pronto."

Estelle walked along the headland that marked the southern boundary of Miramar Bay. The cliff was part of a seaside park and topped by a triangular meadow. A sunset breeze flattened the grass into a shimmering gold-green plate. The drop-off was marked by a rusting fence and danger signs that clattered in the wind. She walked slowly and wished she was capable of appreciating the beauty that surrounded her.

It was only when she started back toward her car that she noticed the structure nestled within a cluster of stunted pines. The branches were fashioned into a fan-shaped windbreak, and within their shadows stood a weather-beaten shack. What appeared to be a grey stone sculpture stood between the hut and the sea. Then she realized the stone was a podium, and the shack was a chapel. A glass-fronted board was attached to the rear wall, detailing sunrise services twice each month. But this evening the place was hers alone.

Estelle settled into a rear pew and bundled herself more deeply into her coat. The shack was open at the front, so that beyond the dais stretched a glorious view of the dusk-clad Pacific. The wind carried a searing bite. The trees sang a hushed melody to the end of day. For the first time since she had arrived in Miramar, Estelle felt a hint of rightness to her journey.

Her Jack would have loved this chapel. Estelle had buried her husband nine months ago. Jack had been the one who urged her to make this trip. If she had known how difficult it would be, how she felt strangled by all the conflicting emotions, she would have refused his dying request. But here she was, and this lonely chapel at the edge of the world was as fine a place as any to remember why she had come.

When the sun finally settled into the blue-gold waters, and the gulls cried a final farewell to the day's end, Estelle spoke the words aloud. "I need help."

It was not much as prayers went. But it would have to do.

CHAPTER 8

Marcela was slender and energetic, with mocha-colored skin and an abundance of soft, dark curls. Her large eyes seemed to be perpetually seeking a reason to laugh. She had been born in Encinitas, but raised mostly in Sacramento. She was married to an electrician who worked for the local cable company. She loved Sylvie and enjoyed her work so much she and her husband were putting off having kids. All this emerged as she showed Connor his station—the restaurant's worst six tables, lining the back wall, away from the windows. Then she led him through the kitchen doors, two of them, spaced well apart. One opened inward, the other out. Connor's mother had always said this was the first mark of a good restaurant, for there would be times when frantic staff forgot to look before rushing through. None of the kitchen staff even glanced his way as Marcela made a loud introduction.

Marcela led him back into the dining room and around the bar. She showed him the alcove holding the glasses and silverware and coffeemaker and spice bottles. Then an older man came over and Marcela introduced him as the headwaiter, Rick.

Connor knew he needed to pay careful attention, that every word and every moment was intended as a test. But just then, his attention was captured by the stage.

Big bay windows, taller than Connor, opened onto the fading sunset. The sea glistened between the rooftops. Gulls wheeled through the sky overhead. The space between the bar and the front windows held a long table with captain's chairs, clearly intended to serve as either a spillover for the bar crowd or to host a single large party. Beyond that, fit snug in front of the bay windows, was a small stage. The left wall contained an alcove shaped like a giant abalone shell, beautifully restored. Tucked inside was a baby grand piano, a Steinway.

Marcela asked, "Something wrong?"

The piano's varnish gleamed ruby-dark in the dusk. Connor said, "I used to play."

Marcela told him, "Back in the day, dance hall girls used to toss their skirts and do their high step up there."

When Connor did not respond, Rick asked, "That makes you sad, seeing the piano?"

"A little." He forced himself to turn away. They were both watching him. The headwaiter was an inch or so shorter than Connor and very narrow. Pronounced cheekbones framed eyes that pierced deep. Connor said, "Music was a dream I let go of."

Rick smiled tightly, as though he understood far more than Connor was saying. "When was that?"

"I haven't touched the keys in seven years." He swallowed hard. "Long enough that I can almost forget the dream ever existed."

Rick and Marcela exchanged a look; then Rick said, "See if the kitchen can use his help." As Marcela led him away, Rick patted his shoulder and said, "Welcome to Castaways."

There was no reason on earth such quietly spoken words would touch Connor's heart. None at all.

* * *

No one spoke to Connor when Marcela left him in the kitchen. Connor knew his tables would be the last to receive customers. On a quiet evening in the middle of the week, he might as well spend it all right here. Being ignored.

A burly red-haired man with a British accent pointed him to a steel bowl filled with fresh spring vegetables and told him to julienne the lot.

Connor waited to see if any utensils would be offered, but no one even looked his way. He gave a mental shrug and asked, "Any chance of an apron?"

The Brit had pecan pies in the ovens separating the pastry station from the main cooking area. The smell of bourbon vanilla was strong. He gestured with his spatula toward a hall at the kitchen's other side. "Pantry."

Connor crossed the kitchen, followed by four sets of eyes. He had no problem with the silence. The stubby hall ended at a steel door, which was propped open, revealing an alley that Connor thought looked remarkably neat. The air coming in was pleasantly cool. A young man with dark hair and tats running down both arms was seated on a cane chair by the entrance, smoking and staring at the gathering dusk. Connor assumed it was the busboy waiting his call to duty.

When Connor started to open the pantry door, he went still for the second time that evening. Directly above the doorway was a segment of varnished wood, on which was branded the message LAST CHANCE SALOON.

Connor felt like he had just collided with a train.

He had no idea how long he stood there. After a time, he felt a hand upon his shoulder. Connor turned to find the red-haired man standing beside him, smiling gently. The Brit asked, "You done time, lad?"

"That's not . . . I haven't. No."

"Ah, well, it's not only inside the cage where the wee dark hours grab hold. You just come along with me."

Connor found himself being led back to the vegetable and garnish station, only this time everyone watched him openly. The Brit introduced himself as Sandy and brought over a paring knife, a sharpening stave, a peeler, and the apron Connor forgot to get for himself. Sandy said, "You know what these are for, lad?"

"Yes."

"Here's a secret you can take to heart. Sylvie doesn't like blood in her veggies. Doesn't make the right impression. So you just wash this lot and hold off until you're certain you won't go peeling any fingers."

"I'm okay."

"Sure, now, of course, you are." Sandy walked back over to the oven and checked his pies. Bruno, a slender dark-haired young man, kept stirring his sauces and preparing plates for the evening rush. Carl, the chef, laid out an array of meats and fish. The computer monitor above the main stove chimed and lit up with the night's first order. Sandy pulled a tray of bread from the warming compartment and slipped it into the main oven. Everybody moved into the next forward gear. All except Connor. He was still getting used to the fact that being slammed at heart level by a simple wooden plaque had somehow earned him a place.

When his hands steadied, Connor started on the vegetables. No doubt the restaurant had a specialist machine hidden somewhere that normally did this job. However, the chore was a valid way of checking out Connor's kitchen creds, for julienne vegetables were not something normally seen outside of high-end restaurants.

Julienne actually referred to the knife he was using, as well as the vegetables themselves. "Julienne" meant to cut into identical straight segments, similar to large matchsticks. When fried, julienne potatoes were often referred to as shoestrings. The term had been in use for over three hundred years, and first re-

ferred to a soup composed of vegetables cut into uniform segments—carrots, beets, leeks, and celery. Added to this would
be minced lettuce and sorrel, and onions cut into thin triangular
slices. The vegetables were briefly sautéed, and then simmered
in chicken stock. Connor could not actually remember learning
these things. He had simply known them all his life. Then he
had forgotten almost everything.

It was far too simple to say an actor's existence required his
single-minded focus, although to a certain extent it was true.
Connor maintained a very discerning palate, even when it came
to ordering takeout. Los Angeles was a very eclectic city, and the
possibilities for ordering in food, or for going out, were endless.
Every section of the globe was represented in the restaurants and
delis and mobile kitchens. None of this was why he almost never
cooked, or spent more than the odd moment reflecting on his
family's heritage.

Connor dried the vegetables, peeled the potatoes and carrots,
halved the peppers and discarded the seeds; then he trimmed the
ends off the zucchini and cucumbers. He cut most of the vegetables
into three-inch segments and four-sided blocks. He sliced them
lengthwise, fashioning long matchsticks about an eighth of an
inch thick. The red and green peppers were trimmed to make
matching segments.

His hands stayed busy, which meant his mind was free to
roam. He could still visualize the block of wood and the words
burned into its surface. They opened the portal to all his carefully repressed memories. Connor had let go of so much from
his early life. His villa in Beverly Flats was equipped with a
granite and stainless-steel kitchen that had cost over a hundred
thousand dollars, which he could not actually afford. Connor
rarely even used the microwave. He had bought a used
Bösendorfer grand piano, but then shifted it behind the plants
in his glassed-in veranda, where it could be both present and
hidden. Just like most everything else from his past life.

The Castaways kitchen reached a natural pause at a quarter

past eight. The first tables were busy with dessert, the later arrivals had their starters and their wine, and Sandy passed around white ceramic mugs of fresh-brewed coffee and portions of a delicate pastry that contained fresh goat cheese whipped to froth and baked with tiny flakes of Spanish ham. Bruno, the assistant chef, introduced himself to Connor and asked about his family restaurant. Connor found himself trying to explain just how impossible a moment like this would have been, because his parents would have been threatening each other with dire bodily harm. No one spoke for a long moment; then Marcela chose that moment to rush into the kitchen with a new order. Sandy pointed a thumb at Connor and declared, "You want my take, he's a keeper, this one."

But the waitress was too busy for Sandy's banter. "We don't have much choice, at least for tonight. Rick has two tables just arrived, my section's almost full, and Sylvie's had one of her attacks."

"No surprise, given the day she's had," Sandy said.

Connor asked, "Attack?"

"Migraine," Marcela said, reading her order notes, typing furiously, and talking at the same time. "Big one."

"And it's all my fault," Bruno said morosely.

"We've covered that ground already," Sandy said. "So stuff it, that's a good lad."

Marcela said to Connor, "Any more customers show up, we're opening your station."

The kitchen accelerated for the second time that evening. Connor was shifted to garnishes; then he helped out wherever an extra pair of hands was required. He prepped dishes for the washer; he stirred soups; he rolled out extra bread. He shucked four dozen clams. Connor regularly made mistakes. Everything took him too long. The rest of the kitchen staff accelerated to a pace he had lost; but the others evidently saw he was trying, so they did not come down on him too harshly.

Sylvie entered the kitchen and walked over to where he scored a crosshatch pattern into six filets of sea bass, then basted the surface with a sauce of rarified butter and chicken stock and white wine, prior to them being flash baked. She said, "Sorry to drop you in the deep end, but Rick and Marcela are super busy, and we have a table of eight that just walked in."

Connor saw how she squinted against the kitchen's overhead lighting, but no one else said anything. Connor replied, "It's no problem."

"Actually, it is," Sylvie said.

Sandy stopped preparing dough for choux pastries. "Not that Hammond git."

"Enough of that," Sylvie said.

"Phil Hammond's got an assassin's charm, I'll give him that much, but he never leaves the hired help a brass farthing." Sandy pounded the dough, shooting up a cloud of flour. "Great git."

Sylvie tried her best to offer Connor a smile. "Consider this your trial by fire."

CHAPTER 9

There were certain elements of stardom that Connor yearned for. Part of it had to do with money, of course. Connor had been broke since his first day in LA. The rise of his acting career had simply resulted in Connor digging himself farther into the debt hole. Even so, if money and fame were the only draw, Connor would be down on Rodeo Drive, enduring the final fitting of his tux and showing off smiles and excitement for the cameras.

What interested Connor most was the chance to design his role.

All supporting actors were basically there to bolster the star and propel the story. They played the foil, the love interest, the villain, the fiend, whatever. Their screen presence was dictated by the lead character. In television, where the pace was constantly frenetic, secondary characters were expected to know their lines, show up early, hit the mark, and bow out. The word that defined most of the roles Connor played was, straitjacket.

Connor heard the party of eight before he rounded the bar. Five men and two women were playing to the older man at the

head of the table. Phil Hammond looked to be in his early sixties and flashed the easy smile of a man well used to center stage.
He was in the middle of a story when Connor approached. The
seven in supporting roles took their lead from the silver-haired guy
and pretended not to notice Connor's arrival. Connor showed
them the easy smile of a journeyman actor, and waited as they
laughed over a joke he had not heard. Connor kept telling himself that his job was the same as usual, play up to the star.

Phil Hammond was a carefully groomed silver fox. He wore
a starched dress shirt open at the neck, gold-and-emerald cuff
links, perfect tan, polished nails. He took his time studying
Connor, then asked, "Do I know you?"

"It's an honor to serve you, Mr. Hammond. Especially my
first night on the job."

"Oh, look," the youngest member of the group said. "Fresh
meat."

Hammond smiled the young staffer into silence, then demanded, "Why isn't my girl over here?"

"Ms. Cassick is unwell, sir. What can I bring you, gentlemen?"

"A single malt for me. Rocks." He beamed at the group.
"And more water for the horses."

Connor laughed because it was expected of him.

Phil Hammond showed the world a regal graciousness.
However, whatever lurked beneath Phil's public mask was
enough to keep the seven others fearfully attentive. When Connor brought their main courses, Phil politely asked him to
bring him another steak, this one cooked as he had requested,
medium rare instead of medium well. Carl made no comment
as he put another filet on the grill. Sandy made do with a single
muttered comment about the old git. Connor did not respond.
He had worked on numerous sets where either the lead actor or
the director would have left Phil Hammond in their egotistical
dust.

As Connor reentered the dining room, Marcela asked him to
stop by the front station when he had a moment. Connor served

the plate, then stood motionless until Hammond took a bite and smiled his approval.

Rick was manning the entry when he arrived. Connor asked, "Is Sylvie okay?"

"She will be. Eventually." Rick pointed at the ceiling. "She lives in the apartment upstairs. She's lying down."

Marcela joined them and scowled at Hammond's table. "Old Phil won't leave you a dime."

"Sandy warned me."

"The one nice thing about Sylvie's migraine is she doesn't have to pretend to enjoy old Phil's company," Marcela said.

Rick said, "Just because he stiffs waiters in his own restaurant doesn't mean he's a bad guy." He added to Connor, "He owns a third of this place."

Marcela said, "He's a snake."

"You don't know that."

"I know, all right," Marcela replied. "I just don't know *why* I know."

Rick asked Connor, "Does that make any sense to you?"

Connor asked, "Doesn't Sylvie have medicine?"

"She took it hours ago," Marcela said. "She says it masks the worst symptoms, but it doesn't make them go away."

Rick told Connor, "Porter Wright just called. The chief wants a late table. He asked for you."

Marcela said, "I can take him if you like."

"No, it's fine. I owe the guy."

Rick said, "Porter waits until the night quiets down and his wife's off duty."

Marcela said, "Carol is a nurse. She's a great lady."

Rick said, "They usually close the place down."

"I don't mind staying late," Connor said.

Marcela said to Rick, "Give the guy my best table. He's earned it."

* * *

Phil's group became steadily louder as the night progressed. By the time Porter Wright arrived, their laughter and shouts punctuated the entire restaurant.

Porter wore his jacket and tie like it belonged to somebody else's wardrobe. His wife was a sharp contrast to the Miramar cop. Carol Wright was athletic and poised and intensely handsome. Her silvery gray hair was cut to draw attention to her striking features. She wore no makeup. She and her husband stopped by one table after another, shaking hands and sharing words. Porter repeatedly frowned at the group beyond the bar. He waited until his wife was seated, then walked over.

The instant Porter appeared around the bar, Hammond went quiet. Porter leaned over, planted one hand on the back of Hammond's chair, and spoke softly. Connor watched Phil Hammond respond with a gracious smile that was utterly at odds with the flush rising from his collar. Porter straightened, greeted several of the bar's patrons, and rejoined his wife.

Ten minutes later, Hammond rose and walked unsteadily toward the exit. Connor stood by the front station and thanked them for coming in. Hammond cast a dark look his way, as though it was Connor's fault that his public mask had been stripped away.

Carol Wright gave no sign that she noticed either the exchange or Hammond's abrupt departure. She had a gentle, knowing smile that she bestowed on Connor like a gift. "Has anyone ever said you look like a movie star?"

"Not recently, Mrs. Wright. Can I tell you tonight's specials?"

"It would be a waste of good breath. I know what I want. Porter, should we suggest this young man take our Celia on a date?"

"Over my dead body," the chief replied.

"Our daughter is struggling to mend a broken heart," she explained, then said to Porter, "I think a night in this young man's company would be just what the doctor ordered."

"If Connor comes within a hundred feet of Celia, he'll need a doctor," Porter assured his wife.

"But you said you liked him."

"As a waiter, sure, I like him fine." He said to Connor, "We'll have the lamb."

"An excellent choice."

Carol said, "Let's order some wine."

"Can't hurt," Porter said. "We walked, I'm off duty, and the night is young."

"I didn't ask for excuses," Carol replied. "I asked for a drink."

Connor said, "I'd like to treat you folks to a bottle."

Carol looked up. "This is new."

Porter said, "Cops aren't allowed to accept bribes."

"You've been a big help," Connor said. "I'd just like to say thanks."

Carol stopped her husband from responding with a hand upon his wrist. "That is very nice of you. Isn't it, Porter?"

"He's still not getting anywhere near our daughter."

"Oh, you. That's very gracious, Connor. We accept."

Rick and Marcela were rushing about, serving other late arrivals. Marcela was the first through the kitchen door. Connor told her what he intended while she punched in the order and apologized to the kitchen staff for making them stay late, as though it was her fault a table had shown up when they did. At first, she gave no sign she had heard him. Then Rick came through the doors, moving faster than Marcela. She said, "Come over here."

"No time," Rick said. "I've got—"

"So do I. And you're going to want to make time for this." When Rick reluctantly moved over, Marcela told Connor, "Say it again."

"It's no big deal. I want to buy the chief and his wife a nice bottle of wine."

"Is that a fact?" Marcela said.

"He's done three big favors for me."

"Has he, now?"

"He found me a place to stay, he gave Sylvie a good word, and he got rid of Phil."

Marcela said, "You get stiffed by your first table, and then you buy the second table a bottle of wine. Not the most profitable way to start your new job."

Rick handed Marcela the keys without taking his eyes off Connor. "Show the new guy around."

"Sure thing." Marcela jangled the keys. "Come on, new guy."

CHAPTER 10

The wall to the left of the entry, just behind the hostess station, was a glass-fronted display case for wine. Connor knew most of these bottles would be filled with colored water and resealed. The bottles on display were drawn from some of California's most expensive vineyards, and were far too precious to be subjected to daylight. The actual cellar was located six steps down the same staircase that led up to Sylvie's apartment. Marcela unlocked the barred entry and stood aside. "The full list is there on the table. You won't be in here, usually, that's Sylvie's job. Or Rick's. But if you do come, be sure and mark whatever you take, and the date."

Connor nodded absently. The chamber was deceptively large, extending back under the kitchen and lined floor to ceiling with shelves. Most of the wine racks were empty. "Where is the rest?"

"This is all we have. Sylvie went broke buying the place and doing it up. Which is why she has old Phil as a partner. Most of what you see here, she bought at auction from another failed restaurant." Marcela scanned the empty shelves. "Sylvie's dream is to build this into something *Wine Spectator* would write about."

Good wine was one of the lessons Connor had carried with him from his family's restaurant. He could rarely afford to drink any, because he had managed to rack up an elephantine amount of personal debt. However, this was different. Tonight he was after a bottle that showed class, something the Wrights would never buy for themselves. He inspected the few shelves holding French reds, and found what he was looking for midway down the right wall. "This is perfect."

Marcela stared at the bottle, then demanded, "What is your story?"

"I don't . . . This is a good wine."

"Yes, Connor. I know it's good. At a hundred and eighty-five dollars, it better be magnificent. And that's not what I meant."

He hid from the intensity of her gaze by bending over the ledger and making note of what he was taking.

Marcela went on, "You're handsome. You're smart. Sandy says you never did time. You're considerate. You stayed polite to old Phil even when you knew he wasn't going to leave you a nickel."

Connor straightened. "I thought with Phil, you know, it's my first night—"

"We're not talking about what I want to talk about," Marcela snapped.

Connor did not reply.

"What are you doing here, waiting tables in Miramar?"

He faced her because he had no choice. She barred the door with a determined ire. Connor said, "Have you done time?"

"No, and that's still not—"

"But you've got your own reasons, right? I mean, the things

you'd just as soon not ever need to talk about. What you've done wrong, why you're here."

Marcela stared at him.

"Not all cages are made of steel," Connor said, repeating Sandy's words.

"So what you're telling me is, you're not telling me."

"Someday. Maybe. Right now . . ." Connor wiped the dust off the bottle. "I'm just trying to get a clear handle on what I've lost. Maybe then . . . I don't know."

"Tell me," she pressed.

If she had stayed angry with him, Connor would have probably deflected. But she was gentle now, and her dark gaze showed a caring nature. Connor had always been a sucker for Latinas with flashing eyes.

He said, "There's something about this town."

"You're right. There is."

"I came here once to escape from a fairly awful weekend up in the hills. Ever since then, I kept thinking about how nice it was, how calm. . . . I got myself into some trouble last week, and all I could think of was, 'If I could just get back here to Miramar, maybe I might find a way out.' "

Marcela's voice gentled further. "What kind of trouble?"

He traced a guilty script on the bottle's surface. "I finally got what I'd been chasing after."

She held him there for a couple of beats. Long enough for Connor to know if she asked, he would answer. Even if it cost him his chance. But in the end, Marcela stepped aside. "Your table's waiting."

The wine was a huge success. Connor decanted the bottle at the table, explaining that it was important for an older wine to breathe in order to fully open the flavor.

Carol confessed she didn't know a thing about French wines. Connor warned her, "I could put you to sleep with stuff that doesn't matter nearly as much as whether you like how it tastes."

"Go on, tell."

"Stop me when you've had enough. In 1855, the French government selected sixty-three chateaux vineyards in the Bordeaux regions and gave them a special status, the Cru Classés. The very best of these are called first growths. Lafite Rothschild, Latour, Haut-Brion, and so forth. Nowadays they sell for thousands of dollars a bottle. There are fifteen second growths, fourteen third growths, ten fourths and eighteen fifths." Connor held up the bottle. "Lynch-Bages is a fifth growth, but it's become known as a 'super second' in recent years because the quality has just gone through the roof."

Carol appeared genuinely interested. "Where did you learn about all this?"

"From my mother. She was passionate about everything that went into making a great table."

"And your father?"

"He worried constantly about what things cost. The only thing he liked about good wine was adding it to somebody's bill."

Carol observed, "They didn't get along, then."

"Like chalk and cheese." He set the empty bottle on the table, held the decanter by the base, and poured a small amount into both of their glasses. "Tell me what you think."

There was a singular pleasure to watching their eyes go round from that first incredible taste. Connor stood there a moment longer, observing them with a genuine satisfaction. When he excused himself to go see about their orders, Marcela caught his eye and nodded. Connor entered the kitchen, buoyed by the sense of having gotten something very right.

When he returned with their plates, Carol had reached

across the table and taken her husband's hand. She was a handsome woman, strong and solid and deeply in love. Carol saw in Porter what others did not. With a simple molten look, she elevated her lumpish husband to a throne of her own making.

Connor wished them a bon appétit and turned away, his pleasantly attentive mask firmly in place. But the way Carol looked at her husband had drawn Connor down a memory lane littered with women whose names he could not recall.

CHAPTER 11

Connor slept fitfully. Every hour or so, he was jerked awake by the image of that simple wooden sign hanging over the pantry door. By dawn, it felt as though LAST CHANCE SALOON was branded into his brain.

His final dream was about Phil Hammond, sort of. Connor stood by the table and looked down at himself, only thirty years older. He woke up knowing what had troubled him about the guy. Phil was smooth, urbane, and played his role well. Just like Connor. The dream's message was clear enough. This was the best he could hope for? Striving and struggling and finally reaching stardom, so his own team of sycophants could crowd around him at a meal they didn't enjoy, giving the king his due?

He gave up on sleep and dressed. His feet ached and his back felt stiff. His left thumb was blistered and he could not remember when he had burned himself. Despite it all, he actually looked forward to performing in scene two.

A little after seven, Connor walked to the diner and was waved into the same booth he had sat in the day before. Connor caught the cook looking his way. The man was obsidian black, with a froth of gray curls covering his scalp. When Connor nodded, the cook gave him a friendly wave. Then the same waitress came over and told him, "Joey says you get the locals discount. Ten percent."

"Joey is the cook?"

"And owner." The waitress was about Connor's age, but she carried herself like a woman much older. Her expression said everything hurt. Her polyester uniform and pale hose and support shoes made her look shapeless. "How'd you land the gig at Castaways?"

"I asked."

She sniffed. "I asked, too. Like, what, a dozen times. Look where it got me. Working for Joey."

Connor had no idea what to say, except, "Could I have a coffee?"

She walked back to the station, lifted the pot, and filled his ceramic mug. "Is it true what they're saying, you bought the cop a hundred-dollar bottle of wine?"

"Who exactly is saying that?"

"Doesn't matter." She sniffed again. "Don't expect it to do you any good. You step out of line, he'll still lock you up."

Connor was still searching for a response when the elegant woman he had noticed in the guesthouse walked over and asked, "Would you mind some company?"

After the waitress filled the woman's coffee cup and turned away, Connor said, "I don't think I understood what it means to live in a small town until just now."

Joey called through the pickup window, "What's the matter, you're not eating?"

Connor started to say something about the waitress being too preoccupied to even ask, but he saw her wince and changed his mind. "What's good?"

"I smoke my own turkey sausage."

"I'll have that and two eggs over easy."

"You got it. Miss?"

"Coffee is fine, thank you." When the cook turned away, she said, "I owe you an apology. I was very impolite yesterday."

"Do me a favor. Take off those sunglasses." Connor watched her hesitate, then fumble the oversized glasses from her face. She was an attractive woman in her fifties, but her gray eyes were hollow. She looked like she had not slept in weeks. Connor said, "You don't need to apologize."

"My name is Estelle Rainier."

"Connor Smith. Nice to meet you, Estelle."

She tightened her lips in what might have been a smile. "Anyway, I'm sorry. I had a shock yesterday."

The waitress chose that moment to return. As she refilled their mugs, Estelle murmured, "Thanks."

"No problem." When they were alone, he asked Estelle, "Do you want to talk about it?"

She turned toward the window. "Sylvie Cassick is my daughter."

Connor wondered if this was another part of small-town life. How every bend in the road, every passing hour, carried the potential to punch him in the soul. "Really?"

"Of course, really. You think I would suggest such a thing if it wasn't true?" She picked up her coffee mug, then set it down, untasted. "She's my daughter and we haven't spoken in nineteen years. I didn't even know where she lived. I hired a detective."

"So when I saw you yesterday . . ."

"I've been here four days and the closest I've come to Castaways is across the street. I watched you go inside. I started to follow you, but then I heard that dreadful Sinatra music—"

"Sinatra is many things," Connor replied. "Dreadful isn't one of them."

She studied the steaming mug. "You're right, of course. My ex and Sylvie loved that sort of music. I felt so excluded. . . . I accused him of making her share his addiction. Which is nonsense. I knew it at the time. But it seems like Sylvie was closer to him than me from her very first breath. I was bitterly jealous."

Connor handed her his napkin and waited until she had cleared her face. "So you heard the music and, what, you left without seeing her?"

"Yes, Connor. I ran away. Can you understand that?"

It was his turn to stare out the side window. "Absolutely."

The waitress set down his plate and announced, "This is on me."

For once, he was grateful for the interruption. "What's your name?"

"Gloria."

He introduced himself, then said, "It's nice of you to offer. But really—"

"Hey, it may not be a hundred-dollar bottle of wine, but still."

Connor showed her his best smile. "That's very nice of you, Gloria, thanks."

When the waitress departed, Estelle asked, "What was that all about?"

"It's nothing. Estelle, why are you telling me this?"

She leaned across the table, her features taut. "I want you to tell me what my daughter is like."

CHAPTER 12

Nowadays Sylvie's life contained few opportunities to watch the sunrise, once her favorite hour of the day. Since opening Castaways, there was always so much to do. However, a migraine and the medicine were always followed by a day where she lived in shadows. Sylvie had built her life on being strong, and she hated this period of enforced weakness as much as the pain itself. She knew from experience that if she reentered full speed too early, she would suffer another attack. So she forced herself to sit by the bedroom's open window and watch gulls dance their silent ballet against the backdrop of shimmering blue. The wind hummed a gentle melody through the cypress and California pines. The clouds sailed great billowing ships across the sky. She felt as though she watched the day through a medicinal blanket.

The old ship captain had lived on the top floor, under the garrets, which now saw duty as her bedroom and walk-in closet and bath. Sylvie often imagined the adventurer seated where she was now, watching sails head into the world from which he had retreated. Sylvie had bought a love seat and matching coffee table, and positioned them so she and Bradley could enjoy a private alcove overlooking the Pacific. That was, of course, before Sylvie had discovered the love of her life had forgotten to mention the wife and three children and Labrador in Santa Cruz. Since that bombshell had landed nineteen months earlier, she went through weekly debates over whether she should burn the love seat in her backyard.

Around eleven, Sylvie descended to the middle floor, entered the kitchen area, and made herself a cup of tea and toast. The entire middle floor was now one great room. The west-facing area had formerly housed four blackjack tables and a trio of roulette wheels. Every shred of that tawdry past had been ripped out. The striped red wallpaper was gone, along with the calico carpet, the fake Art Deco lightshades, and the benches where the fancy ladies had sat and waited to be summoned.

Rick phoned around midday, assuring her he would take over the setting-up responsibilities. Sylvie protested, as usual. Her migraines were part of the restaurant's routine, coming as they did once or twice a month. She liked to think of herself as a woman who thrived on being independent and self-sufficient, but these attacks were a habitual reminder of how much she relied on others. Rick, Bruno, Marcela, and Carl would arrange among themselves to take deliveries and make decisions over the night's specials and do everything she simply did not have the energy to do today.

She drifted downstairs at four-thirty. Her feet seemed scarcely able to find the next step. She made a quick tour of the kitchen, accepted the polite wishes from her staff, then settled onto her stool by the front door. She did not plan on moving one inch more than was absolutely necessary all night.

Ten minutes later, Marcela arrived bearing a carrot cupcake with a single candle. "Happy birthday."

"Shame on you," Sylvie replied. "I had almost managed to forget."

"Hey! Last year, you got your wish, right? You survived that dreadful Bradley. You recovered. You moved on."

Rick stepped up beside her. "We're not supposed to speak his name, remember?"

"Once a year, it's permitted." Marcela lifted the cupcake. "Now wish and blow."

Sylvie looked at the flickering flame. "I still can't think straight. You wish for me."

They both liked that a lot. Rick said, "A guy who deserves you."

Marcela said, "Old Phil gets hit by lightning, run over by a Greyhound bus, and buried in a mudslide. Tomorrow."

Rick said, "You don't think maybe that's a tad overkill?"

"Hey, did I criticize your wish? A guy who deserves Sylvie? Huh. So he walks in and has a meal and leaves? I mean, really."

Sylvie relished having a reason to smile. "So edit the poor man's wish, why don't you."

"You meet the lover who has been looking for you all his life, only he doesn't know it until now. He sees your good heart, and he loves you for the best that you are. He helps you find the happiness you deserve." Marcela lifted her chin at Rick. "Now *that's* a wish."

Rick was smiling too. "I stand corrected."

"You go stand in the corner, is what." To Sylvie, "Girl, the candle is gonna melt away, you don't blow."

Sylvie did so, tasted a tiny sliver of the icing, then set down the cake and asked, "What do you think of our new waiter?"

"I like him," Marcela said. "Connor doesn't talk about himself, which is nice for a change. But the boy's got a past, I weaseled that much out of him."

Sylvie noticed her headwaiter had lost his smile. "Rick?"

Rick replied carefully, "Connor did not put a foot wrong all night."

"So you like him?"

"I didn't say that."

Marcela flashed genuine ire. "What could you possibly have against the guy? He took on everything the kitchen gave him. He stayed polite, and he handled old Phil with a smile. What, Connor spent too much on the wine?"

"Wait," Sylvie said. "He bought wine?"

"For a table," Marcela said. "To thank the chief."

"Connor bought a bottle of wine for Porter? What was it?"

"Lynch-Bages, 2005," Rick said.

Marcela told their headwaiter, "There is no reason on earth for you not to like him."

Rick's only response was to walk away.

Marcela asked, "What is that all about?"

"Maybe he's got a hunch or something," Sylvie replied. "But why wouldn't he tell us?"

Marcela shrugged. "You figure out what makes any guy tick, you be sure and let me know."

The restaurant was surprisingly busy for a Wednesday, but it all remained at a distance for Sylvie. A group from one of the Moonstone Beach hotels filled the long table. Locals chose that night to come in for a meal. A business group decided there was nothing they would like more than a good night out to round off their successful meeting. By eight o'clock, every table was full and Sylvie had turned away three late arrivals. Connor handled his six tables fairly well. He was rushed and he made mistakes, but he apologized sincerely and explained that this was his second night after years away from the trade.

Sylvie mostly sat on her leather-clad stool by the host station. She made just one round of the restaurant, and visited the kitchen only twice. She drifted through the hours. The migraine drug always gave her a sense of being disconnected from reality.

Around nine, she began a mental conversation with her new waiter. The handsome man of mystery. Connor Smith. As she watched him, she wondered what it was that troubled Rick so.

The answer was almost audible, certainly clearer than anything she heard from the outside world. *Rick is afraid you're going to fall in love with me,* Connor mentally replied. *And I'm no good.*

Sylvie walked to the waiters' station and made herself a cup of coffee as she silently observed, *You certainly look like bad news.*

I am. Very bad.

Sylvie remained by the coffeemaker, staring out at the night beyond the window. The imaginary Connor asked her, *And what would you like for your birthday?*

Sylvie did not need to think that one over. *The same three wishes as every year. To own this restaurant free and clear. To know the love of an honest man. And to spend another happy hour with my father.*

As she returned to her station, she saw Connor smile at a table, brightening the lady's night. And right then, Sylvie realized what Rick had seen.

Connor was just going through the motions.

She could easily have put it down to Connor's newness or her own addled state, but Sylvie felt as though her medicinal distance actually clarified things for once. Connor Smith was not really engaged.

He worked the job and he talked the good talk. However, there was a special quality to a good waiter. They might be aloof; they could be utterly cold in their manner. Still, they conveyed a unique passion about their work. They treated it as a profession. They saw themselves as a vital component of the evening. And that was what an outstanding restaurant was all about. It did not merely prepare good food. It created an experience.

Sylvie kept watching, and became fairly certain two of Connor's tables felt the same. They might not be able to say why, but they were not taken with Connor's act.

And that was exactly what it was.

Rick chose that moment to walk over. "You holding up okay?"

"Marginally." Sylvie gave a fractional jerk of her chin in Connor's direction. "I see what you mean about him. He's . . ."

"Disconnected," Rick finished, and patted her on the shoulder. "Leave this with me."

CHAPTER 13

Connor spent much of the shift thinking back over his conversation with Estelle. He was rushed off his feet, and needed desperately to focus. However, even as the restaurant filled up, he could not get the woman out of his head.

Their time together in the diner had lasted all of ten minutes, maybe even less. Connor had tried to explain that Sylvie had not been feeling well, and as a result they'd only spoken a few words. Estelle would not be put off, though. "You had to have said something. She doesn't just offer a job to any fool who wanders in off the street."

"Thanks so much for the compliment," Connor said. "A wandering fool. That's a new one."

"I've got a lifetime's experience of saying the wrong things." She leaned in closer still. "Please."

He wished he had not asked her to take off her sunglasses. Estelle Rainier's eyes were a stormy gray, one shade darker than her daughter's. Her gaze held a desperation that was borderline frantic. Connor had no choice but to reply to her. "Sylvie is gentle and beautiful in a fractured sort of way."

"'Fractured'?" she said.

"I don't know exactly how to describe it. But I had the impression that she didn't just get a crippling headache out of the blue. It came on because she's carrying some awful burden."

"What is it, do you think?"

"I have no idea. What I can tell you is, the people here care for her."

"What people?"

"Everybody." He related his conversation with the stylist. And the way the two front staff almost cradled her when the pain struck. "Miramar's chief of police came in with his wife. I'm pretty sure he wasn't there just for the meal. He came to check me out."

"For Sylvie."

"Right. Everybody around here thinks the world of your daughter. And something more."

"What?" Her soft plea held a desperate edge.

Connor struggled to put it into words. "She's made a home here."

Estelle's tension and the strength slipped away. Her shoulders slumped. Her features ran like wax. She turned to the window and worked hard not to cry.

Connor did not know what to say. "I'm sorry."

Her fingers trembled as she pushed the sunglasses back over her eyes. She fumbled her way from the booth. As she left, she said, "Don't tell Sylvie I'm here."

"Estelle, maybe—"

She pointed an unsteady finger at his head. *"Don't."*

Connor had no choice but to say, "All right. Fine. If that's what you want."

"What I want?" Estelle turned away. "I should never have come."

The waitress had clearly been observing them, because as soon as Estelle was out the door, Gloria was standing over Connor and demanding, "What did you tell that poor lady?"

He shook his head. "What she said she wanted to hear."

At a quarter to ten that evening, Rick pulled Connor into the kitchen. Connor feared he had gotten something terribly wrong. Instead, Rick told him, "I want you to do something for me."

"Sure thing."

"Yesterday was Sylvie's birthday. She mentioned you two love the same kind of music."

Connor watched Marcela slip into the kitchen and step in close. She asked Rick, "Did you tell him yet?"

"I *asked*."

Connor replied, "Like I said last night, I haven't touched the keys or sung a note in seven years."

Marcela asked, "It's kinda like riding a bike, right?"

"Not at all."

Rick wasn't budging, though. "You see the state she's in. It would mean the world."

"We won't count the bad notes against you," Marcela said. "And neither will she."

Rick took his silence as agreement, and said, "Marcela and I will handle your tables. Let's go set you up."

Marcela patted his arm. "This is going to be great."

Connor thought it was going to be anything but that. Even so, he followed Rick through the bar area and climbed up onto the stage. Rick told him, "We use this mostly for weddings that take over the whole place."

That meant the piano was most likely tuned. Unlike his voice. Connor watched as Rick opened a closet built into the alcove and drew out an electronic drum kit, microphone, stand, and mini-amp. Rick shifted them into position and asked, "Will this work?"

"Rick, man . . ."

Rick guided him onto the stool, positioned the mic stand and drum machine, plugged in the cables, then stepped back and said, "It's all yours."

Connor watched Rick retreat from the stage, then set his fingers on the keys. He had always taken pride in his hands. Connor's reach was as powerful as his grip. He had once been able to play with a gentle smoothness, creating the liquid sort of backdrop that his melodies had required.

Now they rested there on the ivory, ten foreigners to a world they had once claimed as their own.

Connor had no idea how he had gotten himself into this. Either he played or he quit. Just get up and walk out and leave the place behind. Connor had seen that unspoken directive in Rick's gaze. The man had not been making a request.

He said softly, "Test, test." He adjusted the mic, turned up the amp's volume, and set the drum machine for a soft swing beat. He had often used a similar machine. The movements came almost naturally, like he had merely been hibernating for seven long years.

He knew Sylvie liked Sinatra. So he started with one of his favorites, the first he had ever reworked into a style that fit his voice.

> *Come fly with me.*
> *Let's fly, let's fly away.*

It had been so easy to stop. Playing once in a while had meant Connor wasn't growing. And he had always aimed high. It was one of his defining traits. When he switched his attention and his energies to acting, the creative draw to music had faded with remarkable swiftness. Initially Connor had assumed he would keep his music as a sideline. Every time he had sat down, though, all he heard was how far he had regressed.

Connor had always pushed himself hard to improve, grow, meet the challenge of drawing in a large audience. He had developed a style to utilize his strengths and mask his weaknesses. He had learned how to arrange the fifties-era ballads into a style more suitable for today's audiences. He had studied the contemporary singers who had made the songs work for them: Norah Jones, Michael Bublé, Diana Krall, Josh Grogan, to name a few.

All lost.

CHAPTER 14

Connor tried twice to rise from the piano and resume his role as waiter. Both times, though, Marcela ordered him back, saying she could handle everything and he was to stay where he belonged. Thirty minutes in, Sylvie walked over and seated herself at the bar. Aubrey, the bartender, poured her a glass of wine, but Sylvie did not touch it.

An hour and a half later, Connor finished with a melody that had taken Nat King Cole to the top of the Billboard charts. As he cut off the amp and drum machine, Sylvie said, "Come join me."

They talked until two. Or rather, Sylvie talked and Connor listened. Whenever she ran out of steam, she would ask him to play again. He sang a couple more tunes, then rejoined her. Sylvie rose from time to time, closing down the restaurant and bidding the staff a good night. Then she returned and started back where she had left off. Easy and natural. Like they had been enjoying such conversations for years.

She talked mostly about her father. "Pop was a true vagabond artist."

Connor asked, "What does that mean, 'true'?"

Sylvie revealed a special smile in response to Connor's question. "You are the first person in years to ask me that. Most people want to know about the 'vagabond' part. What they're really asking is, how was it for me to live on the road. And the answer is, wonderful and terrible in equal measure. I went to eleven different schools in twelve years. I dressed mostly out of Goodwill hampers. The boys who came flocking around were not the sort that interested me. The girls thought I was weird. Their parents suspected I was a bad influence. I spent most of my time alone."

Connor found it was the easiest thing in the world to reach over and take her hand. He said softly, "*True.*"

"All the wonderful parts of my life start with that word. My father was true to his dream. He painted scenes from the Pacific coastline. I was born just north of the Mexican border. My earliest memories were of playing in the Baja desert. When I was nine, he sold an entire collection of paintings to a gallery. He earned enough to take us north. So far north. We lived for two years in the Alaskan wilderness. Then we traveled back down south, staying six months in one place, a year or so in another." Sylvie gazed back over a wealth of memories, the smile as gentle as her voice. "Pop was a man of quiet happiness. My earliest memories are of the ratty camper, the only home I ever knew before we landed here in Miramar. We'd travel until he found somewhere he wanted to paint. When he hunted out a spot off the beaten track, somewhere with good light and a fair breeze. When he'd put on those albums, I knew we'd found another home."

She spoke of the man with a soft yearning, a hunger so tender it made Connor's eyes burn. He had never imagined what it would be like to have a woman speak his name with such gentle passion. "What about your mother?"

Sylvie pulled her hand away. "She left us when I was twelve. That's all you need to know about Estelle."

Connor did not know what to say, or how to recapture the feeling. He thought about the woman lying alone in the guest-house, too frightened to come meet the daughter she had abandoned.

Sylvie's voice hardened with her gaze. "Estelle started these one-sided battles when Pop made enough money for us to head north. My mother had always assumed when the money came in, we would buy a home and settle down. My father refused to even discuss it. He would hide himself away in another painting, disappear with his oils and his palette for days on end. When my mother tried to convince me to go away with her, I took off with Pop. We hiked for six days in the Canadian Rockies, and when we came back she was gone. I received, oh, four or five letters. Each time I wrote back and told her if she wanted to talk to me, she could come home. Mom's last letter said that was the problem, she needed the home Pop never gave her. Three weeks later we moved, and I never heard from her again."

Connor nodded quietly, then asked, "Will you show me your father's work?"

In reply, Sylvie walked to the front door and locked out the night. She took his hand and walked him around the paintings on the restaurant's walls, as though it was important for Connor to meet Gareth in his daughter's intimate company.

Gareth Cassick was a troubadour in oils. He painted with too much heart to ever be called great, but there was a colorful wonder, a quiet fervor, that sang through his every brushstroke. Gareth Cassick captured little of the landscape's precision. Nor did he try. His aim was to paint its reflection within his own heart. These images fashioned the likeness of a man who loved the Pacific coastlands with every fiber of his being.

Five of his oils adorned the restaurant's walls. One was of an Alaskan ice floe with iron cliffs as a backdrop. Another depicted a bear fishing the broad mouth of a river in a snowstorm. In the third, a commercial trawler plowed a golden furrow through a placid sunset. But it was the fourth and fifth that captured Connor.

One was of an abalone shell about a foot and a half tall, nestled in the sand, with a wave's froth lapping the upper boundary. The heart of the shell was painted as a sunset. The colors were one step off gaudy, and no doubt the art critics would have called it maudlin. Connor stared at it and felt as though he greeted the painter himself. Perhaps it was how Sylvie stood there beside him, not speaking, not pressing, content to give him all night if he wished. Finally he moved to the fifth, and by far the finest of them all.

The moon rose over indigo hills. The mountains were shaped like a pair of night-clad hands. They sheltered a collection of lights at their heart. The fingers flowed into the sand, and then the ocean. A mist gathered above the effervescent land. Only the moon shone clear.

Sylvie said, "This was the first painting Pop made of Miramar. We arrived here a few weeks before my sixteenth birthday. Pop had become friends with guys working nets on a trawler. They took us out for a night run. On the way into harbor, I told Pop I didn't want to go back on the road. I wanted Miramar to be my home. For the rest of my life. If he left, it would be without me."

Connor took a slow breath. *Home.*

"He never said, but I've always thought this painting was his way of telling me that he had finally found a place where his bones could rest easy."

Connor walked back to his room through a dense and chilling fog. But it was nothing compared to the daze he felt. As Sylvie had walked him to the door and bid him good night, she had invited him to share in a sunrise walk. Her invitation had been expressed with a shyness that had touched Connor. Now, as he climbed Miramar's main street, he had the sense of being offered a rite of passage. The evening had woken something inside him. It was such a strange sensation, he could not even name it.

He knew full well he was attracted to Sylvie. A blind man in a coma could see that much. What Connor could not understand was, *why now?*

Falling for a woman was the absolute last thing that should happen to him now. And it was not because of Kali, his soon-to-be ex-fiancée. If Connor had gained anything from traveling to Miramar, it was the absolute certainty that ending that marriage before it started was the right thing to do.

His footsteps scraped on the pavement, the sound overloud in the silent night. The fog was so thick he could not see much beyond the next streetlight. Time and again, he returned to the same inescapable fact. How could he be right for any woman, or know which was right for him, until he had a handle on who he really was?

One day, he would very much like to have a woman like Sylvie Cassick say she loved him. A woman whose physical beauty was so natural, it emerged spontaneously from her heart, as instinctive as a blooming rose.

Sylvie was a woman who cared so deeply, even strangers wanted to embrace her. Even a broken wretch from the world of film and lies gravitated to her. Even a Hollywood actor who did not have the first idea of who he truly was, a vagabond who could only say that he was lost. Connor was a wandering idiot who had run from all his dreams, simply because they had come true.

Love a woman like Sylvie Cassick? Hopefully. Yes. Someday. When he deserved it.

Love this woman *now*? The idea was not just absurd, it was dangerous. For both of them.

The fog was so thick Connor almost missed turning into the guesthouse. Then a corner of the sign emerged from the gloom. He crossed the parking lot, let himself into the room, and shut his door against all the vague yearnings that had chased him through the night.

He had not come all this way just to break another woman's heart.

CHAPTER 15

When Sylvie finally slipped into bed, she was not the least bit sleepy. This was another of the migraine's aftereffects. She would be back on a regular schedule tomorrow or the next day. She lay in bed, wide-awake, and rewound the conversation with Connor. Now and then, a refrain from one of the songs Connor had sung for her swam through her mind, and she smiled at the ceiling. His voice was deep and silky smooth. He showed a richness that extended through his entire range. He was rusty, and he made mistakes, and every time he stopped playing, he returned to the bar with the hollow sadness in his eyes. But none of it mattered. Not really.

To call theirs a conversation was entirely wrong. The only time Connor opened his mouth was to either sing or ask a question. Several times, she'd started to inquire about him, but she had stopped. Her words had remained unspoken. Connor's haunted look halted her. The night was simply too fine to make him confess his secrets. There would be other times for that . . . if she wanted.

That was the real reason, of course, why she wasn't sleeping.

She was trying to decide whether she wanted to have this move further. On any level.

Which made her invitation for a dawn walk all the more astonishing. She had not been out for a sunrise stroll with anyone since Bradley broke her heart.

She wondered about the great tragic mystery that had brought Connor here. Almost everyone who arrived in Miramar came with baggage. The stories were often sordid and made for spicy gossip. Sylvie did not mind a man with a past. She liked adventure. She liked the aroma of danger. She loved the idea of dancing a lifelong tango with a man whose history was as jagged as her own.

The one thing Sylvie valued most was honesty. The rarest of wines was nothing compared to this. Candor was a distilled elixir that seasoned the finest day and turned even the hard hours into a delicate feast.

Honesty. Frankness. Integrity. It was a shame that so few men understood what those words meant.

She found herself recalling the day she had driven up to the home where the man she had thought was the love of her life lived. She had sat in her car for almost an hour, watching Bradley play Frisbee with two lovely children and a barking dog. The memory still astonished her. How could a man fool her so completely? And why had he done it? The realizations that had wrecked her hopes for love and a family still rankled. How could she have not even suspected that the man lived a double life?

Sylvie rolled over and shut her eyes. She was no closer to answering those questions, and probably never would be. One thing, however, was certain. She was going to have to ask Connor to reveal himself. Not only because she needed to know his secrets, but more than anything, she wanted to see if Connor would tell her the truth.

CHAPTER 16

Despite the short night, Connor rose from his bed before the alarm went off. He was jerked from sleep and five seconds later from the bed itself, drawn upright by the realization that today was the day. As soon as he returned from his walk with Sylvie, Connor was going to contact Los Angeles.

He made a coffee and drank it, standing at the counter of his little kitchenette. He dressed and descended the hill to find Sylvie waiting for him in front of Castaways. She smiled a welcome that appeared strained in the dawn. The mist had retreated somewhat, leaving a glistening blanket over every surface. Together they walked in silence down the winding hill and joined the beach-front lane.

The path was mostly ground asphalt; but where the rocky shoreline took sudden dips, the passage was linked by rough-hewn wooden planks. The walk was almost two and a half miles long, running from the southern to the northern cliffs that defined Miramar's boundaries. The trail dipped and weaved, a lyrical line drawn between earth and sea.

The morning's ocean and sky were both fashioned from the

same cold steel. They walked to the northern point without speaking a word, and met no one. Even the gulls gave way at their approach. The central coast revealed its link to the Pacific north this morning. Connor recalled the Carolina fogs he had known growing up, great billowing swaths that settled an expectant hush over the world. This was something else entirely. The air was biting, the wind a soft blade against his exposed skin. A massive swell crashed somewhere out beyond his field of vision, blasting froth across the shoreline.

Sylvie was wrapped in a pearl-gray jacket zipped up to her chin, with a matching woolen cap. She walked with the lithe motions of a dancer, scarcely seeming to touch the earth. When they reached the northern cliffs and turned back, she said, "A penny for your thoughts."

"I was remembering a chef in my parents' restaurant." Connor had no idea where that had come from. For a guy who rarely gave time to his past, he found it remarkably good to share with her. And easy. He felt like he could tell her anything. "I haven't thought of him in years."

"Tell me."

"I started running errands and doing odd jobs around the place when I was eleven. The head cook was this guy, Leonard. My dad nicknamed him 'Spock,' you know—"

"The Star Trek guy played by Leonard Nimoy. Sure."

"He actually looked like Spock's evil twin, minus the pointy ears. He was a convicted murderer—two counts of manslaughter, did twenty years. He was out on parole. Man, could that guy ever cook." He smiled at the memories drifting in the mist. "He loved Louisiana French cuisine, the heavy sauces, the dishes that took all day to prepare, but he basically could do anything. He had an encyclopedic knowledge of spices."

"But he carried shadows."

"You can't imagine. Every conversation with Spock that wasn't about food became a walk on the wild side. Here I was, this little skateboarding kid and in-house mascot. All Leonard needed to do was look my way and my blood froze solid. I heard him tell my dad once, his second year inside he found a book in the prison library about cooking. That book was the only reason he made it out alive."

Sylvie's response was to take his hand. They continued on in silence, content to share the morning's immense solitude

Connor found himself calmed by Sylvie's closeness. The worries and fears waiting for him back up the hill, the call to LA, the questions for which he had no answers, all of this vanished in the drifting fog. All disappeared because of this woman who walked beside him.

The light held a cathedral quality, spilling through the ocean mist like heaven's own stained glass. Connor felt as though everything he glimpsed was made diamond-brilliant by Sylvie's presence. It felt as though she filled a space inside him, opening his senses to a level he had never before known.

They left the path and took a winding staircase down to the beach. The ocean's roar was so powerful he felt it in his chest. The sand was blanketed by clouds of sea froth. He could feel the ocean's chill on his exposed skin. Gulls swept past, eyeing them with a calm loftiness. Otherwise, they had the shore to themselves. At the next set of stairs, Sylvie led him across the hard-packed sand. As they climbed back up to the coastal path, Connor was halted by a sudden desire to kiss her.

Connor might have stood there all day, held by that crystal-gray gaze, as brilliant as the sunrise through the Pacific mist. It was there in her open expression, her need to hear the truth from him. If only he knew what that was.

On his way back up the hill, Connor stopped by the general store and bought a cheap phone that contained no GPS chip and five hundred minutes. He returned to his room and put on another pot of coffee while he set up the phone.

Connor poured himself a fresh cup and dialed Kali's number. Then he stopped in the act of making the connection. The bedside clock read half past ten. His soon-to-be ex-fiancée never got up before noon, unless she had an engagement of seismic proportions.

He cleared the screen; then he punched in the number for Kali's assistant. Kali ran through PAs at a ridiculous pace. She referred to the males as "Eric" and the females as "Erica." When the voice mail picked up, Connor identified himself and asked for an appointment to speak with Kali at three that afternoon.

Connor walked outside and sat in the narrow doorway, waiting for his heart to slow down. Estelle chose that moment to walk over and ask, "Can a girl buy you breakfast?"

"Not today. I've got . . . things."

"Terrible thing, things," Estelle said, turning away. "Good luck."

"Estelle." He could say it now, because he was facing his own dreaded truth that very moment. "You need to speak with Sylvie."

She did not look back at him. Instead, Estelle lifted her gaze to the blanket of gray. "The worst part of running away is facing the consequences. Wouldn't you agree?"

Connor did not reply or look up as her footsteps receded into the mist. When he was ready, he went back inside and placed the second call.

CHAPTER 17

Ami Chen was a senior talent agent with CPP. The agency's name was formed from the three original partners, now retired, which meant no one even remembered who they were. New actors who yearned to be added to the CPP roster said the name stood for "Careers Pulverized and Plundered." CPP occupied the top six floors of a premier building on Wilshire Boulevard. The six-lane road separated Beverly Flats from Beverly Hills; or as Ami Chen liked to tell Connor, it split the A-list from the hired help.

Ami managed five A-list stars and around sixteen actors of Connor's status. Plus six directors, three producers, and a half-dozen writers, whom Ami referred to as her in-house menagerie. The exact number of character actors depended upon whom Ami had recently dropped. Ami went through her B-list actors like other women went through cupcakes.

There was actually no such thing as a B-list. There was only the A-list and everybody else. Actors like Connor lived on a knife's edge. This fostered a justifiable paranoia, for most character actors were a single slip away from the long bus ride back to Indiana. Ami Chen was only too happy to show them the exit. She called these dismissals her release valve. Every agent in LA ingested a ton of refuse for every successful deal. Ami had once confessed that these firings granted her a momentary sense of power. Connor hoped Ami had shared this secret motivation as a means of telling Connor that he was somehow special. He, however, had never built up the courage to ask her.

Because his number was not identifiable, Connor's call was schlepped instantly to voice mail. This was standard practice in Hollywood, where there simply was no extra second available for the hordes of desperate outsiders. He identified himself, gave his new number, and then went back out to the parking lot. He could not find enough air in his room. Estelle was seated now in the little park behind the guesthouse, a large coffee set on the bench beside her. She glanced over, then away.

Five minutes of pacing, and then the phone rang. Gerald, Ami's assistant, said, "Is it really you?"

"Yes."

"Which of my four hundred messages and counting did you decide to respond to? I'm only wondering, since I've stubbed three fingers reaching out."

"I bolted. I panicked. I had to get out of LA before it was too late."

"Well, that's hardly the most *original* excuse I've ever heard."

"But it's the truth."

Gerald gave that a beat, then said, "When I couldn't find you, she *shouted* at me. I *hate* shouting."

"I'm sorry. Really."

"You sound like you mean it."

"I do."

"Then again, you're an actor. You're *paid* to sound genuine." There was a strident voice in the background; then Gerald said the words that formed the foundation to Connor's acting career. "Hold for Ami."

Ami Chen was a five-foot-three bundle of fierce intelligence and angry determination. She rammed her way through every blockade Hollywood's film world tried to put in her path. She was considered one of the top agents at making careers. Ami greeted Connor with "Explain why Gerald couldn't track you down."

Not a great one for casual conversation, his agent.

"I ran away," Connor repeated. "I didn't take my computer or my phone. I was too afraid they'd track me. Or that I'd contact Kali in a weak moment."

"Hold one." The line clicked off.

There were any number of reasons for this silence. The first time he had been in Ami's office, Connor had been overwhelmed by the sheer volume of her phone traffic. Ami's granite desk was the size of a small independent island-state and held five computer screens. Two of them were reserved for handling her phones. Gerald fielded all of Ami's calls, then passed those he deemed worthy to the monitor where she could point and click and connect. The neighboring screen held any intel or alert that Gerald might have received in the initial dialogue. Anyone who worked regularly with Ami Chen treated Gerald as a principal ally. Gerald earned more than any junior agent at CPP. It was why he remained in Ami's front office, despite the fact that his boss defined the term "difficult."

The calls Gerald decided to pass through were color-coded. The ones he thought Ami should take instantly were yellow, and those dealing with actual payment were white. Red calls were problems, always with notes attached on screen two. Blues were the ones she took if or when she had the time or felt bored. When Connor had asked what was used for personal calls, Gerald said there weren't enough of those to deserve a color.

The line clicked back on, and Ami demanded, "Are you marrying Kali Lyndon?"

"No."

"This is not some yo-yo exercise, a bit of last-minute jitters that struck in the lead-up to your wedding."

"No yo-yos, and surprisingly few jitters," Connor replied. "At least since I arrived here."

"And where exactly is this 'here' located?"

"A million miles from LA. Farther."

"Strange how you sound like you're in the next room."

"Believe me. I'm not."

Ami did not probe further. She was pure LA. She did not care about such minor issues as love or commitment. Her laser focus was aimed at just one thing.

The bottom line.

Ami was so quiet that Connor thought she had dropped his call. Then she said, "Thinking."

Connor took his phone back outside. Thankfully, Estelle had disappeared. He paced the length of the parking lot. Again.

Finally Ami said, "I have something to tell you."

Connor's heart dropped out of his chest, straight onto the pavement. Splat. He had actually heard Ami use those very words when dumping other actors. Twice. The first time, Connor had been seated in the narrow confines of Gerald's outer office. The second time was in a bar, the night she had confessed the acid pleasure found in such dismissals.

Connor said, "Go on, then."

Ami said, "You are being considered for the primary bad guy in the new James Bond film."

The strength drained from his legs so fast he landed on the pavement. The hand not holding his phone kept him from sprawling backward. "What?"

"It's not a done deal, but they're serious. You'll die, of course, but only after being on-screen for eighteen minutes. Possibly twenty-three, if they go with the script's current draft. They want the film to mark your big century of on-air demises. They think this can be used in the film's advance online promo."

"I thought . . . Never mind."

"You absolutely deserve what you thought I was going to tell you," Ami assured him. "You've been such a bad boy. Have you told Kali?"

"I've asked Erica to set up a call with her at three."

"Let me handle that."

"No . . . I . . . What?"

"I'll prep her PR first, convince them they can use this." Her voice tightened. "You just remember we haven't signed the deal yet."

"Ami, I don't understand a word of what you just said."

"What you're asking for is the kind of service reserved for my A-list. The clients who pay for my place in Bel Air."

"Ami, I haven't asked you for *anything.*"

"Which doesn't change the fact that you need to be handled. Now you apologize to Gerald."

"I already did."

"Do it again, this time with champagne, because Gerald is my handler. Which now makes him yours. So, darling, when Gerald calls, what will you do?"

"Answer the phone."

"Night or day, darling. Whatever he tells you to do, darling, treat it like it's a command straight from God."

It was only after Connor had spoken again with Gerald and sat there on the pavement beneath the steel-gray sky that he realized what Ami had called him.

His agent only had five darlings. Three of them had won Oscars.

CHAPTER 18

Connor left for the restaurant an hour and a half early. His room could no longer hold him. His mind was an electric jumble of conflicting thoughts and emotions. The only word to describe how he felt just then was, disjointed.

Here he was, running away from his life in LA. Only now he was also running from Estelle Rainier, a woman whose most threatening move was to ask questions about a woman Connor hardly knew.

For seven years, he had tried hard not to miss his music. It had been almost that long since Connor had even listened to his favorite artists, for fear of being dragged down into a hopeless reflection of his many wrong moves. Then he had played for much of the previous night, and the clearest impression Connor carried was the smile of thanks from his one-woman audience.

When he had climbed on that midnight bus, Connor thought he had walked away from acting, as well as his soon-to-be ex-fiancée.

But this morning, he had been terrified by the prospect of his agent dropping him. And now he was as excited about the possible Bond gig as anything in his recent life.

He was fleeing a public relations mockery of a wedding. But all he could think of was sharing another dawn with Sylvie.

He repeatedly told himself that the last thing he should be doing was involving himself with another woman. All the while, though, he was held by the memory of those beautiful crystal-gray eyes.

He hurried to a job that had nothing to do with the world he had come to call real. He had slept only a few hours. His eyes felt grainy and his feet hurt.

Still, he was genuinely eager to start his gig, waiting tables at Castaways.

Connor checked his watch. In precisely two hours, his agent would be on the phone *handling* the situation with his soon-to-be ex-fiancée.

Yet, all he could think about was seeing Sylvie again.

But how was that even possible? What was he going to tell her? Everything she thought about him was wrong, and the prospect of telling her who he really was filled his gut with leaden dismay.

That brought him to the greatest dilemma of all.

Connor had spent enough time in the woman's company to know the question that Sylvie most wanted to ask him.

Who was he really?

Connor had no idea how to respond.

Sylvie felt as though her day remained sheltered by Connor's quiet strength. The dawn walk had meant more than she could possibly have imagined. It had been a very long time since she had enjoyed that sense of companionship, where words were unnecessary, and the closeness of a man as natural as breath.

During her childhood, sunrise walks had framed Sylvie's happiest times with her mother. Her father often worked late into the night, sometimes falling into bed with the sunrise.

Mother and daughter had shared countless mornings, chasing gulls and sharing dreams.

Then toward the end, they had spent those hours arguing. Estelle had revealed her plans to leave on one such walk, a bitterly cold May morning with the Canadian foothills lost to a fog as thick as today's.

Sylvie checked her reflection, but saw most clearly the heartbroken girl in the months following her mother's departure, standing outside their ratty camper, knowing she was not strong enough to reknit the fabric of her family. She recalled the shocking sense of loss she had known, hearing Estelle speak about her need to leave them. That was the way her mother had described her state—as a *need.* Sylvie had not thought of that in years. Now it was as clear as the cry of gulls through her bedroom window. She remembered how frigid her tears felt on her cheeks. She remembered how it had started to snow, as though the world wept with her.

Sylvie could not say exactly when Fridays had become cleaning day. There was a certain logic to the timing, however. The weekends were always so rushed; neither the restaurant nor the kitchen was ever fully scrubbed. Monday was their one evening off. The normally slower Tuesdays and Wednesdays often felt as though they would never end. Sylvie spent most Thursdays at the local markets and taking their weekend deliveries. Friday afternoons, everyone showed up early. Carl prepared something special for the Castaways staff and filled the restaurant with the prospect of a fine meal. Today it would be a veal pot-au-feu with baby potatoes coated with olive oil and rosemary and sea salt, then oven roasted. The resulting exteriors were hard and crunchy, while the interiors were cottony and soft, and the flavor exploded with each bite. This was followed up with one of Sandy's trademark desserts, crème brûlée with chocolate-cinnamon biscotti.

Because the scouring took place every week, there was a settled, comfortable routine to it all. Even the brass railings to the outer doors and the bar and the hostess station, the least appealing of all the many jobs, were simply done and left behind. The new busboy's name was Gustavo, and he more or less took every task in his stride. Throughout the initial half hour, as Sylvie helped him remove grease from behind the main stove, she found herself humming snatches from Connor's melodies. He took some of her father's favorite melodies and formed a composite of the modern world. He sang from today's perspective. She could not say it any better than that. The years of not practicing showed in repeated off-key notes, but it had also embedded a rough burr, a sorrow that deepened the emotions. Made it . . .

When she paused to take a new reservation, Rick joined her at the hostess station and asked, "Is Connor coming?"

Sylvie answered, "I forgot to mention it."

Rick shrugged. "I think I met the real guy last night."

"'Real,'" she agreed, thinking that was the word she had been searching for. "You liked his music?"

Rick shrugged. "Not really."

She swiped his arm. "Liar."

"Bruno said it sounded like Whisky a Go Go, only at one-third speed."

"Maybe I was too hasty letting Bruno off the hook for those bad fish." They were both smiling as she said that.

"Are you going to keep Connor on waiting tables?"

The question surprised her. "Of course."

"I just wondered, you know."

"We can't begin to afford live entertainment. Phil would have a seizure."

"Old Phil," Rick said, mimicking Marcela.

"It would be great, you know . . ."

"If Connor could bring that heart to his work." Rick nodded. "I'll have a word with the guy."

* * *

Connor liked how his early arrival was greeted with the simple friendliness of being accepted. Sylvie explained that this was their day to give the entire restaurant a thorough going-over, then assigned him to scour the kitchen's four steel tables. The industrial-strength rubber gloves protected his hands, and the double aprons—one plastic over the white cotton—kept the cleanser from staining his clothes. He hated the acrid stench, but the work was soothing. He had worked all his life. Sometimes it felt as though the need for constant labor was embedded in his DNA. Nowadays when he returned home to Charlotte, his family always chided him for not working hard enough. As though hours of daily labor were the defining trait of a life well lived. His parents had been divorced for over fifteen years, and the restaurant was long gone, but they both still held to this core principle, as did Connor's brother and sister. None of them believed that his acting gigs were true work. They listened to his descriptions of the predawn calls and the weeks of living on four or five hours' sleep, the blistering lights and the acting classes and the rehearsals without pay, the heartbreak and misery that was the fate of most people striving to break in, the bitter jealousy that was the fodder for almost every actor on earth. They heard him out, but they did not believe him. Not really. He could see it in their gazes.

It wasn't that this work was easy, but it was defined. He had a job. He got on with it.

When he was done, he stripped off the gear, found himself a seat on the narrow patio, and ate at the wagon-wheel table with Sylvie and the others. He was one of the team. They joked with him about his choice of music. Bruno asked if he could add a couple of hip-hop numbers. Sandy asked if he knew any by David Bowie. Sylvie caught his eye twice and smiled.

The facts of his double life ate at Connor's heart like acid.

When they finished eating, Rick asked Connor if he'd like a cup of coffee. Something in the question caused all the others to rise and reenter the restaurant, including Sylvie. When they were alone and both cradled steaming white ceramic mugs, Rick said, "Are you sure you want to be a waiter?"

Connor felt that sudden inward jerk, like a corner of his secret covering had just been pried loose. "Of course I do. I'm here, aren't I?"

"Partly," Rick corrected. "You're *partly* here."

"What's that supposed to mean?"

"You're a smart guy. I think you already know."

Connor tasted the coffee, then set it down on the wagon wheel. The sun was half-hidden behind a corona of high clouds and the air held a biting chill. That was not why he shivered, though.

Rick gave him a chance to respond, then went on, "You don't bring enough of yourself to the table."

Connor found himself fighting back a sudden urge to confess, to tell the headwaiter in Sylvie's restaurant who he was, and what he faced. Instead, he clenched his teeth and swallowed it down.

Rick said, "You're going through the motions. You've got all the moves and none of the heart. You do what it takes to get the job done, and then you walk away. Which is fine, long as people are only interested in hearing the specials and getting their glasses filled and having a plate set down in front of them. But if they come looking for an experience they can share in, if they want a night they'll remember, if they want . . ."

Connor could almost see the words hanging in the air before his face. He finished the sentence in spite of himself. "The best life has to offer."

"We represent their entry to a world beyond normal," Rick agreed. "We put a face on their chance to escape the day-to-day."

Connor sensed that Rick had said all he intended. He was tempted to respond by sitting there, waiting the guy out. See how long Rick would let the silence drag out. The words welled up inside him again, stronger this time. Connor said, "I've spent seven years becoming an expert at going through the motions."

To his surprise, Rick seemed pleased by his response. "What, you think that somehow makes you unique?"

"I don't . . ."

"Someday I'll tell you about all the superficial moves I learned to make." Rick had an ancient's piercing gaze. "Was that true what you said, about being raised in a restaurant, your folks turning it into a battlefield?"

"Every word."

"Did it ever occur to you that's why you disconnect?" Rick rose from the table. "Maybe it's time you moved beyond the past. Try for something new. That's what brought you here, isn't it? The chance to start over?"

Connor opened his mouth, but no words came out.

"There's no future in repeating past mistakes." Rick gestured for Connor to join him. "Come on. It's opening time."

CHAPTER 19

Connor's new phone buzzed just as he was pouring wine for his first table. Connor almost dumped a full glass in the lady's lap. He brought their starters, excused himself, and walked outside. The phone's readout gave no name, and the caller had left no message. But only one person had this number. He hit redial, and Gerald answered on the first ring. "How soon can you get back to LA?"

"Tomorrow, I guess. If I have to."

"*Yes,* you have to. Do I strike you as somebody who would ask such a thing because I'm *curious?*"

"Okay, Gerald. Fine."

"Don't you *dare* give me that tone of voice. I have been *slaving* away for *hours.* Now I positively *must* know where you are."

Connor breathed the name. "Miramar."

"That sounds vaguely familiar."

"It's a small town on the central coast."

"Of course. I hear it's quite lovely. How long is the drive?"

"I have no idea. I came up here by Greyhound bus."

"How utterly *dramatic.* PR will positively *die.* I can see the next episode of the cable show now, an opening shot of you boarding the bus—"

"Gerald. Just. Stop." Then Connor heard the chuckle, and realized that had been Gerald's idea of a joke. Connor said, "I can't shoot you. I need you too much."

"Oh, please. You've got to give me my tiny shred of fun, all the trouble you're causing." There was the sound of typing. "The nearest airport is sixty-three miles away. How utterly primitive. All right. I'm sending a car. They'll be there at six o'clock tomorrow morning or I will *shoot* somebody."

"There's a Motel Six at the juncture of the 101 with the Miramar highway. I'll meet the driver out front. Have him ask for Mr. Smith."

"A Motel Six, my, we *are* slumming."

"Can I ask why I need to show up?"

"Ami has worked her magic. That's all I'm allowed to tell you. Ta ta, *darling.*"

When Connor turned around, Sylvie was standing in the restaurant's open doorway. "Everything all right?"

Connor found himself fighting the day's second urge to confess, this one even stronger. But there were customers to be served, and a wall of questions for which Connor had no answers. So he said, "I'm trying to cut off some loose ends."

She nodded, as though that made perfect sense. "Where are they, these loose ends?"

"Down in Los Angeles. I need to travel there tomorrow."

"Saturdays are often our busiest night. Can it wait?"

"No, Sylvie. I'm sorry. It can't."

She hesitated long enough for Connor to know the question before she asked, "Are you coming back?"

"As soon as I possibly can. I'll try and make it back before the restaurant opens tomorrow evening."

"It's a long way to go for a few hours."

"But the hours are important," he assured her. "Vital. If I can't make it back, I'll phone."

"All right, then." A hint of that special smile returned. "I have to cut you some slack after last night."

He did his best to return her smile, though it felt like the day's first lie. "Thank you."

"Only, now you owe me some serious time on the ivories." She gestured for him to follow her back inside. "We're talking hours."

Porter Wright came in a little after ten that evening. The place was winding down after a typically frantic Friday. The police chief wore his tan uniform, as rumpled as the man himself. He approached Sylvie's station, and whatever he said was enough to blanch her features ash-white. Connor tried not to stare, but he feared she was having another migraine attack.

Marcela followed him into the kitchen, where she explained, "The day you showed up, Bruno found ten kilos of coke. In a couple of our fish."

Connor said, "Get. Out."

"Eleven," Bruno corrected. He hammered his cleaver through a lamb shank and buried the blade into the chopping board. "Eleven keys."

Rick pushed through the doors and stopped by Marcela's other side. His expression said he knew what they were discussing. Marcela went on, saying, "The detective handling narcotics is a real piece of work. I think that's probably behind whatever just ruined the lady's night."

Connor asked, "Porter can't bring the detective into line?"

"Different forces," Rick replied. "Major crimes means the sheriff's department becomes involved."

Connor understood why they were having this conversation. "You want me to play for her again. No problem."

They showed genuine satisfaction. "Hold off until things settle down," Rick said.

Marcela said, "I'll finish your tables."

"Thanks. Listen, I may miss tomorrow's shift. I'm headed

down to LA. I'll try to make it back before Castaways opens, but I can't say for certain."

"Sylvie told us," Rick said. "She's arranged for an old pal to take up the slack."

Marcela tightened the distance. "Are you coming back?"

"Absolutely," Rick replied for Connor. "The man doesn't get away that easy."

Sylvie stepped through the doorway. Her features held to that uncommon tight cast. She said to Connor, "Porter wants to have a word."

Porter Wright offered a politician's greeting, cheery and loud enough to be heard by anybody listening, which was almost everyone. "How are you settling in, Connor?"

"Pretty well, thanks."

"Carol is still talking about you and that wine. Really made for a special night."

Marcela stepped up beside them. "Carol can do that all by herself."

"You got that right." Porter's gaze made a lie of his smile, hard and cautious. "Carol was so taken with you, she actually came up with a little gift all her very own."

Connor sensed there were actually two conversations taking place. "Really, Chief, it isn't necessary."

"First of all, I'm Porter to my friends. And second, did I say she'd given me any choice in the matter?" He turned to Sylvie and asked, "Mind if I borrow the gentleman for a minute?"

"Not long, please, we're busy." But there was a mechanical rote to Sylvie's words.

"I'll cover for him," Marcela said. She added to Connor, "See what happens when you bribe a cop?"

"Couple of minutes is all." As Porter passed Sylvie's station, he touched her arm and said quietly, "Remember what I said. You're not in this alone."

If Sylvie even heard him, she gave no sign.

Connor waited until they crossed the street, and entered an empty side lane, to ask, "What's going on with Sylvie?"

"That business is strictly between her and me," Porter replied, unlocking his cruiser and opening his door. "You should be thankful I'm so good at keeping secrets."

Connor slipped into the passenger seat, fairly certain he knew what was coming down the pipe. Even so, his gut took a swooping dive when Porter said, "Carol knows. She said to tell you, she won't be the one to let this particular cat out of the bag. But there's something you need to see."

Porter reached over, opened the glove compartment, and pulled out an iPad whose pink floral cover said it belonged either to his wife or daughter. "These gadgets are beyond me. But Carol said all I needed to do was turn it on and hit . . . Yeah, here we go."

Within three seconds of the screen flashing to life, Connor knew he saw his agent's work. On one hand, he had to admire it as a stroke of brilliance. On the other, it made him sick to his stomach to watch.

Kali Lyndon was at her styled and coiffed and manufactured best. Her rouged cheeks were adorned with tears that glistened like liquid jewels, which they were. Those tears were a special blend of glycerin and microscopic flecks of diamond dust to catch the spotlights.

She was, Connor had to admit, one stunning and alluring lady. Kali was a modern combination of inherited money, daily trainers, and cosmetic surgery. Rich, fit, and voluptuous.

Her eyes were the giveaway. They were a lovely shade of lavender gray, thanks to special tinted lenses. But there was nothing all the specialists and handlers could do about the empty space down deep. Connor stared into that beautiful face and thought of Rick's words out by the wagon-wheel table. He wondered if his own eyes held any more life or heat than Kali's.

Peyton Stein, the cable lollipop, said, "Kali, you've just received word that Connor Larkin has run away from the marriage. How does that make you feel?"

Kali's response was interrupted twice for practiced sobs. When the camera shifted on the second to show Peyton offering a tissue and a sympathetic look, Connor chuckled.

Preston said, "Your fiancée is working on a broken heart and you're laughing?"

Connor replied, "There's no way Kali could have gotten through that much dialogue in one take."

"Wait, you mean this was rehearsed?"

"And still she missed her cue. So they cut over to Peyton. It gives them the chance to keep what she got right and reshoot the rest."

"Man, that is just cold."

"You have no idea."

Kali was saying, "I know if I could just have ten minutes with Connor, even five, I could change his heart."

Peyton said, "You mean, change his mind, don't you, Kali?"

"His heart has to rule this decision," Kali replied. "No matter how afraid he might be, if he truly loves me . . ."

"And if he doesn't, Kali?"

"He loves me."

"But what can you do? Connor Larkin has *run away.*"

Porter said, "Here's what Carol wanted you to see."

Kali said, "I'm offering a hundred-thousand-dollar reward to anyone who helps me locate my Connor."

They bounced that ball back and forth a couple of times. Connor thought Peyton's shock over the reward was totally overdone, especially when they flashed a phone number at the bottom of the screen. This told anyone with half a brain that the whole deal had been set up in advance.

When the segment ended, Porter stowed the device back in the glove box. "I'd give a moth landing on a bug zapper better odds than you."

"The wheels are grinding down in LA," Connor replied, and gave a swift recap of what had happened earlier that day.

Porter shook his head. "Hollywood might as well be circling out there beyond Neptune."

"A car's picking me up at six tomorrow morning from the Motel Six."

"Might be a good idea if you let me take you there tonight. I'll drive you up and book the room, so there won't be any questions from the front desk."

"I'll pay you back."

"You better believe you're paying."

Connor thought of his promise to play for Sylvie. "It could be late before I'm done here tonight."

"No problem. I'm on duty till four." Porter slipped a card from his pocket and passed it over. "Call me when you're ready."

CHAPTER 20

After closing, Connor hung around and played a few tunes. But his thoughts were two hundred and thirty miles to the south. He felt like the lyrics were just lies set to music. Finally Connor stopped playing, but remained where he was, because Sylvie moved over from the bar and settled onto the bench beside him. She sat there, staring at the empty keys where his hands had been, and asked once more, "Will I see you again?"

"Yes."

"You're not just going to vanish in a puff of LA haze."

"I told you. I plan to work tomorrow's shift. Otherwise, I'll call."

Sylvie responded by wrapping one arm around his waist and settling her head on his shoulder. Connor smelled a mix of fragrances in her hair, long hours and restaurant flavors and a hint of old perfume. Her warmth was as exquisite as her scent. "Have you written any songs of your own?"

"A few. But before I quit playing, I was thinking I'd like to take hits from the seventies, eighties, and nineties and rework them in a sort of signature swing."

Swing purists loathed the very idea. The few times Connor had mentioned it, they had called him a traitor to the cause. He had not spoken of it in years.

All Sylvie said was "You should never let go of your dream."

Connor turned to her, hoping to find some way to say how deeply those words touched him. He was met by her rich gray gaze, deep enough for him to dive into and just keep falling.

Kissing her was the most natural thing Connor had done in a very long while.

The moment felt so right as it happened.

And so utterly, terribly wrong the instant it was over.

Connor gently pried himself off the bench. "I have to go."

"Really?"

"Yes. Now." He crossed the restaurant and unlocked the door. "Good night, Sylvie."

Connor packed an overnight bag, phoned the chief, then crossed the parking lot and knocked on Estelle's door. Soon as she appeared, he knew Estelle had not been asleep, and that he was right to come.

Connor told her, "Your daughter is one of the finest people I have ever met."

Estelle pushed open the door. "Come in and tell me why."

"No, Estelle."

"Connor, *please.*"

"*No!*" His pent-up frustration pushed her back a step. "Estelle, you need to *go to her.*"

"I can't."

"You can't let this chance slip away! Sylvie is going through a really rough time. She *needs* you!"

"I'll only make it worse."

Her tears forced Connor to gentle his tone. "Maybe. But you need to take that chance. For both of you."

Estelle wiped her face. "There's a policeman watching us."

Connor picked up his satchel and stepped back. "Promise me you'll speak to her."

"I'll . . . try."

Connor stood there until she shut and locked her door. He walked over to where Porter stood by his car. "Thanks again for doing this."

"No problem." When they were both seated in the cruiser, Porter asked, "Want to tell me what that was about?"

"No." Connor looked back to where the light framed Estelle's window. "Definitely not."

Porter started the engine and pulled from the lot. "Strange way for you to repay a kindness. Refusing to tell an officer of the law something he might need to know about."

Connor responded, "What did you tell Sylvie that got her so upset tonight?"

"That was a highly confidential matter, and none of your business."

Connor waited.

"Are you suggesting that the chief of police trade information with a man he knows to be operating under false pretenses?"

"Absolutely."

Porter took the valley road out of town. "You first."

"Her name is Estelle Rainier," Connor said. "She's Sylvie's mother."

The road dipped and weaved through the night. "I know I've heard something about that lady. . . ."

"Estelle abandoned them when Sylvie was a kid. They haven't spoken in nineteen years."

Porter swung the cruiser over the final rise, then descended into the farm valley. The fields stretched out to the distant moonlit hills. "Does Sylvie know the lady is here?"

"No. Estelle is afraid to approach her. This, after hiring a detective to find Sylvie."

Porter glanced over. "How'd you get in the middle of that one?"

"I have no idea."

Porter's laugh was a soft, comforting rumble. "You're here in town, what, all of . . ."

"Three days," Connor replied. "Give or take an hour."

"You got a job you don't need—"

"I need it," Connor corrected. "Desperately."

"You're in tight with a girl you *definitely* don't need. . . ."

Connor knew Porter was waiting for a comeback, but he had no idea how to respond.

Connor's silence only made the chief laugh once more. "Now the lady's mother is *all over* your case."

"She knows who I really am," Connor said. "Estelle hasn't said anything, but I'm positive she knew from the first moment we spoke."

Porter's laughter bounced around the car. "Carol is going to die, she missed all this."

"You forgot getting rousted by the chief of police," Connor said. "Sort of."

This only made Porter laugh harder. "There ain't no such thing as a sort-of roust. Not with me."

"Your turn," Connor said.

The chief went quiet, then, "You heard about them finding drugs?"

"Eleven keys in the fish," Connor said. "I heard."

"The detective handling the case is not high on my list of good people."

"So I've been told."

"Yeah, well, he's convinced the county prosecutor they should treat Sylvie as their prime suspect. He insists the trawler in question was using Castaways as a conduit for dealers operating around Santa Cruz and Paso Robles."

"You have got to be kidding me."

"I wish. But given the restaurant's history and Sylvie's own past . . . Did she tell you about her upbringing?"

"A little."

"Her dad was arrested a number of times for trespassing, probably parked that old camper on private property and left it there long enough for the owners to bring in the law. Sylvie's got her own sheet—but because she was a minor, it's all sealed. But the records do show how the county repeatedly tried to put her in foster care. There were a couple of court cases, finally dropped because she was fierce about staying up with her schoolwork."

Connor rubbed the sore point over his heart. "She is one amazing lady."

"You got that right." Porter kneaded the steering wheel with two massive fists. "I'd like to wring that detective's neck."

"You told her tonight about the possible arrest warrant because you want her to go ahead and hire a lawyer," Connor guessed. "Which Sylvie can't afford."

"That pretty much sums it up," Porter agreed.

Connor looked back through the wire-mesh screen, out to where the road disappeared over the rise. "There's too much of everything in your town."

Porter glanced over, but he did not speak.

"Too much honesty," Connor went on. "Too many raw emotions. Too many blows coming out of nowhere." Connor turned back around. "Too many reasons to care."

"Welcome to Miramar." Porter slipped into the motel's forecourt and cut the motor. "That's my town in a nutshell."

"Thanks again," Connor said. "For everything."

Porter jerked his chin toward the entrance. "Everything's set up. They've accepted the same story as the Miramar guesthouse because it came from me. You've lost your wallet, you'll be paying cash." As Connor rose from the car, Porter said, "You have to tell Sylvie who you are."

"I know."

"And soon," Porter insisted. "Sylvie needs to hear this from you."

Connor shut his door, then said through the open window, "She's lucky to have you for a friend."

Porter took that as the farewell, nodded, and put the car into gear. Connor stood there as the cruiser pulled out of the lot.

Trucks rumbled along the highway, pulling him away from Miramar. All the people he was coming to call friends. Most especially a woman who deserved to learn the truth about the man she kissed. The mysteries and the questions. All of it belonged to a haven he wished he could stay in a little longer. And come to call his own.

CHAPTER 21

After tossing and turning for a futile hour, Connor rose from his Motel 6 bed and went downstairs to the guests' laundry room. He had once found great comfort in sitting and watching the machines. Tonight, however, the steady rhythm only reflected his churning thoughts. He carried his clean clothes back upstairs and ironed the jeans and T-shirt he intended to wear for the journey south. Finally, around two, he lay back down and eventually drifted away. His dreams were fractured glimpses of a woman's lovely gaze, and lips he probably should never have tasted. But which he yearned to kiss again.

Connor was in the Motel 6 lobby at a quarter to six. After so many disjointed nights, his eyes felt grainy and his thoughts muffled. The night clerk was handing over to his replacement, and their happy chatter drilled at his brain. He stepped through the sliding glass doors into the frigid dawn. He was wondering if he might wake up before he froze, when the car pulled into the lot.

The sight brought both clerks outside. The night clerk was

hefty and the girl on dayshift was a slender waif, both were in their twenties, and both completely agog at Connor's ride.

The guy said, "Is that a *Rolls*?"

"A 1956 Silver Cloud," Connor confirmed. Kali's people had selected it as the car to take her to church, and then launch them into their honeymoon.

The girl said, "That car is bigger than my apartment."

The guy said, "I didn't know they made cars that white."

The girl said, "Are you, like, famous?"

The guy said, "When that cop dropped you off last night, I thought, you know, we had a serious criminal on our hands."

The girl said, "Oh, come on. The Mafia comes to Miramar? Please."

The driver rose from the car and asked, "Is one of you a Mister Smith?"

"That would be me," Connor said.

"Sorry to keep you waiting, sir." The chauffeur scampered around to open his door. "We better get started. You're due on set in less than five hours."

As Connor slipped into the rear seat, the girl said, "Happy trails."

CHAPTER 22

A script in the traditional blue cover embossed with the CPP logo was waiting for Connor. The seat was softest ivory leather piped in gray. The carpet was matching gray silk velvet. There was enough legroom for Connor to stretch out fully. The front seat was backed by a full bar, each item carefully nestled in padded holders. Beside the sterling silver ice bucket was a rack holding bottles of single-malt whisky, signature vodka, Puerto Rican rum, and six hand-cut crystal glasses. The fridge held minis of soft drinks and fruit juices. Connor opened the panel next to the fridge and found a cheese plate, a fruit bowl, and seven sandwiches with rare roast beef and creamed horseradish on rye.

Connor selected one of the sandwiches and poured himself a mug of coffee from the silver thermos. He opened the script and began to read. He went through it slowly and finished in twenty-five minutes. There was a handwritten note on the last page that read, *Phone as soon as you're done, Gerald.*

Connor asked the driver, "Can I borrow a pen?"

"There should be one in the armrest, sir. Along with a lapel mic and battery pack."

"So there is." Connor started over, this time working out his part's tempo and emotional bearing. After the third reading, Connor was ready to make the call.

When Gerald answered, Connor said, "The bridal Rolls? Really?"

Gerald revealed a laugh like a stork. Ack-ack-ack-ack. "I *so* wish I could have seen your face."

"At least you didn't order them to tape white ribbons running along the hood."

"I *tried,* believe me, but the company said the wind would tear them apart. I was *very* disappointed."

Connor asked, "Did you write this script?"

"Well, I *had* to. What they sent over was such *drivel.*"

"This is actually very good."

"Now you're making fun of me."

"I'm serious. You've given me a solid set of lines here. The emotional cadence is steady and builds to a genuine crescendo. You ever want a job writing for soaps, let me know. I'll introduce you to my agent."

"Ha. Ha. This is me, not laughing."

"Really, Gerald. Good work."

The genuine compliment left Ami Chen's assistant at a loss for words. He cleared his throat, then said, "Yes, well. There's a downside to all this, I'm afraid."

"Go on, then."

"The episode is going out live."

Connor leaned back in his seat. It all made sense now. The Rolls had been sent so he would show up for his final act in the limo that would have carried them from the ceremony. The script, the urgency, it all came down to this.

Gerald said, "Helloooo?"

Connor replied, "This is actually a very good thing."

"I'm sorry. There must be a problem with this connection. I thought you just said—"

"It means we do this in one go. No outs, no reworks. I don't have to repeatedly dredge up these emotions for all the takes Kali usually requires."

"Ami said you would like it. I didn't believe her. Kali's people shrieked so loud they set dogs to howling in Tijuana."

"I can imagine."

"The cable people are *swarming*. But really, the *attention* this is getting. The Internet has been on *fire*."

"I think I should go in raw," Connor said. "No makeup, no hair, no rehearsals."

Gerald mulled that over. "What are you wearing?"

"T-shirt, jeans, rope belt, canvas boots."

Gerald played the stork again. Ack-ack-ack-ack. "Kali's people will need oxygen and those paddle thingies to restart what passes for their hearts."

"Tell them my rough state will heighten the impact of my lines. Also, it will show how we were never really meant to be together."

"The perfectly groomed lady and the gardener." Ack-ack-ack-ack.

"Is that a yes?"

"I probably shouldn't say this, but it will be a *pleasure*. You have no idea what a *pain* they have been."

Actually, Connor knew all too well. "Gerald, I owe you big time."

"I have a penchant for vintage champagne and lavender roses. Four dozen is a nice round number."

"I was thinking," Connor replied, "that it makes up for making me show up in this bridal boat."

Ack-ack-ack-ack. Gerald hung up, still laughing.

CHAPTER 23

Sylvie rose early Saturday and went for another walk along the shoreline path. The lane was crowded today with weekend joggers and cyclists, many of whom puffed out greetings as they passed. Sylvie recognized the faces from her clientele. The day was crystal clear, the sky a pale wash of porcelain blue. Sylvie spent much of the walk telling herself that she should not miss Connor quite so much as she did. She tried not to worry over whatever mystery errand had taken him down to LA, or how it might keep him there.

When she returned home, Sylvie made a fresh pot of coffee and opened her treasure chest. The box had been a gift from Rick and Marcela to mark the restaurant's first anniversary. It remained one of her most cherished possessions. The proper name was a Victorian travel writing desk, and it had been designed for use by adventurers exploring the world's far-flung reaches. The top was slanted and covered with an inlaid leather pad. The front folded out to reveal an inkstand and letter holder. One interior drawer held recipes, the other articles on wines and spices. The larger central space beneath the lid contained ideas for redesigning the restaurant's interior and menus from other restaurants she admired.

She had planned to spend the hours as she often did on Saturdays, leafing through her clippings and printouts of menus, working up a new rendition all her very own. She had a leather-bound notebook where she jotted down ideas, fashioning them over weeks and months until she was ready to spring them on her kitchen staff. Carl was the perfect sounding board. He listened well, remembered everything, and rarely commented with more than a nod. Then he would work through the idea and try it on the staff. Together they would incorporate these comments; and if it worked, they would present it as a weekly special.

Her mind kept returning, though, to that vile detective and the prospect of being brought up on charges of smuggling drugs. She hated the resulting sense of helplessness, how little of this was under her control. She had no choice but to wait it out, and hope for the best. The longer she sat there, the more the cloud grew, skulking dark and heavy on her mental horizon.

Finally she stowed away her half-formed recipes and touched the interior sidewall. It gave a little click and came free in her hand, revealing the box's secret compartment. For the first time in nine months, Sylvie pulled out the bundle of pages folded and tied with a lavender silk ribbon. She had started this wish list as a child. Sylvie loved Miramar, and had no intention of ever living anywhere else. However, she was still her father's child, and the urge to wander remained strong within her.

But she did not want to travel alone.

Her father's company had made the road their friend. She wanted this again. She wanted to journey with someone who shared her hunger for new horizons. She wanted . . .

She unfolded one of the oldest items, a stained and faded pamphlet for Machu Picchu, the mystical ruins in the Peruvian Andes. The words were barely legible now, but it did not matter. She could recite the entire brochure from memory. She turned the fragile pages, and thought how nice it might be to share this dream with Connor.

As she retied her ribbon and refit the wooden sleeve over the secret compartment, Sylvie smiled over the recollection of Connor's kiss.

Sylvie had been astonished by how good it had felt.

How rich the flavor of his lips had been.

How she wanted to taste him again.

How she could still feel the strength of his arms as he held her.

How much she wanted to have him hold her again.

And never let her go.

CHAPTER 24

Connor ran through the script a final time; then he stretched out on the backseat. He assumed the dread prospect of what awaited him at the end of this ridiculous journey would keep him awake, but the interrupted nights and hard work and emotional upheaval that had led up to this moment served as a balm. He was asleep in the space of three breaths.

He dreamed of walking along the Miramar shoreline with Sylvie. It was the same as their time together, only much richer. In his dream, they had been doing this for years, sharing hundreds of dawns. Thousands. He talked about himself and his latest acting gig. He shared from one heart; she received with the same heart. They were that bound together.

He was jerked from the dream by the sound of his phone buzzing. Connor fumbled and pushed himself upright, then dry scrubbed his face and struggled to fit his fractured world back together. The luxurious Rolls-Royce and the silent driver and the script on the velvet carpet all seemed tawdry.

The phone went silent. Connor poured himself a cup of coffee. The dream had seemed so real; the loss of connection to

Sylvie left his chest hollow. He tried to tell himself that it was impossible to miss this woman, especially with everything he had waiting for him in LA. However, the dream's impact would not be denied.

When the phone started buzzing again, Connor saw Gerald's number, hit the connection, and complained, "You just woke me from the best sleep of the week."

"Don't you *dare* take that tone of voice. Kali has been running around here *screaming* at people. I *hate* when people scream. That woman has *such* a voice."

"Tell me."

"And the *language*. Between her and the director and that Peyton, I was blushing."

"You're enjoying this," Connor stated.

"Oh, all right. This is actually more fun than Mardi Gras. But don't tell anybody I said that." Gerald released another of his trademark laughs. Ack-ack-ack-ack. "When I told Tony what you were wearing, his shriek broke windows in Burbank."

Tony was the show's director. Peyton and Kali both adored him. The behind-camera crew referred to him as Tony the Toad.

Gerald asked, "How far away are you?"

Connor leaned forward and passed on the question, then told Gerald, "The car's GPS says thirty-two minutes."

Gerald asked, "Some cable executive paraded through here half an hour ago. She claimed we are about to knock *Days of Our Lives* off its ratings perch. I thought Tony was going to have a hernia."

"Sorry I missed that."

"Well, at least you'll be here for the main event." Gerald played the stork a final time, and cut the connection.

Connor opened the central armrest and clipped the mic to the inside of his shirt's lapel, ran the wire down next to his skin, then slipped the battery pack into his back pocket. There was also a fold-out cosmetic mirror, which revealed an uneven two-day growth the color of sunlight through honey. It turned Connor's cheeks as cavernous as his eyes. His hair was tousled; and when sunlight glanced through the side window, he winced. Connor folded the mirror away and poured himself another cup of coffee. He decided his appearance fit the role perfectly.

Kali Lyndon's father had been a nondescript gentleman who wore his pin-striped suits even at the family dinner table. He had lived in the shadows, shunned publicity, and never had anything bad to say about his only child. Kali's mother died when she was seven, and she was raised by a variety of nannies. Her father's empire continued to grow, even after he confessed he wasn't sure why he felt a need to make more money than he would ever spend. They lived in a fine house in a nice area of St Louis. Her father moved in the circles of power when he was forced to, but he preferred to send his associates and remain the quiet, unassuming man he was. He died of heart failure when Kali was nineteen. At that point, his closely held empire of hotels and shopping centers was estimated to be worth over four billion dollars. He left everything to his beloved daughter.

Kali's attendance at the board of directors' annual meeting remained her only contact with the business her father had built.

So long as Connor played second lead to Kali's star, they actually got on great. Connor found her funny and endearing. He ignored her temper tantrums with the same deaf ease he had shown to any number of stars on set. Kali had never met anyone like him. She claimed Connor was the first man who could handle her. Connor thought it might be at least partly true.

Kali Lyndon's world revolved around playing the poor little rich girl. She was seen and photographed at every star-studded opening. She did the latest, wore the finest, was friends with the hippest. She shone for the cameras. But Kali had a problem. She needed to be fed her lines. So long as she was scripted, Kali was in her element.

Which was how her publicity machine came up with the idea for this wedding.

A fake reality show.

The cable network ate it up.

Kali's estate fronted the coveted ninth green of the Bel-Air Country Club golf course. Her home was nestled in three and a half acres of meticulous gardens and fountains and four swimming pools. The mansion itself covered twenty-three thousand square feet and had four turrets. In addition, there were six garages, a poolhouse, two guest cabanas, and servants' quarters. When asked why a single lady needed such a big place, Kali gave one of three stock answers. Because I can. Because it's fun. Or her favorite, I like getting lost and discovering rooms I've never seen before.

The camera crew and tech support and Tony the Toad were clustered just outside the mansion's main gates. Connor stowed the script away, slipped over to the side facing the cameras, and put on his game face.

Showtime.

EXT. GATES TO KALI'S ESTATE. DAY.

ESTABLISHING SHOT: The pale stone wall extends in both directions, topped by black steel spikes. The only entry is a pair of tall metal gates embossed with the initials, KL. The gates are closed. Two UNI-FORMED GUARDS stand by the pillars.

The white Rolls-Royce bearing CONNOR LARKIN pulls up to the gates. Connor's face is visible through the open rear window.

CONNOR
I'm here to see Kali. My name—

GUARD ONE
I know who you are.

Guard One pulls a phone from his pocket. His eyes never leave Connor as he speed-dials a number and speaks softly.

GUARD TWO
Being that stupid is a crime, right?

Guard One cuts the connection and uses a key to open the gates.

GUARD ONE
Some states it's a felony.

The Rolls pulls slowly through the gates.

CLOSE-UP on Connor's face. His expression says this is exactly the reception he deserves.

INT. KALI LYNDON'S OFFICE. DAY.

KALI LYNDON sits at her desk. She is dressed in pastel tights and a pale yellow off-the-shoulder sweatshirt. She looks beautiful, tragic, and utterly vulnerable. A tear rolls down one cheek.

Kali is writing, or at least trying to write. Before her rises a vast pile of engraved wedding acceptances.

CLOSE-UP *handwritten on the card directly in front of Kali are the words GIFT: ANTIQUE SILVER SERVICE.*

Kali's hand holds a silver pen. She has written a few words on a sheet of her personal stationery, but now she is halted by sorrow.

KALI (VOICE-OVER)
Dear Clarissa, Thank you so much for the lovely gift, which unfortunately I must return because Connor and I . . .

The voice stops where her hand has frozen.

CLOSE-UP *as a tear falls onto the unfinished letter.*

INT. ENTRANCE TO KALI'S OFFICE. DAY.

ERICA, *Kali's private secretary, knocks on the open door.*

ERICA
He's here.

Connor's arrival was tracked by a platoon led by Tony the Toad. The cinematographer was on point, aiming his Steadicam at Connor's face. The second cameraman was hidden behind the left-hand column, tracking the Rolls and showing what Connor saw, the house and the grounds and all the wealth he was walking away from.

Outside the camera's view, everything was in frantic motion. Working on so-called reality television meant learning how to ignore the sound boom hovering overhead and tracking his every motion, the constantly shifting lights, the assistants handling the cables and running interference on Tony the Toad, who was busy hissing into his radio and waving his hands at everybody, especially Connor.

The Rolls pulled around the circular drive and halted by the bottom step. On cue, Kali's latest assistant opened the massive front door and stepped onto the veranda. As Connor rose from the limo, the Steadicam operator shifted position so as to show . . .

A catering truck was parked between the main house and the garages built to look like French stables. Beyond them, a work crew was busy dismantling the wedding tent. At a hysterical cue from Tony, the entire catering staff froze in the process of loading bottles and glasses and silverware back into the truck. They all turned and glared at Connor.

From her position on the top step, Erica greeted Connor with a volcanic scowl. When he reached the top step, she wheeled about and led him through the manor's open door.

The third camera guy and the assistant sound guy and their assistants were all on position just inside the portal. Connor stopped midway across the inlaid granite and marble floor, when his foot hit the piece of tape with his name on it. He gave Kali's palace and the life he was throwing away a long, slow look. This allowed the two outside cameras and their teams to rush around the side of the house, fly through the kitchen door, and tiptoe into positions. At another bat-wing motion from Tony, Connor turned to the sweeping staircase and Erica's burning gaze.

Erica's smoldering walk along the upstairs hall was tracked by camera two. Connor followed at a slower pace, holding to the beat structure laid out in the script. His every step was duplicated by a change of camera angle. One step, a survey of the idyllic life he was tossing aside. Another step, back to the camera focused on his face, close-up on the expression of a man wracked by doubt and regret. Connor had no trouble showing those emotions. They were exactly what he was feeling—only not for the reasons the audience expected.

A final close-up on his face, building on the tension and the guilt and the uncertainty, and then Connor stepped past the assistant's blistering glare and stepped through Kali's office doorway.

The Steadicam operator nudged Connor's ankle, and he shifted slightly to the left, allowing the guy to get a full-on shot of Kali almost falling apart. She made a huge effort, maintained a shred of control, and uttered her first line:

"Why, darling? Why?"

CHAPTER 25

The three mics taped to the ceiling of Kali's office looked to Connor like giant black caterpillars. Metal light-stands stood in both corners behind Connor, bathing Kali in perfect illumination. One cameraman crouched by the window. Another stood on a mini-ladder and shot over Connor's shoulder. Cables snaked all over the floor. Tony the Toad raced back and forth between watching the shoot through the open office doorway and studying the monitors stationed in the guest room next door.

Connor knew his shoddy, sleepless state heightened Kali's polished beauty. It suggested that he and Kali had already broken apart, and really they'd had no business being together in the first place. This was the structure of good drama, where the setting amplified the action and the dialogue.

Connor's lines confirmed what his presence already revealed. He was not good enough for Kali. He could never live up to her expectations. He wished her happiness. He hoped she found the man she deserved. . . .

Despite the crowd and the lights and the hollowness of breaking up for the cameras, Connor thought the drama carried a solid punch.

Like most experienced television actors, Connor had developed a mental clock with a precise second-by-second counter. He could also see when Kali forgot the last bit of dialogue she was supposed to deliver before they left the office. As a result, he completed his line by inserting the first word of her own. In response, she flashed him a tiny hint of the mischievous Kali, the lady who in private moments had referred to the reality charade as a playtime for adults. He had always been genuinely fond of her spirit, and seeing it now added an extra spice to their final exchange. As they left the office hand in hand, and walked the hall and down the stairs and across the palatial foyer, Connor sensed that the entire team was delighted.

They arrived outside the front door within five or six seconds of perfect. Connor had hoped they might have a private moment, but it was not to be. The second and third camera crews had slipped out the side entry and were now ready to track his departure.

The Rolls was gone. His satchel sat forlornly in the middle of the drive.

This was definitely not scripted.

That could only mean they had intended to catch his surprise on live camera. The significance was clear enough. Connor had arrived care of Kali's money. He left on his own steam.

Tony the Toad at work.

Connor gave them five seconds to register his shock for the audience, then turned and looked up to where Kali stood on the top step. He gave his final lines, "Good-bye, Kali. I'm sorry."

"I'm sorry, too. More than you will ever know."

The script had him descending the stairs and walking to the car, where he was to pause for a final, sorrowful glance at the woman and the wealth and the life. Then the camera was to track the car to the gates, pausing there for the guards to offer a caustic farewell. Connor figured it would work just as well if he hoofed it.

Kali, though, interrupted the beat structure by going totally off grid. "Connor, wait."

The sound technician had already started descending the stairs with Connor, and he swung the boom back fast enough to have taken off somebody's head. With a rare flash of genuine emotion, Kali said, "Tell me *why!*"

Connor was enough of a pro to give the Steadicam operator time to get them both back in frame. He replied, "This is me, Kali."

"I *know* that."

"No. You know the me I was for you. But *this* is me. And the truth is, I don't belong in your scene."

"You said you loved it!"

"I did, for a night. Or a weekend. But all of this, the house, the PR machine, the parties, the people—I just don't fit."

"I could change!"

He had to smile. "I believe you would."

"Really, I mean it."

"For a night, sure. Or a weekend. But for good? Kali, I want the life your dad loved."

That stopped her cold.

"The small town. The real people. The simple life."

"You'll stop acting?"

"Not unless I have to. Your dad stayed a businessman. I hope I can do this, too. Hold on to some kind of balance."

Kali struggled with that. "Why are you only telling me now?"

"I just figured it out. That's what came from running away."
He climbed back up the steps and kissed her cheek. He tasted
salt, and realized these latest tears were real. "Good-bye, Kali.
Be happy."

Tony the Toad said, "And we are off air."

CHAPTER 26

As they approached the Saturday afternoon opening time, Sylvie became filled with the sense of a storm building beyond the horizon. She knew from her GP that some patients with migraines had attacks whenever there was a big low coming. Apparently, the most sensitive patients were so impacted by changes in atmospheric pressure they could not get on a plane. Thankfully, this had never been an issue for her. Imagine predicting bad weather with a headache. Even so, Sylvie repeatedly checked the horizon as she prepared for work. But the sky remained blue, the wind mild and off the sea.

It was only when she arrived downstairs that she realized how right she had been about an approaching tempest.

Two of them.

Porter was seated at the otherwise empty bar, cradling a kitchen mug with his two scarred hands. Rick and Marcela stood together on the bar's other side, as though they needed one another's company. They all three shared the expression of funeral directors waiting to greet the recently bereaved.

Sandy came bustling in from the kitchen, bearing a plate of

fresh pastries. "They're called petticoat tails. Don't ask me why. My mother swore by them. Said there wasn't a thing that couldn't be put straight by a few of these and a proper cuppa."

"Nix on the tea," Rick said. He reached under the bar and brought out what Sylvie referred to as her hidden stash, a bottle of sixty-year-old Bas-Armágnac she'd found during the renovations. He set a snifter on the bar and poured a liberal splash. "Sylvie, come sit. Now drink."

"That's meant for celebration," she replied.

"The lad's right," Sandy said, pushing the plate toward her, "and have a few of these to mop up the alcohol."

"I'm not the least bit hungry."

Marcela said, "Eat."

Sylvie knew she had no choice, not really. They carried bad news, something so terrible she needed to be dosed. One look at their collective expression convinced her that resistance was futile.

She tossed back the Armagnac and ate two of the tails, or whatever they were. The brandy drew a line of liquid fire down her throat. "All right. Tell me."

Porter waited until Rick refilled her snifter. Then he said, "The prosecutor is bringing formal charges against you. I convinced them to let me bring you in for the arrest and arraignment on Monday, rather than create a scene here. Possession with intent."

Sylvie was very glad for the stool's support. "That's insane."

"They've come up with nothing that will hold up in court," Rick agreed. "Not a single definite lead. This is a face-saving measure. They have to know they can't bring a verdict against you."

"But if I'm indicted I'll be tried and convicted in the court of public opinion," Sylvie protested.

"If people around here didn't care for you as much as they did, I might agree," Porter said. "As it is, this town will definitely think otherwise."

"This is awful."

"It's not good." Rick unbuttoned his shirt pocket and drew out a sheet of paper. "Officially, Porter can't recommend a lawyer."

"Rick . . ."

"Hear me out." He unfolded the sheet and flattened it on the bar between them. "These three are the region's best defense attorneys. I have it on best authority."

Sandy said, "A gutter brawler in your corner is just the ticket."

Rick went on. "I've had an unofficial word with all three. You need to contact them tomorrow. They'll take your call, despite it being a Sunday. Make your choice and sign them on."

Sylvie asked weakly, "How much?"

"All of them ask about the same," Rick replied. "I know because I checked. They'll want a retainer of twenty thousand and another fifty if you go to trial. Which, in my opinion, you won't. Not if you come into the initial arraignment with your guns blazing."

Sylvie pressed both hands to her middle. There were only two places where she could get that kind of cash. Neither was the least bit appealing.

She had falsely assumed such bad times were relegated to her past. Things were different now. She was a citizen of the town she loved. She cared for the town and the people. Somehow that should have been enough to protect her from this sort of calamity. Because that was what it was, really. Everything she made went to paying off the loans she had taken out to first buy and then renovate this beautiful place, her restaurant.

Now she just might lose it.

She realized with a start that they were all silent. Waiting. Sylvie took her time, inspecting each face in turn. It turned out to have been the exact right thing to do at that moment. There in their expressions was the confirmation of all the rightness this place held for her: the caring concern, the friendship, the offering of strength when she was at her weakest.

It granted Sylvie the ability to say, in all truthfulness, "I'll find a way through this."

"Of course you will," Marcela said. "And we'll help."

Sylvie told herself it was utterly unbecoming for a boss to break down and weep, especially in front of the police chief and three of her employees. "I can't tell you what this means. But I couldn't possibly ask you . . ."

"One step at a time," Porter said. "Choose your attorney. Get them up to speed."

"I don't know what to say."

"Good," Marcela said. "At least that's settled."

"Done and dusted," Sandy agreed.

Rick tapped the rim of the snifter with one fingernail, making it ting. "Now get ready for round two."

"What?"

Marcela nudged the glass closer. "Drink."

The only sensation Sylvie had from the two stiff brandies was a muffled distance from her surroundings. She observed the fact that she could not stop leaking tears. She saw how the grim demeanor they shared only grew more severe. The one comforting note was how they all shifted closer to her. It was as though they were determined to shelter her the very best way they could. Their concern only further clouded her vision.

Sylvie wiped her eyes and watched as Marcela drew a tablet from her purse and set it on the bar. Rick reached across the bar and took Sylvie's hand. Sylvie actually had difficulty hearing precisely what Marcela said. Something about Marcela's neighbors, two mad old ladies who loved Marcela and her husband to bits and made them all kinds of superfattening delicacies from their native Argentina. How the two old ladies were addicted to the daytime telenovelas. Only, they had gone on and on, this week, about some celebrity wedding. . . .

Sylvie was not clear on exactly how things proceeded from

that point onward. Something about the way they were all clustered about her, so close she could feel their unified strength and support, left her unable to focus intently upon anything.

Then she was struck by the sudden realization that Connor must have traveled south to Los Angeles for this wedding. There had to have been something terrible. . . .

It could only be one thing: a traffic accident.

Marcela's words became a faint buzz. All Sylvie clearly understood was how sorry Marcela was to be the one to have to tell her this.

Sylvie took a hard breath, and asked, "What happened to Connor?"

In reply, Marcela turned the tablet around, brought up the YouTube website, and hit play.

Some artificially bright cable personality was going on and on about . . . Sylvie could not understand what she was hearing. How could this woman be so falsely happy?

Then the scene shifted. And there he was.

The sight of Connor's face appearing in the back of a white Rolls-Royce and speaking to the guards filled Sylvie with an icy calm. When Connor emerged from that ridiculous car and started toward the gaudy palace, she said, "Turn that off."

"I'm so sorry," Marcela said.

"It doesn't matter." Sylvie rose from the stool. "I'm going back upstairs."

"I'll come with you," Marcela said.

Sylvie started to object, then remained silent. She knew the reason they had all gathered about her had less to do with Connor's actions than the betrayal she had endured nineteen months earlier. Connor was a mere shadow of that awful time. She had only known this actor for less than a week. There was no way he could have any impact on her. No. What she felt was merely the sensation of being returned to the nightmare she thought she had finally left behind.

Or so she tried to tell herself.

She started to thank them for coming together and support-ing her. But the words remained stuck somewhere inside her. The whole thing was absurd. How could she feel hurt and dis-appointed by a man she clearly did not know at all? How could Connor possibly wound her?

When Marcela came around the bar and took hold of her arm, Sylvie protested, "I'm fine."

"Of course you are. You're the finest person I know."

Sylvie felt a momentary burning from the words and the concern behind them. But she pushed that away as well. She had gotten through such an awful revelation before. This was noth-ing. The actor she knew as Connor Smith was of no importance whatsoever.

CHAPTER 27

A Lincoln Town Car waited for Connor around the first bend. When he opened the door, he was astonished to find Ami Chen seated in the back. She was dressed in what Connor had come to think of as standard agent chic—black silk slacks, black one-ply cashmere turtleneck, black suede pumps, dark purple pearls, and matching fingernail polish. Ami Chen was nothing if not predictable in her garb.

She had the laptop open on the central armrest. Her phone earpiece was slightly larger than Connor's thumb and had a two-carat diamond in the lacquered surface, a gift from her husband. She gestured for Connor to enter, then went back to scrolling through a contract on her tablet. "No, no, no, I can live with clause four. The fifth is out of the question, strike it out utterly.... Raymond, I am not making requests here. Shall I proceed? Thank you ever so. The next two clauses are acceptable, the last . . . Hang on and I'll ask." Ami turned to Connor. "Can you ride a bike?"

"Yes."

"I'm not talking about the kind with pedals."

"I figured that. My answer is the same."

Ami was just one-quarter Mandarin, but she liked to say it was the only part that mattered. She held to a distinctly Asian manner of tension and brusque command. Her small form reminded Connor of a black firecracker with the fuse lit. She leaned forward and asked the driver, "Why aren't we moving?"

"I'm still waiting for somebody to give me a destination, ma'am."

She said to Connor, "So tell."

"My house."

"Beverly Drive, south of Wilshire. Now go." To the phone: "Yes, Raymond, he knows bikes. All right. Hang on." She turned to Connor. "Raymond wants to know if you can do some of your own stunts."

"Absolutely," Connor replied. "Who is Raymond?"

"Casting agent and your new best friend. But only if what you claim about bikes is true. Raymond says that if you can't ride well enough for high-speed close-ups, they will void the offer."

"Tell him you'll call back in twenty minutes with everything he needs to know about me and bikes."

"Did you hear that, Raymond? How should I know? Evidence of one form or another, I assume. No, you're certainly not holding. I need to speak with Connor about other matters. No, you are only the center of the universe once we have a signed contract and a deposited first payment." Ami cut the connection. "You have to love the Raymonds of this world. There are too many to shoot."

Connor asked, "That was Bond?"

She pointed to the driver, shook her head, and asked, "Gerald told you about the Web traffic?"

"And the studio executive."

"Your breakup with the lovely Kali Lyndon could be the highest audience ratings the cable network receives this year. In the middle of the day." Ami showed a rare smile, the expression of a contented cat. "How did it go back there?"

"Between Gerald's redraft and the fact that we went out live, pretty good."

"Gerald watched the feed. He said you did quite well. Any regrets?"

"Absolutely. I wish I had never started down that road with Kali."

She surprised him by slipping off her glasses and revealing her piercing gaze. "Is my Connor growing up?"

"I sincerely hope so." He hesitated, then decided there would never be a better time to speak of what had come to him on the ride south. "Can I ask you something?"

"Go ahead and we'll see."

"If there was one thing about my acting that you'd like to have me change, what would it be?"

"Oh, now, that's a dangerous one."

"What, you don't think I can take it?"

"Oh, I suppose it's possible. The question is, do you *want* to go down that road? After all, you've made a highly successful career for yourself."

"Playing the bad boy."

"A particular *kind* of bad boy—the one who doesn't care. Your characters are so utterly detached they can laugh as they're tossed off the cliff."

The words struck deep, as Ami clearly knew they would. Connor needed a moment before he asked, "You don't want me to change that?"

"Of course not, darling, not if that is what the role calls for. Your audience *adores* this. But, well, let's face it. You're coasting. This type of role no longer challenges you."

"So you'd like me to . . ."

"Grow a heart. But only if you can keep playing these uncaring characters when they're called for. Just expand into new directions." She tilted her head, examining her impact. "Was that a horrid thing to say?"

Connor rubbed the skin over his chest. "Only because it's true."

When the limo pulled into his drive, Connor found himself studying the house with uncommon intensity.

Ami asked, "Something wrong?"

"No, it's just . . ." Connor suddenly felt foolish confessing. "I feel as though I haven't been here in years."

She tilted her head, examining him from a new angle. "What happened to you up there?"

"So much." But now wasn't the time to start on that.

Ami let Connor hold the front door for her, waited while he coded off the alarm, then moved slowly through his home's public rooms. Although Connor was pressed by the ticking clock, he did not rush her. He felt as though he saw it with her, the two of them studying a stranger's house. Then he excused himself and went upstairs for a quick shower and change of clothes.

Connor had bought the house on a whim. A friend who had tried his hand at acting and failed was now a realtor. When Connor had first begun to earn serious money as a television bad guy, the realtor had urged Connor to sink his new funds into this place, and to do it swiftly, because it would not remain on the market for more than a few hours. In fact, the house had not even been officially listed and Connor's was the first of a dozen offers that same morning. His bank manager was well accustomed to the swoop-and-dive incomes of LA actors, and had the mortgage details completed in ninety minutes. Before he even wrapped his head around the idea, Connor owned a home and a mortgage large enough to give him nightmares.

The same realtor referred Connor to another former actor, now a contractor specializing in home reconstructions. The place certainly had needed a great deal of work. The home was late Craftsman, a movement shaped around a rejection of both Victorian foppery and the mass-produced housing that was swamping much of America. The house had been built in the forties, expanded haphazardly in the sixties, again in the seventies, and then once more in the early nineties. The contractor had proposed to tear out much of the interior and bring the entire structure to its original style. After Connor had signed onto another massive load of debt, the contractor had merged the rooms with broad-planked flooring, using oak when the original eucalyptus and teak proved impossibly expensive. The windows were rimmed with stained glass from a local artist, who also supplied all the downstairs light fixtures.

When Connor returned to the living room, Ami announced, "Gerald would positively die to live here. He's bid four times on Craftsman homes and lost."

"I'll have him over for dinner when I get back."

"It would please him no end." She followed him through the living area and into the kitchen. "I am impressed."

"Thanks."

"And surprised. Two words I don't use often." Ami poked him in the chest. "Seeing this place, I think you just might be able to pull off the change in character."

"'Grow a heart,' " Connor said.

"Right." She glanced at her watch. "Now show me what's going to convince Raymond."

"This way." Connor led her through the kitchen and opened the door leading to the garage. When he had returned from his most recent and profitable journey to Japan, Connor had celebrated by buying two new toys. He turned on the lights, used the kitchen panel to reset the alarms, then shut and locked the door.

Ami still stood on the top step, surveying his pride and joy. "Oh, my. Wait, wait, I want to record this. I'll send it as a link to Raymond and blow him out of his argyle socks. All right, tell me what I'm looking at."

"This is a 1989 BMW M6, known in Europe as the M635 CSi," Connor said. "Mine was the next-to-last model to roll off the assembly line. It was sold to a collector, who drove it less than two thousand miles."

Ami smiled from behind her phone. "A perfect bad-boy car."

Connor hoped the camera did not pick up on how those words stabbed him. "Original black diamond-flecked paint, black Recaro leather seats and interior. BBS racing rims. Modified M88/3 engine, the second-fastest BMW ever built."

Ami lowered the phone a notch. "I admit it even makes this agent's heart go pitter-pat. But why should Raymond be convinced of anything?"

"Because the car is not why we're here." Connor stepped to the second bay and swept off the dustcover. "*This* is."

Ami cried, "What is *that*?"

"Ducati Multistrada. This S model is the fastest street-legal bike in the world." Connor strapped his satchel onto the back. "Liquid-cooled, twelve hundred cc, ninety-degree twin with desmodromic valve actuation and variable cam timing. Multiplate clutch. Pirelli Scorpion racing tires."

"I have no idea what you just said," Ami told him.

"The people Raymond needs to impress will get it." Connor walked over and hit the control raising the garage door, then pulled a helmet and quilted leather jacket from the wall rack. "Trellis-style tubular steel frame. Sachs shocks. Ducati Skyhook suspension. A pair of three hundred mill Brembo brake discs up front. A single two-sixty in back."

Connor pushed the bike outside, waved Ami to join him, then hit the control to lower the garage door. "The S model comes equipped with a Bosch-designed inertial measurement unit, or IMU. It gauges the bike's lean angle and interacts with the antilock braking and throttle management to bring it out of any high-speed skid."

Ami demanded, "Wait, you're leaving?"

"I promised I'd be back in time for my gig tonight in Miramar."

"What gig?"

"Long story. Not acting."

"I'm your agent. You need to keep me informed of all gigs!"

"Soon." Connor strapped on the helmet, then lifted the face mask and asked, "Are you still recording?"

"Yes."

"Good." He hit the ignition and raised his voice. "One last thing. Zero to sixty in three seconds flat."

CHAPTER 28

In the five months since Connor had last been on his bike, he had often dreamed of riding. The dreams always began with the sound. There was nothing like it on earth. The structure of a racing bike drew the rider down to a high-kneed crouch, the best position for an aerodynamic passage. The sound was monstrous. In his dreams, Connor first heard the bellow from a distance. The shifting gears took the bike through curves and dips; then Connor swooped in, drawn into the position of control. Or rather, as close to control as any human could be atop this much force. His dreams carried him through a few heart-swooping moments, before the end came. Connor either lost control or simply steered his bike partly around a corner and then turned *away* from safety and flew out over the cliff. His dreams always had the same end.

Connor had started riding at seventeen, using earnings from his music to buy an old Suzuki. He had ridden racing bikes owned by friends. He knew the danger rush, and he was ready for something that took him to the edge.

That became the problem.

There were secret clubs all over the LA basin. The website passwords were given out only after the group personally accepted the newcomer. They usually met after midnight, with a route planned out in advance. Two, three hundred miles of empty moonlit terrain.

They flew. Fifty, sixty bikes, racing for the pure unadulterated rush.

Most racers spoke in a slow, careful cadence, totally at odds to their action on the bikes. They didn't care where their mates came from. They never discussed the outside world. They rarely asked who the other riders were. They were uninterested in what jobs others held, what else they owned. When they met, there were only three topics.

The machine.

The road.

The speed.

Focused.

Connor had seldom tested his limits in the daytime, much less on a road as public and monitored as the 101. So he kept it to the limit observed by most high-end cars, just under eighty-five, for the first hour. Then he came upon three other racers. Two rode BMWs; the third was a woman on the new Harley racing beast. They exchanged a quick set of hand signals, enough to show that Connor belonged and needed to hurry.

They joined together . . . and they flew north.

Early on, Connor had realized that like the majority of racing bikers, he lacked the fear factor that served as an inhibitor for most people. The only time Connor became afraid was *after*. When he stepped off the bike, and came to a physical halt, and his heart still had wings, and his mind was perched out there . . . beyond. Only then did he realize how close to the final boundary he had come. It left him feeling exquisitely alive and achingly vulnerable.

At least it had once. Then about five months ago, everything had shifted.

The moment of change had been as definite as the crystal stars and the frigid night that had surrounded him. Connor had stood on top of the cliffs overlooking Rancho Mirage. He had made the solitary climb with his lights off, the silver moonlit asphalt illuminating curves with no guardrail. The ride done, Connor had stood there by his ticking bike and realized that he had not gone looking for a thrill. He had taken the ride without lights, alone, because life no longer held meaning. Live or die, he did not care anymore. The night had become filled with the jarring recognition of how much he had lost. The hollow void at the core of his being had grown so vast it threatened to consume him totally. He had ridden slowly back to LA, parked in the garage, pulled on the dustcover, and had not touched his bike since.

Until now.

Connor did not race to Miramar in order to be there in time for his job.

He was chasing after some small shred of everything he had lost.

The answer was there. In Miramar. He was absolutely certain. The town held his last chance at life.

CHAPTER 29

Sylvie made it easily up the stairs to her apartment. Marcela hovered just behind her, like she expected Sylvie to collapse at any time. The idea was ridiculous. How could anyone possibly think that a man she had only known for four days could impact her in such a way? Even so, her mind felt partially disconnected from her legs, which remained somewhat reluctant to obey her instructions. When she entered her apartment, Sylvie looked around in confusion. Now that she was here, she could not remember what had seemed so important to bring her upstairs.

Marcela asked, "Do you want to lie down?"

"Of course not," Sylvie replied calmly. Talking seemed like such a bother. She started toward the chaise lounge by the front windows.

Marcela continued to shepherd her. "What can I get you? Another brandy? Something to eat?"

"Tea would be nice," Sylvie decided.

"Tea it is."

Sylvie waited as Marcela bustled about and tried to fill the apartment's empty spaces with her chatter. When Marcela brought the tea, Sylvie said, "Connor is *engaged.*"

"He was until a few hours ago," Marcela corrected.

"He was going to be *married.* What kind of man cheats on his fiancée the week of their wedding?"

"A total louse," Marcela said sadly.

"I feel like a complete idiot." Sylvie lifted the cup, set it down. "Did you see how beautiful that woman is? And famous? And—"

"A total airhead. I saw."

"Connor was *toying* with me."

"I liked him," Marcela said softly. "A lot. So did the others."

"We liked Bradley, too."

"No, girl. *You* liked Bradley. Everybody else watched and worried."

"Why am I only hearing this now?"

"We told you, like a hundred times. You were too much in love to hear."

The care and concern in Marcela's gaze almost undid her. "You are a dear, sweet friend."

"Is that your way of saying you'd like to be alone?"

"It is indeed."

Marcela set Sylvie's phone by the saucer. "You need, you call."

"Thank you."

When Sylvie heard the downstairs door click shut, she rose and walked unsteadily to the corner that served as her office. She unplugged her laptop from the charger and brought it back to the chair. Before sitting down, she opened the front windows.

Just in case.

She had no trouble finding the YouTube link. The latest so-called episode, the one that had gone out live on the cable channel, was less than three hours old and already had more than two million hits. She watched the entire tawdry incident; then she found the link to the previous installment. She sat through the engagement party and Connor's disappearance and Kali Lyndon's tearful appeal; then she turned off the computer.

She forced herself to drink the tepid tea. There on the blank screen, Sylvie found herself watching a replay of events from nineteen months ago. She overlaid the cable personality's absurdly cheerful voice and relived the last time a man had pretended to be someone he wasn't. The last time Sylvie had allowed herself to fall in love.

She had been with Bradley for eight blissful months. He traveled a great deal, he claimed for his work. He kept a small apartment overlooking the northern cliffs. Or so he had claimed. She had since learned that it actually was owned by a former friend. They had met when he had entertained clients at Castaways. Bradley had returned the next night to continue their conversation. He was handsome, intelligent, a good listener, beguiling.

Everything he had told her had been a lie.

Sylvie had only learned the truth when regular customers, a couple from Santa Cruz who spent almost every weekend at Miramar, observed her with this man from their hometown. This man whom she loved and planned to marry. This man, they revealed, who was nothing like the person he claimed to be.

And now it had happened all over again.

Only this time, things had not gone nearly as far with Connor. Instead, her friends had come to her rescue. She turned and looked over to the silent kitchen, and the empty space where Marcela had stood. There was no telling how long it would have taken her to discover the truth, had it not been for those dear friends.

Then, far in the distance, she heard a motorcycle.

The engine made a distinctive racing roar. The noise was exquisitely refined. The driver kept the revs up to a screaming level as he powered through the curves leading into Miramar.

Long before the engine's bellow rushed down Main Street, before it slowed and burbled to a stop below her window, Sylvie knew it was Connor.

Sylvie rose from her chair and looked out the window just as he pulled off his helmet and unlimbered from the ride.

She stared down at him for a long moment. As he eased himself to a full upright position, a pair of ladies on the opposite sidewalk slowed for an appreciative glance. His hair glinted dark and honeyed in the late-afternoon light. His weary features looked sculpted. He was not merely handsome. He carried the magnetic quality of a star.

Not that it mattered any. Sylvie turned from the window and uttered the same words she had spoken as she'd risen from the car and crossed Bradley's front lawn, "Let's get this over with."

CHAPTER 30

Connor was still vibrating from the ride when Sylvie appeared in the doorway. As usual, he only felt the impact of the ride and his tucked-in position now that he was off the bike. His thighs and lower back ached somewhat. His neck and shoulders were stiff. He stretched back, then forward. The adrenaline rush granted the moment a crystal precision.

This meant that the instant Connor saw Sylvie's face, he knew it was over.

There was little to her outer appearance to suggest anything wrong. She wore a lovely pearl-gray jacket and slacks, clearly ready to greet the weekend crowds. But there was no welcome for Connor. No greeting.

"Sylvie, I'm so sorry—"

"Don't be silly. What on earth do you have to apologize for?"

He felt as though the ground continued to move beneath him. Thankfully, the bike's handlebars were there for him to grip for stability. "All this has been such a terrible mistake."

Her smile was merely a professional reflex. "I couldn't agree more."

Connor could see that discovering who he was had erased something very fragile inside her. Something very precious was no more. "If I could go back and stop—"

"Oh, please." Her voice was almost cheerful. "There's no need for such drama."

Connor breathed in and out. He tasted the salt in the air. He heard the gulls cry. His clarity was sweet agony. This, he knew, was how it felt to break a heart.

Two of them.

Sylvie seemed to find exactly what she wanted in his silence. "There was nothing real between us. So there is nothing for you to apologize for. Not *really*."

Connor did not speak because he had nothing to say. His body hummed to the realization that he loved her, and that she would never be his.

"Please don't come back here anymore."

Connor saw Marcela and Rick both watching from the restaurant's front window. Sandy and Bruno stepped up behind them. It was only fitting that they be there to watch him crash and burn.

Sylvie scalded him with another cool smile. "Have a good trip back to LA."

She turned and walked back into her restaurant.

CHAPTER 31

There was no reason why Connor should choose to push his bike the three and a half blocks uphill from Castaways to the guesthouse. But something about the fragile quality of his heart seemed to require this labor. By the time he rolled into the parking lot, he was puffing hard. He set it onto the kickstand; then he just stood there. His hands rested on the controls. His limbs still vibrated, but he suspected it was more from the impact of Sylvie's words than the road. He could feel the aftereffects from his toes to fingertips.

Connor had no idea what to do next. Stay in Miramar or return to LA? The question had no meaning.

Then Connor spotted the light framing Estelle's window.

He walked over and stood by the door, long enough for the night to gather strength. He had no logical reason to involve himself further, but this was the only act that felt the least bit right.

He knocked softly and waited.

When Estelle opened the door, he knew the answer before he asked, "Have you spoken with her?"

"I tried. I told you I would." Estelle's voice was scarcely a murmur. "I failed. Again."

Connor had no idea what to say.

"I'm leaving tomorrow. Would you ..." Estelle breathed hard. "Tell me about my daughter. Please."

Connor nodded slowly. Coming here made sense now. "I'll meet you in the coffee shop around the corner. Fifteen minutes?"

Connor crossed the lot and took the satchel off the back of his bike. He showered and changed into his only remaining clean shirt, the white knit pullover he had bought for the job. He put on the second pair of new black gabardine trousers; then he settled on the edge of his bed to put on socks and shoes. The leaden weight of his heart threatened to plant him there. Connor tried to tell himself that it was ridiculous to hurt this badly. He had only known the woman for four days. What was going on?

The only answer he came up with, no matter how little sense it made, was to walk down to the café and settle into the seat across from Estelle.

She asked, "What will you have?"

"Americano, black." When she returned and set the cup before him, he cradled it in both hands. He saw Sylvie in the steaming liquid. He tried to describe Estelle's daughter, and failed. So he started at the beginning. Not of his own journey, but from the moment he had heard the music and let himself be drawn into Castaways.

Connor described his own feelings, along with the events. He left nothing out. He named every song he had played for Sylvie, and did so in proper order. He related what Sylvie had told him about her past. The only thing he left out was the cold manner in which Sylvie had spoken about her mother. Connor did not once feel that he was breaking confidences. This was her *mother*. But as he reached the point where they had kissed, he finally realized the true purpose behind the talk, at least for him. Connor was trying to determine the precise moment he had fallen in love.

As he related that horrible confrontation this afternoon, as he described being gutted on the street, Connor reached the answer to at least one mystery.

His heart had been captured from the very first moment he had laid eyes on the lady.

Estelle drew him from his painful reverie. She reached across the table and took hold of his hand. When he looked up, he found himself met by a truly sympathetic gaze.

Estelle said softly, "You poor kid."

Connor clenched his jaw against the sudden upwelling. The power of his emotional upheaval was shocking. He was a man known for feeling nothing. Yet, he was on the verge of sobbing here in public.

Estelle went on, "I suppose you'll be heading back to Los Angeles. I'd like to give back my rental car and catch a lift to the airport."

Connor swallowed hard. "I'm on my bike."

"It's been a while, but I used to enjoy the occasional ride."

As he started to agree, he found himself struck by a realization. He needed to stay in Miramar.

Connor had no idea why he felt so certain, but to have clarity of any sort was far more important than logic. Nothing about his entire sojourn in this place was sensible. He said, "Don't go."

"I told you. I've been here eight days and the closest I've gotten to my daughter is across the street." She smiled sadly. "At least that was true until tonight."

The passing moments only intensified the awareness that he was not going anywhere. Not yet. And neither should she. "Stay one more day."

"What for, Connor?"

"I have no idea," he replied. "But I think it's important."

CHAPTER 32

The one thing Connor could say for certain about Miramar, it was not a place made for easy nights. The best sleep he'd had all week had been in the limo riding south. Despite his hard days and broken nights, he spent most of those dark hours pacing. Sylvie's act of final closure was only partly to blame for his restlessness. There was a hunger to understand what was happening—a need to see himself moving beyond the confusion. He had no reason to stay in Miramar and every reason to leave. Down in LA, he was freed from the shackles of a PR-driven marriage. His star was on the rise. His agent had laid down a challenge for growing his abilities as an actor. And yet . . .

Every time he opened his door and glanced at his bike, he grew increasingly certain that his time here was far from over.

Around midnight, he lay down and slept a few hours, repeatedly jerking awake from images strewn like leaves blown by a careless wind. A little after four in the morning, he rose and put on a pot of coffee. He took his mug out to the bench where Estelle often sat. The night was utterly still, the stars a great silver sea. An owl greeted him. A car passed. Otherwise, the hour was his.

It seemed as though the idea grew with the dawn. Connor remained where he was, long after the chill worked into his bones. The concept was so fragile he was not certain he could shape it into words. He feared if he rose he might allow the doubts and sorrow to seep in and wreck it. So he waited until the tremors shook him; then he went inside and took a long, hot shower. He lay back down and must have dozed off, because daylight greeted him when he opened his eyes.

Connor rose and stretched and made a fresh pot. He stood by the kitchenette and studied his room. Today was to have been his wedding day.

Their honeymoon was to have been a three-week extravaganza. Week one was to have been spent in a mahogany palace built on stilts above its own private atoll in the Maldives. For week two, they were booked into a seven-hundred-square-foot tree house in the virgin forests of New Zealand. Week three was in the royal suite of the Paris Ritz.

Connor looked around his little studio. The recent redecorations had not removed its basic flaws. Beneath their coats of fresh paint, the concrete walls dimpled and cratered. He could easily have reached up and shifted the popcorn ceiling tiles. The air conditioner rattled. His view through the old slatted window was over the central parking area. The soundproofing between rooms was almost nil.

There was no place Connor would rather be.

What was more, he knew what he needed to do next.

He still could not make sense of it all. And the heartache from yesterday's confrontation with Sylvie rendered him hollow. This new direction felt right, though. He clung to that simple fact. It had been a long while since he could say that about any of his moves.

Connor poured a fresh mug and went through his clothes

from the previous day. He found the police chief's card in the back pocket of his ride-stained jeans.

Porter Wright answered, "Do you know what time it is?"

"A quarter past nine."

"A quarter past nine, on my Sunday off," Porter corrected.

"I need to ask you something, and I don't think it should wait."

Porter sighed. "Hang on a second." There was a rustling sound, a pause, then, "All right. What is it?"

"That problem you told me about—Sylvie and the drugs. Is that still an issue?"

Both Porter's sleepiness and his ire completely vanished. "Why are you asking?"

"I want to help."

"Connor . . . you need to understand, whatever you do won't repair the damage."

He had already reached this conclusion, but having Porter slam the door shut on his last shred of hope was tough. "You heard about yesterday?"

"The town's favorite lady discovers her mystery waiter is a Hollywood star on the lam from his own wedding. She strips him bare on Main Street. He pushes his two-wheeled red rocket up to the guesthouse and disappears inside. Yeah, I heard. I expect most of the town spiced their Saturday dinner with speculation over why you're still here."

"I told you. I want to help Sylvie."

"You mind if I ask why?"

It was the first time Connor had spoken the thought aloud. "I can't make things right. I accept that. But I want to try and make things better."

Porter went quiet. Then, "Can you come up with twenty thousand dollars?"

The simple answer was no. Connor was as deep down in the debt hole as he had ever been. Just then, it seemed as though his attitude toward money was basically one more splinter from a broken life. Connor saw no need to tell the cop what he was thinking, so he merely asked, "This is for Sylvie's lawyer?"

"She needs one, and I know for a fact she's dragging her heels because of the money issue. Sylvie is afraid she'll wind up owing Phil Hammond more than she already does. Rick and Marcela are trying to raise the money in town. A lot of folks will probably want to help out, but there's not much time to go find them."

"Give me a couple of hours," Connor said. "I have an idea."

"Son . . . I don't think she'll accept any help coming from you."

Connor opened his door and looked over to where Estelle sat, isolated and lonely in the sunlight. "As far as Sylvie is concerned, I won't be doing a thing."

CHAPTER 33

Estelle agreed to Connor's idea while he was still in the windup. "I'll do it."

"I can help."

"You already are. I've received a . . . What is the word for unexpected funds dropping into your lap?"

"Every actor's dream," Connor replied.

" 'Windfall.' That's the word. My second husband recently passed away. He had an insurance policy he never told me about. I want to use these funds to pay for Sylvie's lawyer." When he started to protest, she said, "This is important to me."

Porter kept them waiting by the phone for almost three hours. Then the chief called to report the attorney would give them twenty minutes of his Sunday afternoon, but only if they could work to his schedule. Connor gave Estelle his helmet and made do with wraparound shades to protect his eyes from the wind. The two-lane roads held to Sunday afternoon sleepiness. Connor pushed it hard. The thirty-nine-mile ride from Miramar to San Luis Obispo took thirty-one minutes. When Estelle slipped off the rear seat, all she said was "Oh, my."

"You need a minute?"

"No, I'm . . . Actually, that was rather fun."

"You have a lovely smile," Connor observed. "You should show it off more."

As they entered the attorney's office building, Estelle replied, "Funny, I was thinking the same about you."

Sol Feinnes was a soft-spoken teddy bear. His broad features showed a gentle demeanor, but the hand that swallowed Connor's held a well-padded strength. He led them through a warren of empty offices and settled them into a conference room overlooking a tree-lined street. "I'd offer you coffee, but my wife and secretary both assure me my cooking is offensive."

Estelle said, "We're fine, thank you."

"Then I'll come straight to the point. We must establish a clear means by which you came to know about a pending arrest that has not yet been made public."

"Two nights ago, in front of the entire restaurant, Chief Wright warned Sylvie this might be happening," Connor replied.

"This is Sylvie Cassick, the defendant." Sol made swift notes on the cover of a manila folder. "And her restaurant is Castaways, correct? Good. Which brings us to the next point. What exactly are your interests in this matter?"

"This is Estelle Rainier. She is Sylvie Cassick's mother."

"That will certainly satisfy any questions the judge might raise. And you are . . . ?"

"An interested third party," Connor replied. "For all intents and purposes, I am not here."

"Your name?"

"Connor Larkin."

Feinnes leaned back in his seat. "The actor."

"Correct."

"You have an ID?"

Connor passed over his driver's license.

"Mr. Larkin, you are here because . . ."

Connor found it impossible to respond. The answer that

came to mind was . . . he was learning how to care. Which made no sense whatsoever. Thankfully, Estelle came to his rescue. She set her check on the attorney's desk and replied, "Connor is part of a group that wants to help Sylvie."

Sol Feinnes examined the check. "Ms. Rainier, you are covering this from your personal account."

"I am, but Sylvie isn't to know."

Sol Feinnes paper-clipped the check to the file's inside flap. "And this is necessary because . . ."

"Sylvie might not accept this help if she knew I was involved."

The attorney examined her over the top of his reading glasses. "May I ask why?"

"We haven't spoken in quite some time."

He made another quick note. "All right. I think it is safe to assume that the DA is moving so swiftly because they intend to blindside my new client. Their case is at best a charade, and at worst an abuse of the legal process. They are apparently being pressed to make an arrest. Sylvie Cassick's role is to play the rabbit they pull from their legal hat."

Connor asked, "So you can stop this?"

Feinnes kept his gaze on Estelle. "My goal tomorrow will be to annihilate them both. I intend to thrash them in a highly public manner."

Connor thought the gentle manner of his speech added an extra flavor to his words. "Excellent."

Feinnes slipped a document from the folder and passed it across the table. "This names me as Ms. Cassick's legal representative. Have her sign and scan them and email as an attachment to me here. I will notify the judge and arrange for a private meeting in chambers in advance of the formal questioning and arraignment. Ms. Cassick should be at the courthouse no later than ten-thirty. You, Ms. Rainier, are obviously welcome to attend."

"And the trial?"

"I can assure you, madame, that if I have my way tomorrow, there will be no trial. What they are intending is outrageous.

My objective will be to make the judge agree with me, and then respond with savagery. Unless they spring some astonishing bit of new evidence to support their case, by the close of business tomorrow this entire episode will have vanished in a noisy blast of cordite."

Estelle showed Connor another rare smile. "It sounds as though we came to the right place."

CHAPTER 34

Sylvie kept the list of attorneys on the counter that separated her kitchen from the dining area. She resisted the temptation to shift it to her desk, where it could more easily be ignored. That had been one of her father's favorite tactics. Gareth's response to every unpleasantness was the same. Whenever a court summons or an eviction notice or an IRS demand or another letter from child services landed in their lives, Gareth stuffed it in the cupboard over the ratty camper's sink and did his best to forget it existed. Once her mother had left, Sylvie had taken over handling all such issues. This was a big reason why she had grown up as fast as she had. Settling in Miramar had basically been her responsibility. At sixteen, she had obtained a fake ID and started waitressing. The funds had mostly paid for their apartment.

All those hard days, all that determination and sweat, had brought her here. Standing by her kitchen window. Trying to decide which attorney to phone. Knowing the expense would probably mean losing outright control of Castaways. Of course, that was the real reason she was tempted to follow her father's example. Shove the list of attorneys in a drawer and pretend the problem could not touch her.

She was dressing for the Sunday rush and still circling the paper on her cabinet when Porter phoned. "You called one of those lawyers yet?"

"Still trying to decide," Sylvie replied, which was at least partly the truth.

"Don't do anything just now. This may be taken care of."

"You mean, they're not going to arrest me?"

"I wish, but no."

"Then what's happened?"

Porter sighed. "If I'd known this call was going to be so tough, I would've refused. I should have."

"You are making no sense at all," Sylvie pointed out.

"Your mother has arranged for a lawyer. There, I've let the cat out of the bag."

"*What?*"

"I don't know how to say it better than I already did."

"But . . . I haven't spoken to her in years."

"I know all that. But she's here. She heard about this mess. She offered to help."

"Wait . . . my mother is in *Miramar*?"

"Right now, she's on her way back from San Luis Obispo. She met with Sol Feinnes, the first name on my list. He's agreed to take your case. Estelle has some papers you need to sign and scan and email back to his office."

Only when Porter hung up did Sylvie realize she was seated on her kitchen floor.

As Connor lifted his hand to knock, Estelle opened the door and said, "I can't go through with this."

Connor stepped back. "I understand."

The absence of any argument deflated her, as Connor had hoped it would. Estelle wrung her hands. "What if I've got it all wrong?"

"Then you leave. But at least this way, you will have known you did what you came to do."

"That's what I've been trying to tell myself all day."

Connor remained where he was, two steps removed from her tension and fear. "Here's what I propose. I will walk you down the street. We'll stick to the same side as Castaways, because I can walk with you almost to the doorway and she won't see me."

"You won't leave?"

"No, Estelle. I'll stay close by for as long as it takes." He spoke in the calm monotone employed by most good directors, keeping their own egos contained, allowing the actor to insert the required emotional energy. "I'll find someplace I can watch the doorway without being seen. When you're done, come out and start back up the street. I'll join you and walk you back here."

She lifted her hands and pressed hard against the bridge of her nose. Then, "How do I look?"

"Just fine. Great, in fact." And she did. Estelle's hair was like her eyes, a shade or two darker than Sylvie's. She had bound it back, but left two long strands to flow over both shoulders. Her silver-and-turquoise jewelry caught the gray strands in her hair. She wore rough silk trousers the color of jeans, with an Indian-print sweater.

Her features were bloodless, and her gaze terrified.

Connor reached for her hand. "Ready?"

"No." However, she took his hand just the same.

Her fingers felt like ice.

CHAPTER 35

When the woman appeared in the doorway of Castaways, Sylvie's first thought was, there was not room in this one weekend for another such shock.

Sylvie instantly recognized Estelle. Her mother's silhouette released a torrent of conflicting emotions. Then Estelle stepped forward, out of the light, and there she was. Nineteen silent years erased in one step.

Sylvie had no idea what to say. She certainly wasn't going to speak the word "Mom" or "Mother," the very idea was repulsive.

"Hello, Sylvie."

When she had told Marcela and Rick what was happening, Sylvie had the distinct impression that they already knew. Sylvie could only assume Porter had told them. That was another thing she did not want to deal with just then. Miramar was not a place for keeping secrets—she had known that since her early days. For the first time in years, Sylvie wished it were otherwise.

When Sylvie remained silent, Marcela walked over and asked, "Hello, I'm Marcela. You must be . . ."

"Estelle Rainier."

"Very nice to meet you, Estelle. Can I get you something?"

"No, thank you."

That galvanized Sylvie into action. "Marcela, take over and seat the early tables, please." Sylvie was glad to find her legs remained capable of functioning. "Let's step outside."

Estelle hesitated, as though reluctant to leave the place, or perhaps she feared Sylvie was going to order her away. Sylvie had to admit that was tempting. Instead, she led Estelle over to the wrought-iron tables and chairs occasionally used by bar patrons or customers waiting to be seated. Estelle said, "Your place is lovely. It is yours, I take it."

"Mostly." Sylvie seated herself, grateful for the emotional numbness. At least the weekend's endless shocks had that one positive effect. She observed, "You seem so calm."

"I was thinking the same about you," Estelle replied. She glanced around, as though searching the perimeter. "I was a total wreck before I arrived. Now I feel . . ."

"Detached," Sylvie replied. "Observing this from a distance."

"Yes. Exactly. I've been here in Miramar for nine days, trying to work up the courage. This after paying a detective to track you down."

Every word seemed filtered through a mental confusion. Sylvie's strongest desire was to demand that Estelle take back the money she had paid the lawyer. Was it even possible that Estelle thought she could buy herself into a relationship with the daughter she abandoned? However, something in Estelle's face left Sylvie unable to utter those words.

Instead, Sylvie asked, "Why did you come?"

"To apologize, Sylvie. I won't say I was wrong to leave. I honestly don't think it would have been possible for me to have stayed."

Sylvie had no idea what to say.

"I kept writing you until six letters in a row were returned. I knew Gareth had moved on." Estelle's lovely features were creased by old sorrow. "I had no way of finding you. It was the most painful thing I have ever endured, losing that last thread of contact with you."

For years, Sylvie had imagined this reunion. These mental confrontations had always involved rage, tears, shouting, fury, and rejection. Instead, she heard herself say, "Can I offer you something?"

"Thank you so much, dear. That is very kind. But no." Estelle paused. "Am I allowed to call you 'dear'?"

Sylvie replied slowly, "I don't know."

"Then I won't." A silence settled over the table. A breeze drifted up the street, spiced by the sea. A car passed. Somewhere a young girl laughed. Finally Estelle said, "I am so sorry, Sylvie. So very, very sorry."

Sylvie could not work out a response. Should she say it was okay? Offer forgiveness, when she felt nothing of the sort? What was the protocol for meeting a mother who had abandoned her?

Estelle asked, "Can I see you again?"

The initial shock was wearing off. In her absence, Sylvie had given this woman an image much larger than life. She was the mother who had abandoned her family. But Estelle was nothing at all like Sylvie had imagined. She was an attractive woman, both familiar and a stranger at the same time. She looked kindly. And sad. And surprisingly ordinary.

Sylvie realized Estelle was still waiting for her response. "Yes, all right. Tomorrow."

"Thank you, Sylvie." Estelle reached into her purse and set a folded document on the table between them. "Your attorney needs you to sign these. Scan the signature pages and send them back tonight as an attachment. You need to be at the courthouse tomorrow at ten-thirty. His name is Sol Feinnes. He seems to be a good man."

There was no way she was going to taint this moment with some false expression of gratitude. "I'm having trouble accepting your help."

"I understand that, but you need a lawyer to represent you in this. Sol hopes he can make all this vanish before the actual arraignment."

Sylvie nodded slowly. "I suppose I should thank you."

"No, Sylvie, you shouldn't." Estelle rose from the table. "Thank you for speaking with me. It means the world. I . . . Until tomorrow."

CHAPTER 36

Monday morning, Estelle suggested to Connor that they take her rental car down to San Luis Obispo. She thought Connor's motorcycle might draw the wrong sort of attention. Connor did not object. He seemed incapable of arguing. He merely asked if Estelle was certain that he should come at all.

The longer Estelle was in his company, the more certain she became that Connor Larkin truly loved her daughter. Yet, he completely accepted that Sylvie would have nothing more to do with him. He clearly felt that he deserved nothing more.

Even so, here he remained. Deeply concerned. As involved as Sylvie would permit him to be.

Estelle was actually more comfortable with San Luis Obispo than Miramar. The beachside enclave was too isolated for her taste, too set apart from the rest of life. San Luis Obispo served as the commercial center for much of the central coast. People came here to shop the big stores, get their teeth fixed, and jump through all the legal hoops of modern life. Cal Poly was based here. A spiderweb of roads spun out from the city, joining together a wide array of towns. As a result, San Luis Obispo reminded her of her previous home in Wilmington, North Carolina. Both held to the vibrant, go-ahead energy of much larger communities.

If Connor noticed any of this, he gave no sign. He did not speak much during the journey. Estelle pulled into the parking garage adjacent to the county courthouse and parked next to a police cruiser. Estelle recognized the Miramar police chief as he rose from the car, talking on his phone. The policeman waved in their direction and headed off. When she cut the motor, Connor said, "I'll wait here."

"What if the lawyer needs something?"

"Give me your phone." He coded in his number, then handed it back. "Just make sure Sylvie isn't around before you ask me to come over."

His attitude baffled her. "Connor, I really think—"

"This is how it has to be." He checked his watch. "You better hurry."

The courthouse had the nondescript functional style of many California government structures built in the eighties. Estelle entered by the main doors, passed through security, and found Sol Feinnes already in discussion with Sylvie. Estelle thought her daughter looked exhausted. The police chief was talking with two people Estelle recognized from the restaurant. He motioned for her to join them.

Estelle walked over and greeted them with, "It's so nice that Sylvie has friends like you at such a time."

Porter introduced himself, then asked softly, "Where's our boy?"

"In the car."

Marcela asked, "Who?"

"Doesn't matter." Porter gestured to where the lawyer was still talking intently with Sylvie. "Sol has requested a meeting in chambers. If the judge agrees, Sol hopes they can wrap this up without it actually moving to a formal arraignment."

Estelle said again, "Sylvie is very fortunate indeed."

Porter pointed to a uniformed deputy who had stepped into the hall and waved to Sol. "Looks like we're on."

There was nothing for Sylvie and the others to do except wait. Rick and Marcela went off in search of coffee. Estelle settled next to her daughter on a wooden bench.

Sylvie said, "I didn't sleep a wink."

"Hardly a surprise." Estelle found herself recalling what she had not thought of in years. Such events had marked her own worst times, being tracked down by some court official and dragged into yet another bureaucratic nightmare. As far as the courts were concerned, they had been homeless. That meant too many judges treated them like cannon fodder. All Estelle said was, "I'm so sorry you have to go through all of this."

Sylvie directed her words down the long, empty corridor. "If I was able, I would have refused your offer of help."

Estelle nodded. "I understand."

"Why are you here? I mean . . ."

"Why now and not before? I buried my late husband nine months ago." Estelle watched her daughter work through the news that she had both married and lost a man Sylvie had never known. "Jack made me promise to try and find you. He'd been after me for years. I always said too much time had passed, that you wouldn't want to see me. . . . Jack was a very good man."

"So this was his dying wish, you coming here?"

"Yes, in a way, I suppose that's true." Estelle hesitated, then decided Sylvie should hear the rest. "The money for your attorney came from a life insurance policy I didn't even know Jack had. He would be very happy to know how it's been used."

Sylvie leaned her head against the wall. "What a weight."

Estelle had no idea how to respond. She sat there. Breathed in and out. Beside her daughter.

Sylvie asked, "Do you have other children?"

"No. Jack and I wanted. We tried. But . . . no."

The silence lingered. Finally Sylvie asked, "Where are you staying?"

"The motel up the street from your restaurant."

"Is it . . . nice?"

"It's fine."

Sylvie took so long in shaping the next words, Estelle could guess what was coming. "Is . . . he still there?"

Estelle decided if a little white lie was ever needed, this was it. "If you mean Connor Larkin, I can't say for certain where he is."

Sylvie sighed. Shut her eyes. Sighed again.

In that instant, Estelle realized that Sylvie was in love with Connor.

Estelle took advantage of her daughter's closed eyes to inspect Sylvie. Perhaps this was what it meant to be a mother, having an ability to see with utter clarity the emotions that Sylvie tried so hard to deny.

Rick and Marcela returned bearing coffee and a box of Dunkin' Donuts. Marcela said, "We were on our way to the cafeteria when old eagle eye spotted this across the street."

"Grease and sugar and caffeine," Rick said. "Nothing better for the blues."

"Nothing legal, anyway," Marcela said. She opened the box and held it out to Sylvie. "I know you're on a permanent diet. I asked for broccoli donuts, but they were fresh out."

Estelle found their feelings for her daughter very touching. It confirmed everything Connor had said about the powerful effect her daughter had on others. They set everything aside in order to be there for her. They expected nothing in return. And this included Connor. Estelle blinked away the burn and smiled her thanks as she selected a donut.

Sylvie ate a mouse-sized portion of donut, just enough to show appreciation for the gesture. She set the remainder on the bench beside her, checked her watch, and pulled out her phone. "Excuse me a minute."

As she stepped away, Estelle asked, "What is she doing?"

"The delivery van should have arrived," Rick replied. "The fleet went out last night."

"Fleet?"

"Fishing. The seas were calm, so there should be . . ."

Sylvie chose that moment to turn back and say, "Bruno says there's been an excellent catch of halibut today. I told him to buy the lot. We'll do a trio of daily specials."

Estelle listened as the three of them discussed possible recipes. Her daughter showed a remarkable mixture of fragility and strength. Despite everything she faced, Sylvie maintained her calm poise. Estelle clamped down on a sudden upsurge of emotions. She had never been more proud of anyone in her entire life.

When Sylvie seated herself once more, Marcela said, "Call Bruno back, tell him to be sure and check the fish for packages. Sorry. Terrible joke."

Sylvie managed a narrow smile. "Awful. You should be ashamed."

"Mortified," Marcela agreed, winking at Estelle.

"Heads up," Rick said, pointing to where Sol appeared in the doorway. "Here comes the posse."

Estelle had the impression that a dark cloud accompanied the attorney down the hall toward them. Sol stopped in front of Sylvie and said, "I have some bad news."

Estelle remained distinctly separate as Sol Feinnes related how the judge refused to even consider his request to drop the charges before they were officially filed. Instead, the judge accepted the prosecutor's claim that there was adequate grounds for proceeding, and again refused when Sol demanded they reveal there in chambers what supporting evidence they might hold. Estelle watched as Rick and Marcela moved in closer as Sol explained the arraignment process, Sylvie's need to respond with a declaration of not guilty, and the probable bail requirement. Estelle trailed well behind them as they moved down the corridor and entered the courtroom. She seated herself in the back row, maintaining a clear distance. When Sylvie glanced back, Estelle smiled briefly. Since her daughter did not motion for Estelle to join them up front, she remained where she was.

How did she feel about this? Being here, living the dream she had carried for so long. Despite all the hardship this moment carried, Estelle was still playing a role in Sylvie's life. Not even the barriers that separated them could impact what she felt, which was . . .

Joy.

CHAPTER 37

Connor did not mind sitting inside the parking garage. The place was quiet and dark as a man-made cave. Occasionally a tire squealed or someone walked past, but no one noticed the lone male in the Chevrolet parked nose out. His recent days had been so intense and his nights so interrupted. Having a chance to reflect was very useful. The mysteries did not plague him so fiercely, though the answers remained unclear. Even so, Connor had the distinct impression that he was closing the door on his years of wrong moves.

If only the turning did not hurt quite so much.

Half an hour later, Porter arrived, bearing a steaming cup of coffee. Connor unlocked the door and Porter slipped inside. "Black, right?"

"Yes, thanks. Shouldn't you be inside?"

"I said my piece and decided to make myself scarce. They're in court. Things did not go like we hoped. Sylvie's being formally charged with felonious possession with intent to distribute."

"That's nuts."

"Everybody agrees with you, except the three who matter—the judge, the prosecutor, and the detective handling the case. Sol intends to lodge a formal complaint. But it's all after the fact now."

"Sylvie isn't in there alone, is she?"

Porter glanced over, then away. "Rick and Marcela are with her. Estelle's camped out at the back of the courtroom."

"What happens now?"

"She'll get bonded out and get on with her life." Porter tapped his fingers on the side window. "Something is going on here. I can smell it."

"What possible good could come from charging an innocent woman with a felony?"

Porter nodded slowly. "That's the question we need to answer."

Connor liked being included in the hunt for a solution. "I still want to help. Long as you keep my name out of it. I don't want to embarrass Sylvie or add to her troubles in any way."

"Which it would, if she ever found out you're involved in this." Porter gave him the sort of stare perfected by cops, level and direct and unflinching. "You're sure you don't want to head on back to the bright lights and the big city? Forget about a lady who doesn't want to have anything more to do with you?"

Connor felt no need to hide the truth. "I can't help but hope, even when I know it's useless. But that's not why I'm staying." He shrugged. "Miramar is where I need to be right now."

Porter just waited.

"I've been sitting here, trying to remember the last time I helped somebody without expecting to get something in return."

"Feels good, doesn't it?" Porter opened his door, started to climb out, then said, "Why don't you come up to the house tonight and join us for dinner."

"Thanks, Porter, I'd like that a lot." He was struck by an idea. "Is it okay if I bring Estelle?"

Porter seemed to find that humorous. "Always room for a lady with a story to tell. Last house on Little Bear Road. Six o'clock."

Reflecting on his odd mixture of emotions, Connor watched the police chief lumber away. Porter was right. It felt better than good to help Sylvie out.

Even when it hurt.

CHAPTER 38

Sylvie had been home less than an hour when Rick called to her from downstairs. She walked over to the top of the stairs and said, "I thought I told you to go home."

"Good thing I didn't," he replied. "Harold Reamus just showed up."

She winced at the thought of adding another burden to her day. Harold served as Phil Hammond's attorney. "What does he want?"

"No idea. I tried telling him he could call and make an appointment like everybody else. He says he only needs a moment of your time."

Sylvie was tempted to agree, but she knew it would only be putting off the inevitable. "I'll be right down."

"After the day you've had," Rick protested.

The attorney stepped up beside Rick. "Which is precisely why I'm here. At Mr. Hammond's personal request."

Rick snorted softly, then stepped aside as Sylvie descended the stairs. Harold Reamus was dressed as always, in a Brooks Brothers suit and narrow club tie and round gold spectacles and polished cordovan shoes. He thanked Rick and smiled as Sylvie led him over to the bar. Everything was very normal about Harold. However, Sylvie often suspected that given the right motivation, the top would spring open to his tight little box, and out would pop the evil clown.

She asked, "Would you like something?"

"Thank you, I won't be staying long."

Rick pushed through the kitchen doors, saying, "I'm just in here if you need anything."

When the door sighed shut, Harold said, "Mr. Hammond has heard of your current dilemma and wishes to offer you his full support. Which is quite considerable, I assure you."

"That's very kind, but—"

"Please hear me out. He asks that you reconsider your choice of Sol Feinnes as your legal representative in this matter."

"How did you hear about this?"

"Your legal troubles are now public record. As I was saying, Feinnes is quite adequate for most of his local clients, but his expertise is extremely limited. He has handled less than a dozen drug-related trials."

"I didn't have anything to do with drugs!"

"Which is precisely what Mr. Hammond said when he heard. It is a sham situation, but the ramifications are dire. If you are convicted, you face a long incarceration and the loss of your restaurant."

Hearing her worst fears stated in such a calmly precise manner left her nauseous. "Why are you here?"

"Mr. Hammond wishes to provide you with the services of the finest trial attorney in California. A man at the top of the state's legal empire, with the power to call a battery of witnesses and deal this case a crushing blow. In exchange, he merely asks that you reconsider his offer of four months ago."

"'Merely' sell him a controlling interest in my restaurant," Sylvie said. "'Merely.'"

"You continue to miss the big picture," Harold said. His

voice was as slick as his hair, a tight sheen that was completely immune to Sylvie's growing ire. "Mr. Hammond is expanding into large-scale hotel and restaurant ventures. He wants you to run the entire division."

"See, Harold, that's where you and Phil miss *my* big picture." Sylvie swept a hand around the restaurant. "This is what I want to run. For the rest of my days. Not Phil's empire. *This.*"

"Alas, Ms. Cassick, your current attitude risks costing you everything. Not just this restaurant. Your life here in Miramar. I urge you to reconsider your position on the matter."

Sylvie swallowed hard, shoving her immediate reaction down deep. Phil Hammond remained her partner in Castaways. There was nothing to be gained by telling his attorney that she found the prospect of working for him repulsive.

Harold seemed pleased by her silence. He slipped from the stool and said, "Thank you for your time. I'll see myself out."

Sylvie was still standing at the bar when Rick's head appeared through the kitchen doorway. "Everything okay in there?"

"Sort of." She actually felt a lot better than she might have expected. Having Phil's lawyer lay things out had eliminated that option. She would never work with the two of them. It simply was not in her genetic makeup. But that was not what held her at the bar. Sylvie felt captured by the most foolish, nonsensical, impossible thought.

She wished she could talk with Connor. She missed him terribly. She positively ached for the chance to see Connor again.

Which was ridiculous, considering that the Connor she wanted hadn't really existed in the first place. He was just a figment of her imagination, wasn't he? So pathetic . . .

She entered the kitchen, chatted with her staff, then ordered them all to go out and enjoy what was left of their day off. Sylvie assured them she was fine, and knew they did not believe her. Her reflection as she locked the front doors showed deep lines that could well last the rest of her life. She worried over what her friends and employees must have thought of this wild-eyed woman who saw them off with a Kabuki mask of a smile. No wonder they had all stayed as long as they did. Sylvie thought her reflection did not look quite sane.

She walked around, turning off the last lights and setting the alarms. Then she seated herself at the bar. Just another lonely woman, staring at another empty night. She felt the weariness like a weight that bound her into place.

Her gaze came to rest upon the piano. She heard the soft refrain of a man inviting her to fly away. Singing the same words her father had hummed for years. The melody came to her now, sung by a man whose arms she could still feel.

Sylvie forced herself to rise and turn away and climb the stairs and prepare herself for bed. The melody did not leave, nor the voice, nor the memory of his kiss.

CHAPTER 39

Porter Wright's home was on the eastern side of the ridge separating Miramar from the farming valleys. His home occupied a natural plateau two-thirds of the way up the slope. The ledge covered five or six acres, most of it given over to a fenced pasture holding three saddle horses. One in particular caught Estelle's eye as she pulled into the drive, a palomino with a snow-white tail and mane. A young woman in her late teens or early twenties was currying a dappled gelding as they cut the motor. She waved an easy hello and called something lost to the evening breeze. Estelle waved back, then turned toward the policeman and his wife standing in the door. "Thank you so much for letting Connor bring me along."

The house was a comfortable ranch that carried the easy grace of Porter's wife. They grilled steaks on the bricked patio positioned between the house and the paddocks. The hillside below was densely wooded with cypress, eucalyptus, and California pine. A fragrant wind whispered and sang through the branches. Sparks rose and joined with the stars overhead. The daughter's name was Celia, and she had her mother's natural strength and easy manner. From several things that were said during the meal, Estelle guessed Celia was recovering from her own bout of loving the wrong man.

Mother and daughter peppered Connor with questions. Nothing was said about the canceled wedding or the woman he had left at the televised altar. Instead, Connor spoke of life as a journeyman actor. When pressed, he described some of the stars he had worked with. Whatever awe the young woman might have felt over being in the company of a man she recognized from television was soon lost. Connor talked of how actors at his level were excluded from the places and parties where the A-list gathered. This meant he only knew them from work, and even there the real stars maintained barriers designed to keep others out. In Hollywood, he explained, even the most casual contact could result in someone handing over a script or pitching an idea.

Celia had seen Connor in a number of his episodic death spirals. Connor showed a detailed and precise recollection of each set and story line. Toward the end of their meal, he had them all laughing over a drama he had recently filmed outside Delhi. In the final scene, he was supposedly bitten by a fake scorpion. Only, a real scorpion had crawled into his bed and Connor almost didn't make it out alive.

They spoke a little about Sylvie and the legal proceedings. Estelle could see how hollow Connor's expression turned even hearing her daughter's name. However, she had no other place to turn for real information. Porter explained about the debts Sylvie had run up while remodeling the restaurant, and how Phil Hammond had come in as a silent partner. At the time, it had seemed like pennies from heaven, Porter said, but Phil's charm had not lasted. There had been several run-ins, most recently when Phil had declared his intent to purchase the restaurant outright. Estelle had many more questions, but the evening's mood had been darkened by the discussion. She did not object when Celia asked Connor if he'd like to see the horses.

Together they left the house and walked to the paddock railing. The three horses trotted over, snuffling their hands for treats. Celia ran to the stables and returned with a sack of apples. Porter sliced off segments and handed them out. Estelle had never spent time around horses. She found their size and obvious strength a little frightening. Yet, they acted like eager children, stomping their feet and nudging the family when they weren't fed fast enough.

Estelle watched the four of them smile as Connor fed the white-maned palomino and rubbed its nose and declared, "This is the most beautiful animal I have ever seen."

Celia asked, "Do you ride?"

"No, and I probably should learn. There are a lot of roles that require it."

"I could teach you," Celia said.

Estelle found it very touching, how they both then glanced over, seeking Porter's approval. All the chief said was "Long as there's no quid pro quo on the man's two-wheel rocket."

"It's called a Ducati," Connor said.

"Call it whatever you like. It's still off-limits. Celia knows what I think of motorcycles, don't you, daughter?"

"We were talking about horses," Celia replied.

Connor said to her father, "No bikes."

Carol pulled her cell phone from her pocket and said, "Celia, sit on the railing. Connor, go stand beside her. Okay, Celia, put your arm around his shoulders. Great, now smile."

Celia said, "I can think of about a dozen ladies who are going to keel over in a dead faint when they see this."

Porter said, "Connor, unhand my daughter."

Celia said, "Daddy, how often does a girl get her very own Hollywood star to help her forget a guy who did her wrong?"

"Connor's helped you all he's going to. Now climb down."

As they walked back to the house, Carol pulled her husband on ahead. Estelle held back, so she was able to observe and overhear as Celia said, "Tonight has been great."

"For me as well," Connor said. "I feel . . ."

"What?" When Connor did not reply, Celia nudged him. "Haven't you heard? Miramar sunsets are made for sharing secrets."

"I feel like I've found a home." Connor sounded subdued. "It woke me up last night. I haven't felt that way about a place in a long time."

"What about LA?"

"I have a nice house," he agreed. "But this is different. I came up here looking for, I don't know. Peace, maybe. A way out. Something. What I found was . . ."

"Tell me."

"A second chance. Which is a really big challenge for me. It means learning how not to make the same mistakes all over again." He lifted his gaze to the sunset vista. "I'd really like to stay here."

"You mean, like, buy a house?"

"I'm so far in debt, buying a shed is pretty much out of the question. But, yeah, I'd love to find a place I could call my own." He addressed his words to the night's first stars. "I don't suppose you folks know of a place that might be on the market."

Only then did they realize that Carol and Porter were both watching and listening. Porter said to Connor, "Why don't you and me take a little drive."

Celia said, "I'm coming, too."

"You don't even know what we're—"

"You want to show him the Kaufmans' place."

Carol laughed. "She's got your number, honey. Looks like we're all coming."

CHAPTER 40

Porter's personal ride was a Chevy double-cab pickup with a six-liter diesel. Connor sat up front and the three ladies were comfortable in back. They descended to the valley floor, then drove another winding lane up the opposite ridge. Connor did not say anything during the ride. Estelle was beginning to think that this was his natural state. She decided the silence suited him.

The road ended at a set of tall metal gates. Porter opened his glove box and drew out a key, which caught the light in a remarkable fashion. When he saw Connor's expression, Porter held it up and said, "Gold alloy."

"He and his wife moved in here on Valentine's Day," Carol explained. "He had the keys specially made."

"Is that romantic or what," Celia said.

Porter checked a sheet of paper, then rolled down his window and punched a code into the keypad. Lights came on along the graveled drive and the house's forecourt. Porter took it slow, granting them time to inspect a Japanese garden replete with fountains and several groves of miniature cypress and fruit trees. The entire fenced-in plateau was less than an acre, and its size suited the meticulous garden. The home itself was simple in the extreme, a long flat roofed rectangle that stretched the entire length of the mini-plateau. The interior held to that same Oriental-inspired concept. Everything was done with a rough-hewn precision. Hand-painted shoji walls were framed in thick redwood beams. The floors were teak and tatami. Carol touched a panel by the entrance, and seasoned wood shutters rolled up. The rear wall was almost entirely glass. The western view showed the full sweep of Miramar and the Pacific.

The home was fully furnished, and appeared to Estelle as though the owners had stepped away for an evening. A lovingly polished Baldwin baby grand stood in the front parlor's far corner.

They let Connor take his time. He wandered through the place on his own. Every time he came into view, and then vanished down another corridor, the Wrights exchanged smiles.

Finally Connor emerged and said, "I'm listening."

Carol said, "The Kaufmans were our dearest friends. Last year, Jamie had a stroke. They moved to Minneapolis, where their daughter and her family live."

Celia said, "They call every week. We exchange gossip, then they talk about putting this place on the market."

Carol said, "Selling their home means accepting that Jamie will not get better."

The words only seemed to make Connor sad. Estelle asked, "What's the matter?"

In response, Connor turned to Porter and said, "You want me as your neighbor?"

Celia walked over and hugged the actor. "Daddy's right," she said. "You're our kind of people."

* * *

On the drive back across the valley, Estelle's mind returned to Sylvie and the dilemmas her daughter faced. When they pulled up in front of the Wrights' home and Porter cut the engine, Estelle asked, "What happens with Sylvie now?"

"You were there in the courtroom," Porter replied. If he found anything odd about her abrupt change of subject, he gave no sign. "The judge agreed with Sol's request for a speedy trial. He had an opening in his calendar starting next Wednesday."

"That poor girl," Carol said.

Estelle felt the dampening effect her words had on the entire car. "I'm sorry for bringing it up like this."

"You're her mother," Carol said. "It's the most natural thing in the world."

Estelle asked, "So Sylvie needs to come up with the other payment, what's the word?"

"'Retainer,'" Porter said. "Fifty thousand dollars."

Connor shifted in his seat, but he did not speak.

Estelle said, "I can manage a little over half of that."

Celia said, "The whole thing is just crazy. Why are they picking on her?"

"That question has me wondering, too," Porter said.

"You're the chief of police, Daddy. Go out there and stop it."

"My powers end with the arrest, honey. It's in the court's hands now."

Celia huffed and crossed her arms. "Well, I don't like it."

Carol said, "None of us do, sweetheart."

Connor shifted again, like the seat could barely contain him.

Porter asked, "You got something you want to say, spit it out."

"I've got a lot that needs saying," Connor replied. "Only not just yet."

Estelle sensed there was more to Connor's intense silence than the house and the evening with a fine local family. She waited until they said their farewells and were driving back into Miramar to ask, "You liked the Kaufmans' place, didn't you?"

"What's not to like," Connor said. "It's beautiful, and the view is nothing short of stupendous."

"Why didn't you ask the price?"

"I need to work out some things first. If I ask, they'll have to talk with the Kaufmans. And that means the couple will have to confront some very hard questions."

"That's very considerate of you," she said. When Connor did not respond, she asked, "Can you afford it?"

"I'm paying a pretty sizeable mortgage on my place in LA," he replied. "I could sell it and move up, then rent somewhere when I have gigs. Or . . ."

"Or what?"

"I'm up for a big role."

"Big enough to pay for a place like that?"

"It's not just the one role. If I land it, and if I do well by it, my career elevates to a whole new level."

"Can I ask what the role is?"

He hesitated, then said, "I'm being considered for a major part in the new Bond film."

She slowed and put on her blinker and pulled to the side of the road. The news was not what had stopped her. Connor seemed to be utterly disconnected from his words. She struggled to find the right thing to say, and settled on, "When did this come up?"

"Apparently, it's been in the works for a while. I received confirmation that it might be moving forward while I was down in LA." Connor rolled down his window and looked up to where the darkened house was invisible against the night. "I could make a home there."

It hit her then. Sitting by the side of the main road leading into Miramar, Estelle realized what Connor was thinking. Any place he called home would remain empty without Sylvie.

And not only that.

She knew what she had to do.

Estelle saw with utter clarity the act that would bind her to her daughter and take a step toward healing the rift of nineteen years.

If only she could figure out a way to make it happen.

CHAPTER 41

When the phone rang on Tuesday morning, Connor was drawn from the most remarkable dream. He had difficulty recalling where he was, what day, why he was sprawled on this lumpish bed, why his hand couldn't find the phone and make the buzzing stop. . . .

"Hello."

"I woke you, didn't I?"

"Gerald?"

"I'd apologize, but I'm not the *least* bit sorry."

"What time is it?"

"Almost nine. Don't they have clocks up there?"

"I slept until nine o'clock?"

"Well, apparently so."

"Give me five minutes to put on coffee."

"Give *Ami* five minutes and you won't need any."

"Wait, Gerald. Just wait." He heard Gerald squawk, but he put the phone down, anyway. Half a minute later, he picked it back up and said, "I can't talk to Ami without pants."

Gerald played the stork again. Ack-ack-ack-ack. "A half-dozen ladies on this floor just entered meltdown. Hold for Ami."

Ami greeted him by saying, "The Bond gig is almost yours."

Connor threw open his door and made a barefoot and shirtless circle of the parking lot.

"Are you there?"

"Trying to find enough air to say thank you."

"They want a screen test. I told them no way, you've played enough roles of this kind for them to forgo such ridiculousness. But they insisted. You'll be happy to know I exacted my pound of flesh."

"Tell me."

"They have agreed to a pay-or-play clause in your contract."

A screen test was standard ops for anyone but the biggest stars, and even they might agree to one if the role was out of their standard mode. To have Ami negotiate *anything* in return for Connor testing meant he was, for the first time in his life, being treated as a star.

Pay-or-play was another item restricted for top actors. Once the contract was signed, Connor would be paid *even if the film was never made.*

"Ami . . . thank you so much."

"That's my boy."

Connor scrubbed his face, trying to force his mind to wake up. "Before the shoot, I need to work through the script with my coach."

"They'll scream over the very *idea* of an outsider seeing their precious screenplay."

"Can you make it happen?"

"Stay by the phone. It looks like the test will be set for tomorrow morning. Gerald will call with the time and contact your coach. The studio will insist you go through the screenplay on set. No way will they allow you to take it home. I assume you can find your way back to Los Angeles?"

"In a heartbeat."

"Now that I've seen your bike, I almost believe you. Come on down this afternoon. They will want you on set bright and early."

Connor showered and dressed. He grabbed a pad and pen and walked over to the diner. Gloria was busy with other clients, and motioned for him to take the booth by the window. Connor waved a greeting to Joey, the cook and owner, and ignored the looks cast his way. Gloria came over with the pot of coffee, poured him a mug, and said, "Joey wants to know if cooking your breakfast will get us part of the hundred-thousand-dollar reward."

"Time's run out on that one."

"Shame."

A shrug at the cook grinning through the kitchen portal, and that was it. Gloria took his order and drifted away. Attention at the other tables returned to whatever had occupied them before Connor showed up. He was left alone.

Connor opened his pad and started writing. The Bond gig was a huge feat. It could potentially elevate him into the rarified status of a character actor who was also a bankable star. There were only a few such people in each generation. Stanley Tucci had been one of Connor's favorites since childhood, precisely because he accomplished what Ami had challenged Connor to do. Only it was now, after the upheaval of the previous few days, that Connor was beginning to realize what it actually meant. Such an astonishing range of roles would only remain believable if the emotions were real. Connor wanted to use this role as a target, and then begin aiming for the same breadth. And flexibility. And heart.

But that was not what his list was about. At least, not directly.

He worked through breakfast. Over a last cup of coffee, a familiar voice asked, "Mind a little company?"

He waved Estelle into the booth. "Not at all."

She smiled at Gloria, said coffee would meet her every need, then asked Connor, "What are you doing?"

"Trying to cement everything I've gained here. I've gotten through the next hoop on this Bond gig."

"So you'll be going back to Los Angeles."

"If the earlier Bond films are anything to go by, they'll build their interiors and custom sets both at the MGM lot in Century City and Pinewood Studios in London. But the on-location work will be shot all over the place."

"Is that answering my question?"

He smiled across the table. "Not really."

"So what happens next?"

"I'm heading back to LA for a screen test."

"And so the list?"

"Right."

"Will you buy the house?"

"If I can manage the cost, if it's available, if we can work things out with my bank." Connor glanced down at his notes. "But the house . . ."

"It's not what the list is about. I understand. You want to anchor yourself in the changes you have started working through here in Miramar."

He liked that about Estelle, the ability to grasp the unspoken, and gently nudge her way into the sensitive areas. "I'm trying to build a list of next steps. I don't want to get back into the rush and the grind and the hype, and then one day discover I've lost it all again."

"You won't."

"I wish I could be so sure."

"Let me be sure for you. You're going to make it."

Connor saw she was studying the large blank space at the center of his list, the place where a woman's name might have become the focus of actions and questions. If she was willing to even speak with him. If he had any idea what to write.

When Connor remained silent, Estelle said, "We have to help Sylvie. We can't let her lose the restaurant."

"I agree." Connor leaned back. "I am in debt up to my eyeballs. Otherwise, I'd—"

"No, Connor. It's sweet of you. But I'm thinking, well . . ." She took a long breath. "I was wondering if maybe we should hold a silent auction, where Sylvie's friends donate prizes."

Connor had a remarkable experience of hearing not just Estelle's words, but the formation of his own question. It was the one that had remained unasked, because he had no idea what exactly he wanted—other than being with Sylvie, which he knew was not going to happen. The issue that remained there in the empty portion of his list was: what should he do? Estelle's idea was not what rocked him back in his seat. He still did not know the answer to his dilemmas. But for the first time, he saw clearly the question he needed to ask next.

What could he do as a means of healing the rift? That was the issue he had to focus on. How could he apologize in a way that went beyond words and actually revealed . . .

His heart.

Connor realized she was still waiting for his answer. He said, "It's a great idea."

"You really think so?"

"Estelle, it's better than great. Everybody I've met around here cares about Sylvie. A silent auction would give them a chance to show her they're in this with her."

Estelle allowed her own uncertainty to show. "But raising fifty thousand dollars . . ."

"Right. The prizes need to be big."

"Something that will get people talking."

And that was it. The first part of his answer slipped into being as he spoke. Fully formed. Ready for action. Suddenly the booth was no longer able to contain him. He rose from the table and signaled to Gloria for the check. He looked down at

Estelle, who was clearly taken aback by his abrupt departure. "Make one of the prizes that I'll play."

"Play?"

"Music. A private concert. Ask Rick or Marcela, they'll explain. It's what drew me into the restaurant that first day. I've loved swing ballads since before I could talk. My mom used to put on one of Nat King Cole's albums when I wouldn't stop crying."

"That's it," Estelle whispered. Her eyes glistened. "This is . . ."

Connor nodded. When Estelle did not speak, he finished the thought for her. "A headline event. Tell you what. See if a reporter for the local rag wants to come down and interview me in LA while I'm doing the Bond screen test. Use that to announce your silent auction."

Estelle wiped her eyes. "You really are a good man."

"No, I'm not." He folded up his half-finished pages. "But I'd like to be."

CHAPTER 42

When Connor entered the police station, a couple was shouting somewhere in the distance. The uniformed woman at the front desk smiled a pinched welcome and said that Porter was busy with a complaint. The woman introduced herself as Maud. She was in her late forties or early fifties, and had the strong, well-worn look of a woman very comfortable in her own skin. She told Connor, "You can go on back or you can sit here and have me pepper you with questions."

Connor was still getting used to the small-town attitude of familiarity. "How about I sit here and quietly work on something?"

"Oh, I seriously doubt that will happen. Celia and my daughter are besties. At breakfast, I heard all about your evening. There is nothing in the world that would please my daughter more than to know you and I had ourselves a real heart-to-heart."

"Do I have any say about my life becoming an open book around here?"

"Not in Miramar. How about I ask one question, then I leave you alone?"

"Doesn't sound like I have much choice." Then two voices, one male, the other female, rose to a near bellow. "What's going on back there?"

"Domestic," Maud replied. "The next-to-worst part of our job."

Connor had no interest in knowing what was worse than enduring that level of rage. "So ask."

"Are you going to buy the Kaufmans' place, and if you do, will you leave LA totally behind?"

"That's two questions, but I'll answer, anyway." As if he had any choice. "I loved the house, but I am up to my eyeballs in debt already. And the house looks extremely expensive. So I have to think very carefully about my next step. Which will probably include going to my bank manager on my hands and knees. As for LA, I want to keep acting. What that means about where I live, I haven't gotten that far yet."

"You like Miramar." She held up one hand. "That's a statement, not a question."

"I like it very much. Everything except the speed with which gossip spreads around here."

"Haven't you heard? Gossip is a small town's version of reality TV."

A beefy woman and a stumpy, red-faced man came storming down the corridor and across the front office and out the main doors. Porter followed them, his expression weary. "Remind me why I didn't just shoot them both."

"Lompoc State Prison is nasty. Plus, we'd miss you when they locked you up." Maud winked at Connor. "And Celia would go off to LA on the back of Connor's bike."

"All good reasons." He asked Connor, "You waiting for me?"

"I'd appreciate five minutes."

"Are you here to register a domestic complaint?"

"Not today."

"Then come on back."

Porter's office was fairly nondescript, highly functional, and uncluttered. The photographs lining one wall were all of his daughter and wife. Connor slowed enough to view Celia as she grew from a smiling toddler to a lovely young woman. When he turned around, Porter waved him into a seat and said, "Those two ladies make even the worst hour manageable."

"They are two great women."

"Yeah, Celia's lucky she took after her mom."

"You must have a lot of bad hours in this job."

"Some days. But I can't imagine acting is all bluebirds and buttercups." He shifted his weight, causing the chair to squeak. "What's on your mind?"

"Phil Hammond," Connor replied.

"Old Phil."

"What's his story?"

"Not much I can tell you beyond Miramar's city limits. You know the story about him and Sylvie?"

"Marcela told me a little. He owns a minority share of Castaways, right?"

"And two of the beachfront hotels. He's a developer from Santa Cruz. That's pretty much it." Porter picked up a pen and spun it between his fingers. "I don't deal in rumors, you understand."

"Sure."

"I don't know anybody who's willing to offer a good word about the man."

"Is he a criminal?"

"When he offered to come in beside Sylvie, I checked because she asked me. The answer is, he's never been arrested. More than that, I can't say."

"Has he ever tried to buy Castaways outright?"

Porter spun the pen between his fingers. "Where are you going with this?"

"Just wondering."

"Well, the answer is, old Phil doesn't ask. He tells. And, yes, about four months back he *told* Sylvie he wants to take over

Castaways. He's offered to make her vice president of his hotel and residential group, or some such. Major pay raise. Lots of perks. Sylvie needed about twelve seconds to turn him down. She tried to be polite about it. Phil didn't take it well."

Connor sat there a minute, trying to fit the puzzle together. He liked how Porter clearly felt no need to push or pry or run on to the next thing. It was oddly comforting, even seated in a chair that was still warmed by the warring couple. "Miramar is nothing like what I expected."

"What do you mean?"

"I thought I'd come here, have a quiet few days, get my head sorted out, go back, rejoin my old life, like that."

"And that hasn't happened."

"There is not one single item that's worked out like I expected," Connor replied. "Starting with the idea that Miramar is calm."

"But you like it here."

"I do. A lot."

"Mind if I ask why?"

"I've found exactly what I needed," Connor replied, rising to his feet. "Thanks for your time."

"Don't mention it. You just be sure and let me know if you ever move past wondering about old Phil."

"You bet."

Porter waited until Connor was almost to the door before adding, "I thought we were going to be talking about the Kaufmans' place."

"We will. Soon. I hope."

"You're wondering about that, too, huh?"

"Oh, no," Connor replied. "I'm way past that."

CHAPTER 43

Estelle left the diner and drove her rental car down to the southern seaside cliffs. She would have preferred to walk, but she could almost hear the ticking clock. Water beaded on her windscreen as she pulled into the parking area. She left the car and walked out to the point. A lazy mist drifted over the water, like clouds too heavy to rise to their proper station. Pillars of sunlight fell here and there, their reflection off the water almost blinding. After a time, she walked back to the open-fronted chapel. A middle-aged couple were seated on the back row. Their eyes were closed and they gave her approach no notice. Estelle settled on a bench where the roof sheltered her somewhat. Her thoughts drifted with the mist.

She had no need of Connor's written list, though she admired him for making the effort. She had carried her own dilemmas for so long they felt imprinted in her DNA. This cliffside refuge seemed an ideal place to prepare herself for what she intended to do next.

Estelle knew she was about to step over an invisible line. This was no longer about helping her daughter from a safe distance. She proposed to take an active role in Sylvie's world. Estelle had no idea how her daughter would react, or whether she was doing the right thing at all. There was every chance she was making a terrible mistake.

When she felt as prepared as she might manage on this tumultuous day, she rose from her place and stepped out to where she would not bother the other penitents. Her whispered words were a simple repetition of the same fractured plea. "I need help."

As she returned to the car, she was certain she had been right to come.

Estelle phoned Marcela from the cliffside parking area. When the waitress came on the line, Estelle asked, "Could you please spare me ten minutes of your time?"

"What's this about?"

"I have an idea about how we might help Sylvie."

"She sure needs it. Look, I told Rick I'd help them prep today. Let me go check in, then we can meet."

"Could you please not mention this to Sylvie?"

"Oh, sure." The woman's good humor shone over the phone. "There's no one who likes being helped less than your daughter. Tell you what, why don't you go up to the café by your motel and I'll meet you there. Less chance of being caught out by the house detective."

Estelle drove back up the hill, parked by her studio, then walked to the café. By the time Marcela arrived, Estelle's nerves had almost taken control. She confessed, "This is probably a bad idea."

"Why don't you buy me a latte and let me decide."

When Estelle brought back the drinks, she took a hard breath and launched straight in, but Marcela did not allow her to get past the first few sentences. "Hold it right there."

Estelle nodded miserably. "I told you it was silly."

"You want to hold a silent auction and ask the town to chip in with prizes and then come and bid? And all the money goes to covering Sylvie's legal fees, so she doesn't have to sell out to old Phil?"

"Something like that. I suppose I—"

"Girl, this is brilliant."

"Really?"

"Of course, really. The whole town is already talking. There are a lot of people who would love nothing more than a way to *do* something. How much does Sylvie need?"

"Fifty thousand dollars. On top of the twenty I already paid."

"Wow." Marcela sobered. "That's a lot."

"Tell me."

"You'll need some major prizes. Something big enough to pull in the valleyites."

"Sorry, who?"

"That's what we call the rich people who have the estates back behind the ridgeline. They're a big part of why Castaways is a success. You'll need a real whopper to get their attention."

"Connor has offered to play."

"Play?"

"As a prize. A private concert with Connor Larkin, star of the next James Bond film."

"Wait . . . *Our* Connor?"

"He's headed down to LA this afternoon for the screen test. A reporter from San Luis Obispo will be meeting with him on set. Connor offered them a scoop in return for promoting the silent auction."

Marcela surprised her then. She turned her face to the late-afternoon sunlight and sat there in silence for a time. Estelle thought the woman defined Latina beauty, the honeyed skin, the full lips, the soft curls, the dark and soulful eyes. Finally Marcela said, "It's such a shame."

Estelle nodded, but did not speak.

"Sylvie won't even talk about him anymore."

"Which is why we need to keep this quiet until . . ."

"Until it's too late for Sylvie to call it off," Marcela finished. "When were you thinking about holding the event?"

"This coming Monday. I've spoken with the police chief."

"Porter. He's great."

"Right. He's arranging for us to use the town hall. It doesn't give us much time to put together the prizes and get word out."

Marcela bundled her things together and rose from the table. "Leave it with me."

But midway across the café, Marcela came to an abrupt halt. Estelle asked, "Something wrong?"

Marcela turned. "I've just had the most delicious thought."

"'Delicious,' as in, 'bad'?"

"Oh, no. It's a lot worse than that. This is just terrible."

"Do you want to tell me?"

"Best you don't know. It'll give you, what's the word?"

"'Deniability.'"

"Right." Marcela shivered. "This is going to be fun."

CHAPTER 44

For once, Connor remained the model driver his entire journey south. Twice he was passed by other bikers, who slowed to observe him and then fly on, clearly thinking unkind thoughts about a rider who could afford a Ducati and apparently didn't know what to do with it. But Connor liked having the time to put everything away, except for the road and the daylight and the ride. The drive forced him to focus down on the moment. He had the sense of developing a clarity that he could then apply to other things.

Twice he pulled off the highway and leaned against his saddle and watched the ocean. Both times he drew out his list and worked through a couple more points. When he arrived home, Connor parked the bike in his garage and sat there, waiting until the next item crystalized in the sunset. He went inside and showered and changed, then rode down to his favorite deli. He did not so much work through the meal as reflect on what he had written, and what it all meant. Then he returned home and went to bed. Twice in the night, he rose and studied the list and thought about his next moves. There was no sense of pressure, or really even of a possible next move. Just the same, the fact that he was thinking about these things left him at ease in his own skin. Given his state just a week or so earlier, Connor considered it a remarkable achievement.

The next morning, he pulled into the MGM studio gates at seven-thirty. Connor gave his name to the guard and was directed to a nondescript office building about halfway down the central lane. When he entered, his coach was nowhere to be found. Instead, Gerald said, "Don't you *dare* give me that look."

"Where's Mavis?" Mavis was his acting coach and a dear friend.

"Sick. Chest. No voice. I've heard cement mixers that sounded better."

"Gerald, what are you doing here?"

"I'm trying to rescue the moment, is what. Although Ami couldn't *possibly* survive a day without me, she's agreed this is important enough to try. And you are *thrilled* that I'm here. Go on. Say it."

Connor knew complaining would get him nowhere. "Thank you, and thank Ami. It's good to have a friendly face in my corner."

"On the next take, you can try and put a little more feeling into your gratitude." Gerald pointed Connor toward the aide waiting with visitor badges. "Go. Scoot. We have to hurry and get started before the suits upstairs change their minds."

The studio would only release the full script after Connor signed a confidentiality form and agreed to work alongside Christopher, one of the film's assistant directors. Christopher dressed like most film school snobs—stovepipe pants and black shoes with absurdly long toes, like they were about to curl up and turn purple and fit the clownish gestures that Christopher made constantly. His dress shirt had French cuffs, which flopped like starched wings around his fingers because Christopher wore no cuff links. His hair was waxed into a precise bird's nest. Christopher greeted every comment Connor made with an eye roll and a dismissive smirk. Normally, working alongside a film school snob made Connor's days crawl as slowly as a receding glacier. Today, however, Gerald handled Christopher with astonishing ease. Gerald made little insider jokes that left Connor completely baffled. If they had been speaking Farsi, he would have found more reason to laugh. Gerald asked Christopher for his opinion at every step. Gerald treated the AD's responses as solid gold. Christopher gradually left his arrogant attitude behind and worked with them.

When they had completed three read-throughs, Connor declared himself satisfied. Christopher left to phone the director and make arrangements for the set and crew. Connor and Gerald remained seated at the back of an unused soundstage, surrounded by the normal assortment of crates and cables and light stands and mic booms.

Gerald said, "You were almost human there at the end."

"I am in the presence of a master," Connor said.

"I hope you were watching," Gerald replied. "You can't expect me to show up every time they throw an AD at you. And the higher you go in this business, the more often they'll assign you a Christopher."

Gerald was a study in physical contrasts. He was aged in his late forties and wore his graying hair cropped military short. He was not unattractive as much as simply unremarkable. Connor had never seen Gerald wear anything other than conservative three-piece suits. He had once told Connor that nothing hid a multitude of sins so well as a tailored waistcoat. Today's outfit was gray herringbone, offset by a starched shirt so glaringly pink the shade could almost be called violent. His wingtips were polished to a mirror shine and his fingernails were always buffed. Gerald could easily have passed as a midlevel accountant, fussy and precise and short-tempered.

"You are as good a coach as I've ever worked with," Connor replied. "And I'm not just talking about the script."

Gerald was still forming his response when the makeup artist came for Connor. The role called for him to have been disfigured by a previous assault, one where acid had scarred the left side of his face. The film's producers wanted to view Connor in full character, and Connor had overridden Gerald's objections and readily agreed. This level of cosmetic makeover was new to him. Connor wanted to see how it affected his speech and his facial expressions. He suspected it would result in a more stifled emotive response, a sort of uniform deadpanned expression. A good deal of their work that morning had centered upon fashioning a character that suited the scar.

Christopher returned, accompanied by a reporter and photographer from the *San Luis Obispo Tribune*. After the introductions were made, the AD announced that the director had become tied up in a meeting with studio executives and could not make the shoot. Christopher fumbled the news so badly, Connor was certain he had known about this all along.

Most actors loathed working with an AD in control of a scene. With many high-powered directors, the AD was little more than a glorified gofer. Shooting a screen test was the director's way of offering the AD a bone. The problem was, doing a scene with Christopher risked having the director insist upon a redo. Connor could see that Gerald was preparing to baste the AD and serve him up well done, but Connor cut him off. "Actually, I'd prefer to work with you."

Both Gerald and the AD gaped at him.

Connor went on speaking. "All the director told you was, he wants me to be suave and deadly. And scarred. Right?"

Christopher jerked a nod. "Pretty much."

"Okay. We've crafted this into an urbane killer whose good looks were part of his allure. His trademark. Then came the last gig before the film opens. This was the first time my character ever failed. And the failure cost him his beauty. So why doesn't he go in for surgery and have it repaired? Because the scars constantly remind him of failure's cost. It's brilliant. It's a role I can grow into. Thank you."

Christopher looked from one face to the next, as though expecting someone to laugh and reveal it was all a joke. When the room remained silent, he said feebly, "I had better go make sure everything is ready on set."

When the door sighed shut, Gerald lifted his hands and applauded silently. Connor smiled, then turned to the reporter and asked, "What would you like to talk about?"

The shoot lasted almost three hours, far longer than was really required. Christopher insisted on multiple takes and constantly fussed over everything. Connor grew weary of the process, and the heavy facial makeup began to itch terribly. Even so, he found the delays actually fit the event. Connor chatted with the reporter; he positioned himself for the news photographer; he introduced himself to the behind-camera crew. Most important of all, he experienced what it was like to work at star level.

When they were done, Connor was standing in the MGM parking lot, seeing off the reporter and her photographer, when his phone rang.

Porter said, "You've made me go and break my own rules. I've meddled in something that's none of my business. Again. Carol says it's just part of growing old, but I have my doubts."

Connor replied, "You do realize you're not making any sense."

"I went ahead and asked the Kaufmans if they're the least bit interested in selling."

Gerald stepped into Connor's field of vision and pointed at his watch. Connor lifted one finger. Wait. "What did they say?"

"They're not ready to sell. Yet. But they'll rent. For a year."

Connor watched a golf cart hum past, an aide driving a star

to the set. He felt himself become distanced from everything that surrounded him, the studio lot and the screen test and Gerald's impatience and the electric aftereffects of an on-camera performance. "Tell them yes."

"Don't you even want to know how much?"

"Is it a fair price?"

"More than, for around here."

"Then I accept. Who can do up the lease?"

"Carol got her realtor license a while back."

"Ask her to get things ready, I'll swing by tomorrow." Connor thanked the chief, then cut the connection and said to Gerald, "There's something I need to show you."

"Ami is *dying* back there. She *hates* answering her own phone."

"Gerald, you really want to see this."

Connor drove back from the studio with Gerald following in his own car. He opened the front door, cut off the alarm, then stood back and let Gerald take it all in. The man moved with the slow, drifting walk of an art lover entering a new gallery.

Ten minutes later, Gerald found Connor in the kitchen. "It's lovely, and I am *terribly* jealous."

"Thanks." Connor opened the door to what appeared to be a second pantry. Inside was a wine room, crafted when the subcontractor redid his home, and one reason why the kitchen had cost him so much. The chamber was almost completely empty. Connor had nicknamed the room, Someday. He asked, "Will you take a glass?"

"If it's nice, I might even have two." Gerald showed a rare smile. "It's a perfect day for a stroll back to the office."

"White or red?"

"Red is too somber. We're celebrating." Gerald lifted his phone. "Ami just texted. The studio and director both love your take. Houston, we have liftoff."

"In that case, we need something special." Connor selected one of the few really fine bottles he owned, a gift from a star who had shone more brightly because of Connor's work. He opened the Montrachet, filled one glass, and poured a trace into a second. He lifted the second and said, "Here's to meeting new challenges."

Gerald clinked glasses, drank, then declared, "Marvelous. You're not imbibing?"

"Can't. I need to head north. You should take this bottle with you, share the rest with Ami."

"Not on your life. This little bottle and I are soon going to be best friends." Gerald sipped again, hummed a note, then said, "All right. I'm listening. Who do you need murdered?"

Connor replied, "I want you to come live here."

Gerald knocked over his glass. "I'm terribly sorry."

"Don't worry about it." Connor reached for a towel. "It's only wine."

"A *Montrachet*? Only *wine*?" Gerald watched Connor refill his glass. "Could you possibly ease me into what is coming next?"

"It's hard to explain."

"Well, at least *try*."

"I'm not happy here. I mean, in LA. At least I haven't been."

"So you've found your nirvana on the central coast?"

"Not hardly. I just feel . . ."

"What?"

"Like I've finally started asking the right questions."

Gerald drained his glass. Set it down. He tapped the rim with one fingernail. As Connor poured a refill, Gerald asked, "So that means what, exactly?"

"Friends have found me a house I'd like to rent up there. And possibly buy. If the current owners decide to sell, and if I can afford it."

"With the Bond money."

"Right. But for now, it's a tryout. And to swing it, I need to rent this place." Connor gestured toward the house. "Ami mentioned your love of the Craftsman style. Find out what this would rent for. Knock off twenty percent. Let's do a twelve-month trial run."

Gerald took exaggerated care in setting down his glass. "I positively *insist* upon paying you fair market value."

"Come on, Gerald."

"Oh, all right. Ten percent below. You are *such* a hard bargainer."

"Write up a lease. Include a clause that if I sell, you get right of first refusal."

Gerald turned and stared at the sunlight falling upon the sliding glass doors. After a time, he said, "When Ami took you on, I told her I thought she was making a terrible mistake. Ami said you merely needed one thing to bring your full potential to the table."

"A heart," Connor said.

"Actually, she said you needed a reason to move beyond your comfort zone. But I suppose a heart will do." Gerald smiled at the sunlit glass. "When I tell her she was right and I was wrong, Ami will crow. I hate crowing."

Connor gave that a beat, then said, "I need to ask your help with something."

"It's not often I utter this word and actually mean it. Anything."

"I need a detective. Somebody who can hunt out dirt on a person, and fast."

"Is the individual you want investigated here in LA?"

"Central coast."

"Let me make a few calls."

"Thanks." Connor slid over an envelope he had prepared while Gerald had toured the home. "Keys to the house and alarm codes."

Gerald looked down, but did not touch it. "You don't mean to say that I can move in *now*?"

"Whenever you like. Long as you don't mind me coming back for my things. I'm packing a couple of cases and hitting the road."

Gerald was still standing there, staring at the envelope, when Connor returned from the bedroom, set his suitcases in the Beemer's trunk, and set off. As he drove north along the freeway, he reveled in the sensation of having gotten at least one thing right.

CHAPTER 45

On Thursday, Connor signed the lease and then slowly toured the Kaufmans' home. They wanted to rent their place with all the furnishings, right down to the antique Baldwin baby grand piano. While Connor was making a mental list of the things he wanted to bring up from LA, his new phone rang. So few people had the number he was obliged to answer. "This is Connor."

"I hear you need a hunter."

The voice was heavily accented and carried a raw, dark edge. Connor asked, "You're a detective?"

"Your guy said you needed information fast."

"My guy," Connor said, "was right."

"Then no detective." The man was definitely Slavic of some persuasion, with a gravelly voice scarred by vodka and harsh black tobacco. "Your detective, he is most interested in building up the hours."

"Hours I don't have," Connor agreed. "You're Russian?"

"Me? No, man, I'm from Alabama."

"Do I get a name?"

"Sure. Jones. How's that?"

"Jones works for me. How much do your services cost?"

"That's between me and your guy. He says call, I call."

"I don't like involving him in my business."

"What business. This is a favor I do for a friend. Nothing more. No payment, no paper trail. I do this, I go back to being a happy Jones in Alabama. Now tell me what you need."

Connor realized he had just two choices: accept the man's terms or hang up the phone. He said, "There is a guy in Santa Cruz. At least I think he's based there. His name is Phil Hammond."

"Spell the name." When Connor had done so, Jones said, "There are many Hammonds in this city. Nine with first names Phillip or P. What else can you tell me?"

"He owns part of two motels on Ocean Drive in Miramar." Connor spelled the name.

"He a big shot?"

"Phil definitely likes to think so."

"Okay. Here. Phillip Jackson Hammond. CEO of Hammond Enterprises. They are . . . Okay, they own parts of many companies. He's rich, this guy. Big bucks. Wait, let's have a look at his IRS filings. . . . Okay, last year he paid Uncle Sam one point three mil."

"Do you see among his holdings a restaurant in Miramar—"

"Castaways. Thirty percent."

"That's our guy," Connor said. "But why would somebody that rich worry about owning a restaurant?"

"You like, I give you his number, you make the call. Otherwise, you ask questions I can answer."

Connor paced down the main hall and across his living room.

"You still there?"

"Thinking." He rounded the kitchen's center island, then retraced his steps. "What else does he have going on around Miramar?"

"Okay, that I can work with. Hold on." There followed several minutes of furious typing. Then, "Lots of activity, this guy. He thinks this activity is hidden. You meet this Hammond fellow, you tell him to hide better next time."

"What?"

"Oh, yeah. This company owns another, and that company has permit requests, okay, so many. Two new hotels, one oceanfront and a big development inland. Complex with name of Rancho Santa Maria. Hotel spa. Two hundred houses. Big."

Connor felt a subtle adrenaline rush. It was nothing like the nuclear high he experienced on his bike, or before the first take of a new film project. This was a different sensation, something so unique it took him a moment to fashion a name. He was moving toward an answer to the core mystery plaguing Sylvie. He was doing right by a good woman, a lady who deserved better. Connor said, "Tell our guy you just earned your check."

"That's all you need?"

"Oh, no. We're just getting started."

"Then you make a terrible negotiator, saying that now." But he sounded like he was enjoying the exchange. "Me, I listen to clock. It says, ticking."

CHAPTER 46

Sylvie passed the next three days wrestling with a dilemma. She was tempted to retreat into the sort of haze that her father had lived in much of his life. Throughout her teenage years, as Sylvie had gradually taken on more and more responsibility for structuring their home and lives, she had often accused him of living in a blind bubble of his own making. But now, she thought that perhaps she had gotten it completely wrong. Maybe there was a point beyond which an individual simply could not cope, and her father's tolerance level for crises had simply been lower than most people's. Whatever the reason, his response to the bad times had been to immerse himself in his work. But instead of using his art to express his anger and frustration, as did so many of his fellow artists, he used his palette to heal his heart. Sylvie wished she could speak with him now, discuss the clarity that had come through her current impasse. No doubt her father would have enjoyed hearing her apologize. He relished anything that closed a distance between them. He would have heard her out and said something about how much he admired her. Then they would have selected an album, and their home would again be filled with the smooth sounds of swing.

The music that Connor had performed so very well.

Throughout Tuesday, Wednesday, and Thursday, as she debated over her next step, Sylvie found it impossible to dislodge the man from her thoughts.

Each day, Porter came by to check on her as she was opening up the restaurant, then again as she ushered out the last patrons. Sylvie had to fight against the burning urge to ask about Connor.

Sol Feinnes called daily and assured her he was doing everything possible, which was not a great deal.

By Friday, Sylvie had the distinct impression that many of the Miramar locals were caught up in some secret drama. Everywhere she went, she felt eyes tracking her. But her internal debate isolated her. She had a decision to make. Whatever it was that had people so worked up would just have to wait.

As Sylvie descended the stairs on Friday evening, she finally accepted the inevitable. Thankfully, the front room was empty, so no one was there to see her as she walked to her favorite painting.

She stood there a long time, studying the hands fashioned from the sea and the hills and the night. She remembered the day he painted it, and what it meant to know they would both be calling Miramar their home.

She reached out and lifted the painting from the wall. "Sorry, Pop."

Sylvie carried it back upstairs and set it on her desk, where she could visit with it at the end of the shift, and again over morning coffee. Gradually growing used to the idea that one more fragment of her former world was gone.

CHAPTER 47

When Sylvie returned downstairs, the empty space on the wall was mirrored by the void at heart level. She found Rick and Marcela and Aubrey and their stand-in waitress, clustered around the bar. They straightened at her approach, and must have seen something in her face because Rick demanded, "What's the matter?"

She knew she couldn't tell them without bawling. That she was going to sell her favorite painting, the only one worth real money, in order to pay for a lawyer to protect her from going to jail for a crime she didn't commit.

But she was also not going to lie to them. These were her friends. They were as close to family as she had these days. They deserved to know.

Only not now.

"More of the same," was all she said. "If you don't mind, I'd rather not go into details."

"Sure thing," Rick said. "Where's the painting of the bay?"

"I moved it upstairs. Just temporarily." That was most certainly true. "What were you talking about when I came in?"

"We've invited Estelle for dinner," Marcela replied.

"What? Here?"

Now that the news was out, they seemed genuinely thrilled by the prospect of Estelle coming for a meal. Sylvie found herself unable to process their reaction. She endured their chatter as long as she could, then excused herself. She walked to her hostess station, gripped the sides of her podium, and inspected the night's bookings. Sure enough, there it was. A reservation for one, booked by Marcela, with the note that she wanted Estelle to have her finest table.

Throughout that busy Friday evening, Sylvie grew increasingly certain that she was the clientele's primary topic of conversation. She felt eyes track her every time she passed through the restaurant. She saw half-hidden smiles and heard discussions quickly stifled at her approach.

Then Estelle appeared, standing in the doorway. Sylvie thought she had prepared herself. Even so, crossing the floor required a special effort. "Welcome to Castaways."

"Thank you so much." Estelle was dressed in a pleated skirt and jacket of pale gray with narrow lavender stripes so subtle they were almost invisible in the restaurant's lighting. "This is such a thrill. I can't tell you how delighted I was to hear you wanted me to dine here. I've so wanted to see what you've created."

Sylvie was still digesting the news that Marcela had included her in the invitation, when the waitress rushed over and embraced the older woman. "You're here! Great! I've got an order waiting. See you!" And she was gone, leaving Sylvie to follow with an embrace of her own. Then she picked up a leather-bound menu and started to lead Estelle through the restaurant.

Only to be halted by yet another surprise.

Everyone seemed either to know Estelle or know *about* her. Table after table rose and introduced themselves. Time and again,

Sylvie saw groups of locals smile and invite Estelle to join them. Sylvie realized the subtle excitement was rising up now, revealing itself. She had no idea how *involved* Estelle had become in this community.

Sylvie felt distinctly threatened by this realization. Miramar was *her* town. Her *home*.

By the time she seated Estelle by the window, Sylvie felt as though the power of choice had been taken from her.

She stood and smiled as Marcela went through the night's specials. Estelle then said, "You decide. They all sound wonderful."

Sylvie said, "The fish is especially nice."

"I would love that."

"What about some wine?"

"Just a glass, please."

Sylvie went to the bar and returned with something, she had no idea what, a glass of the first open white she had seen. She then stepped back as Rick stopped by Estelle's table. Sylvie returned to her hostess station and watched Aubrey go over and shake Estelle's hand. Then Marcela returned with a starter. The three of them laughed over something.

Sylvie's resentment grew steadily as the night progressed. Why did Estelle have to come to Miramar, now of all times? Sylvie had spent her entire life building a home for herself here. And now these people all assumed she would make room for the woman who had abandoned her? This was *her* decision. *Not* theirs. And *certainly* not Estelle's.

Sylvie did her best to suppress the evening's hidden tempest. Every time Sylvie returned to Estelle's table, Rick or Marcela or Aubrey was already there, chatting away like old friends. This was good in a way, as it allowed Sylvie to stand beside them, poised and smiling, humming little notes in response to a conversation she could not hear over the noise in her head.

As closing hour approached, Estelle rose from her table. Sylvie walked over and asked, "Are you sure you won't have dessert?"

"No, thank you. I'm not one for sweets." She turned and surveyed the restaurant. "Sylvie, this place of yours is simply marvelous."

"You're very kind." As Estelle was granted a final round of farewells from her staff and the few remaining customers, Sylvie held to her smile and waited. Finally she walked Estelle through the main doors and out into the night. When they were alone, Sylvie asked, "So what are your plans?"

The night shattered.

Sylvie could almost hear the sound of crystal breaking. She saw the broken shards appear in Estelle's gaze. "I just meant . . ."

"I know what you meant." Estelle's voice had resumed the soft sorrow it had held on that first awful meeting. "I'll leave Tuesday. In four days. If that's acceptable."

"Stay as long as you like," Sylvie said feebly.

"Thank you. That is very kind. I think Tuesday." Estelle's voice strengthened with each word. Only now it carried a flat, metallic note. "That way you have one less distraction going into the trial, yes?"

"Whatever you think is best."

"Good night, Sylvie."

She stood and watched Estelle climb the hill. Logic told Sylvie she'd done the right thing at the right time. But she was chased back inside by an echoing refrain. How much she wished she could take back what she had said.

Only when she locked up for the night did Sylvie realize that she was the only person Estelle had not embraced in farewell.

CHAPTER 48

Two hours later, Sylvie carried her turmoil upstairs. She had a dozen perfectly good reasons to let the situation with Estelle remain as it was. A hundred. The days were already too full. She needed to focus on getting through this crisis and finding some way to pull her life back on track. Maybe then, she could reconnect with the woman who had abandoned her. Right now, the only thing she really needed . . .

Sylvie seated herself in front of the painting. She missed her father with a visceral longing. He rarely had offered any answer to the problems they had faced. And there had been a lot of problems. But he had always made her feel better. His painting glowed softly in the room's lights, a gentle communication passed through all the years and experiences that separated him. Sylvie knew he would want her to make peace with Estelle. This made her feel even worse about how the night had gone.

As she climbed the stairs to her bedroom, she found herself wishing yet again for the chance to talk things over with Connor. The sheer impossibility of the yearnings did not free her from the simple fact that she missed him. Despite everything. She wondered what it would be like to rely on a man's strength again. She had been alone for so long, faced so much on her own, gone so far. Sylvie tried to tell herself that it was ridiculous to wonder about such things with Connor. The man who had lied to her about almost everything. The man who could not be trusted. Especially now.

But that night Sylvie found no peace in sleep.

She dreamed that she was downstairs in the restaurant. Once or twice each week, she had a nightmare where she stood at the hostess station and searched for a reservation that she herself had taken and then forgotten to write in the book. Sylvie would start to tell the group of eight or ten or even an entire wedding party that she had made a mistake, and there was no room for them. Then she'd glance down and realize she had forgotten to put on pants.

Tonight's dream was very different indeed.

To start, the restaurant was almost empty. For another, she stood by the long table and stared at the stage. Her mother was seated in a chair by the tall bay windows. She smiled as Connor played the piano and sang.

Sylvie almost recognized the melody, but she could not place it. Estelle nodded her head and tapped her fingers in time to the song. They were so wrapped up in the moment they did not even notice Sylvie. It was just the two of them, and they were happy.

Abruptly Sylvie became lanced by the conviction that they both knew she was there, but chose to ignore her.

There was nothing she wanted quite so much as to join them. As she started forward, another person leapt in between her and the stage.

Sylvie faced herself. She was an angry, vindictive, bitter woman who looked thirty years older. Aged and desiccated and filled with a lonely, burning rage. The fury left no room for any goodness. Or love.

The second Sylvie fought with vicious ferocity. The harder they struggled, the more Sylvie wanted to be up there. With the two of them. However, she could not break through. She could not . . .

When Sylvie woke up, she was standing in the middle of her bedroom floor.

CHAPTER 49

A brisk wind blew from the northwest when Sylvie emerged Saturday morning. Normally, these were her favorite days. The air carried a special bite that was only found along the Pacific Northwest. The cloudless sky was a piercing blue, the sunlight strong enough to defy the day's chill. Sylvie loved taking a few indulgent hours where she could revel in a place that was, for her, unique in all the world.

But after such a fitful night, Sylvie rose to a breakfast of regrets. She knew she had to act. She walked up the main road to the guesthouse and found her mother seated on a bench, reading the newspaper. Estelle started at her daughter's appearance and hid the paper away, like she had been discovered doing something wrong.

Sylvie said, "I've come to apologize."

"There's no need."

"I shouldn't have spoken like I did. I . . ."

Estelle studied her for a long moment, then asked quietly, "Would you like to sit down?"

Sylvie settled onto the bench and searched for something more to say. But now that she had apologized, she felt deflated.

"I was sitting here, wishing I could speak with my Jack," Estelle said. "I need to tell him he was right to make me come and find you."

Sylvie opened her mouth to shape words, which she would probably never speak, about wishing to know a man she had not even been aware existed.

Estelle turned to her. "My darling daughter, you never need to apologize to me for anything. And certainly not for last night. The very thought is, well, it's absurd is what it is. I *abandoned* you."

Sylvie watched as Estelle swung about and aimed her face at the sun, as though drawing in enough strength to maintain control. Sylvie wished she knew how to reach across the impossible distance and offer comfort. But all she could manage was, "There's so much in my life right now."

Somehow, for once, she had said the right thing. Estelle calmed enough to say, "And the very last thing I want to do is add to your burdens."

"You're not," Sylvie said. And only as she shaped the words did she realize they were true. "Really. I'm fighting against . . ."

When Sylvie could not find the proper word, Estelle offered, "Shadows?"

Sylvie could not think of a better word, so she nodded agreement. It wasn't exactly what she'd had in mind, but somehow the word fit comfortably in the space between them.

They settled back and sat through a most uncommon time. The sun warmed the silence, and even knitted together the wounds, at least enough for Sylvie to say, "Would you like to take a drive with me?"

* * *

The journey to Paso Robles took just under an hour. Sylvie spent much of the time regaling Estelle with stories from her teenage years. Back then, the regional farmers' markets had been a highlight of Sylvie's week. San Luis Obispo, Santa Maria, even occasionally Santa Cruz, all of these had shaped her knowledge of the region she called home. Her favorite was Paso Robles, an inland town with two very distinct faces. The old section dated from the same era as Miramar's founding. Back then, Paso Robles had been a center for the state's cattle and sheep industries. Nowadays the local agriculture was dominated by grapes. The central coast was California's second-largest wine producer after Napa.

The region was also home now to thriving organic farms; as a result, Paso Robles held a prosperous, go-ahead air. The central coast had not been quite so hard hit by the drought as farther inland or to the south. The result was a lingering trace of the easy high-octane life that had characterized Californian farming communities until the reservoirs dried up. Shopping at these markets had been Sylvie's introduction both to the region's oldest families and to healthy cuisine. She had obtained her first waitressing job from a chef she had met here in the Paso Robles market. From that experience, she had been drawn into the artistry of food.

Her father had painted any number of the markets. Many old-timers still held on to sketches and pastels Gareth had traded for produce. Nowadays their children greeted Sylvie as one of their own.

Sylvie's ride of choice was a Ford F-150, with a covered rear compartment and two oversized coolers. As she parked in the market's overflow lot, she asked, "Is it bad, my talking about times with Pop?"

"I doubt very much that a rule book has ever been written to cover this situation," Estelle assured her.

"I mean, do you mind?"

"It hurts," Estelle confessed. "A little. But I also like it very much. You're filling the empty spaces."

The oddest things seemed to impact Sylvie these days. She needed several minutes to swallow down the emotional burn. They were almost at the market's periphery when she managed to say, "I want you to stay."

Estelle stopped, causing the foot traffic to veer around them.

"Don't leave on Tuesday," Sylvie told her. "Even if you were really planning to. I mean, before I said what I did. Leaving now would only make it worse, going into the trial." She gave herself a mental kick. "That sounds so selfish."

"No, Sylvie. It sounds so human," Estelle replied. "You are facing one of the worst episodes of your adult life. You are absolutely justified in being selfish."

"Then you'll stay?"

Estelle said slowly, "There's something I need to tell you."

"What?"

"Let's wait until we've enjoyed this outing a little. Please. It's such a special moment for us both."

"So . . . it's bad, what you are going to tell me?"

Estelle bobbed her head from side to side. "It's hard for me to say. But it needs to be discussed. Afterward, if you ask me again, I'll be here with you through the trial."

"But I have to tell you a second time that I want you to stay," Sylvie said, wanting to get it right. "After you tell me your secret."

"Right."

"Which you won't say now."

"Right again."

"What if I insist?"

"Don't," Estelle pleaded. "This is a dream come true for me. Just let's enjoy this time together, all right?"

In truth, Sylvie was grateful for the chance this offered to leave the painting in the truck's rear compartment and pretend the day did not hold such a hollow ache. As they started walking toward the market, Sylvie said, "I hate knowing a secret is out there worse than anything."

"Of course you do." Estelle slipped her arm through Sylvie's. "It's part of being a woman."

CHAPTER 50

Everyone in the Paso Robles market, traders and customers alike, seemed to know about Sylvie's problems. She and Estelle were stopped every few steps by yet another person who assured Sylvie of his or her support. Sylvie had no idea how to respond, especially when these folks included Estelle in their greetings. Word had spread so fast, she assumed it had something to do with the secret Estelle insisted upon putting off.

They passed the art gallery that formed the horrid purpose for this journey. The owner was a regular at Castaways and had repeatedly offered to buy the painting in Sylvie's truck. Sylvie's step turned leaden at the thought of carrying the oil inside. Then they were past it, and another couple greeted them, and Sylvie found herself in no great hurry to do anything more than enjoy an hour with Estelle.

At the market's heart was a makeshift food court, with over a dozen food trucks offering everything from Szechuan to Honduran specialties. From a family that remembered serving Sylvie as a child, they selected tortillas of spicy pulled chicken and coriander. They had found a table somewhat removed from the others and ate in companionable silence. Then Estelle bundled up the waste and said, "Thank you for sharing this with me. It means more than I can say."

Sylvie took that as her signal. "Will you tell me whatever it is you've been holding back?"

"I'll do better than that," Estelle replied. "I will show you."

It seemed to Sylvie as though Estelle moved with exaggerated care. Every gesture carried a sense of dramatic tension. Sylvie realized Estelle was struggling against her own anxieties as she drew a newspaper from her purse, unfolded it, and set it on the table between them.

On the front page of the *San Luis Obispo Tribune,* Connor Larkin stared up at her from four different photos. One showed a terrible scar covering almost half his face. Then she read the caption, though the words seemed scrambled in her brain. Something about a starring role in the new James Bond film.

Even more surprising than being confronted by Connor, and realizing that Estelle not just knew but had participated, was Sylvie's internal reaction. She was not nearly so shocked as she might have expected. All the smiles and furtive discussions made sense now.

So, too, did the dream.

She stared down at Connor's pictures and read how he was backing a regional appeal to cover her legal costs. She read the response from Sol Feinnes, who declared the entire court proceedings a travesty, as bad a case as he had ever seen in his three decades as a trial lawyer. Then there was the paragraph quoting Estelle, who expressed an unqualified confidence that with the support of Sylvie's friends along the central coast, her daughter would emerge triumphant.

She lifted her gaze and watched the market crowds stream past their table.

For one incredible, impossible moment, it felt as though her father was seated there with them. Sylvie stared across the table at Estelle, the woman whose efforts meant she might just possibly be able to rehang the painting back on the restaurant wall.

Sylvie confessed, "I had a secret reason of my own for this trip. I have one of Pop's paintings back in the truck. My favorite. A gallery owner here in Paso Robles offered me forty thousand dollars—"

Estelle said sharply, "Don't you dare."

"I thought I didn't have any choice."

"Well, you do." Estelle reached across the table. "You have faced so much. You have done so well. Now you need to let others help you."

"That's very hard for me," Sylvie said, "letting others be strong."

"Well, of course it is. You had no one else to count on for so long except yourself." Estelle's face crimped tight. "And I am largely to blame for that."

It would have been so easy to remain silent, to allow the harsh truth to punish Estelle for abandoning her. But just then, in that sunlit moment with her father so close she could almost hear his voice, Sylvie found it easy to say, "But now you're here."

Estelle squeezed her hand once, then let go, leaned back, and used her napkin to clear her eyes.

Sylvie lingered there, knowing all along that there was a fourth person who needed to join in their moment. Finally she spoke the word aloud. The name she had vowed never to utter. "Connor."

"He's a good man," Estelle said. "Yes, he's made mistakes. A lot of them. But he's trying to make amends."

Sylvie found a delicious pleasure in fashioning the name again. "Connor. He lied to me."

Estelle nodded. "Yes. He did."

"I hate liars worse—"

"Worse than living alone?"

Sylvie took a long breath. "There was a man . . ."

"I know. Bradley. That wretch."

"Who told you?"

"Rick and Marcela. I'm so sorry."

"The two of them are in on this?"

"Up to their eyeballs." Estelle smiled. "They are wonderful."

"Yes, they are." She resisted the urge to speak his name again. Instead, she said, "I don't know what to think."

"I understand."

"You say that a lot."

"Do I?" Estelle toyed with her cup. "My late husband Jack was a very good man. He helped me see that the first thing that I had to do, if I was ever going to know any sort of happiness, was to forgive myself."

"That must have been hard."

"Very."

"I'm sorry. That sounded terrible. I didn't mean you . . . Actually, I don't know what I meant."

Estelle's smile was mostly sad, but not entirely. "You don't know, you can't imagine, how wonderful it is to be sitting here and talking to you."

CHAPTER 51

On Friday, Connor hired a U-Haul and drove back down to Los Angeles. He finished loading up on Saturday, tucked his bike into the rear hold, signed Gerald's one-year lease, accepted the man's fumbled thanks, and joined the heavy northbound traffic with a smile on his face. On Saturday night, he slept in the Kaufmans' former home. Twice he woke in the night and padded through the rooms, taking it all in.

On Sunday, he was joined by forty-seven of his new best friends.

What happened was this.

At dawn, he went out to the east-facing Japanese garden and discovered a rough-hewn wooden bench tucked into an alcove of miniature cedars. The bench was situated so the sunrise would reflect in the ornamental pond. Now and then, Connor caught glimmers of liquid gold flashing in the water as giant koi rose and joined in his salute to the new day.

Then he went back to bed and slept until almost noon. He woke and stretched and showered, filled with a luxurious sense of languor. Connor drove his Beemer into town and enjoyed a late brunch at the diner. When Gloria asked a couple of questions about Hollywood, several tables turned to hear his response. It all seemed to carry the idle curiosity of small-town life.

Connor left the diner, crossed the street, and stopped by the guesthouse office to thank the matron and check out. When he entered the rear parking area, he was greeted by a dozen or so people milling about the small patch of green. The lot was jammed with cars and pickups. Estelle waved and continued with her conversation as Marcela walked over and declared, "I don't know whether to shoot you or hug you."

"I deserve the first, but prefer the second," Connor replied.

"Don't we all." Marcela shook her finger at him. "You bad boy. Why didn't you *say* something?"

"You saw the shape I was in when I showed up here." Connor saw others shifting in closer. "I needed . . ."

"A reality check?" Marcela offered.

"A chance to step away and take a good look at all the wrong moves." He asked, because he needed to, "How is Sylvie?"

"Hanging in there. Barely." Another finger shake. "You hurt a good woman."

Connor dropped his gaze. Nodded to the pavement. Guilty as charged.

Marcela stepped forward and hugged him. The woman's embrace was as intense as her smile. "That's for everything you're doing to make things right."

It burned his throat, but he said it, anyway. "If only I could."

She cocked her head, with her dark eyes glistening. "Is it true, you're moving into the Kaufmans' place?"

"Signed the lease Thursday, slept there last night." Connor could not ignore the people any longer. "What's going on here?"

"We were planning to use Estelle's studio for sorting the auction goodies and making preparations."

Connor observed, "You'll never fit all those people into her studio. Much less the items."

"I know. Our auction has grown from a minnow to a whale. But we can't get into the town hall until tomorrow." Marcela started ticking off her mental list. "We need to set up the program. We've got volunteers supplying lots of finger food, but they need a kitchen. The beverage service that supplies the restaurant is donating a ton of drinks. We've got almost a *hundred* items to be auctioned, and turned down almost as many. We need to set up—"

"You can use my place," Connor offered.

And that was all it took. Five minutes later, he was at the head of a car train that stretched back almost half a mile. Estelle was seated beside him, and spent the journey describing her time with Sylvie in the market. When they arrived, they jammed the drive and spilled down the narrow lane. Marcela took charge with the ease of a born general, showing the newcomers the same mix of brisk authority and warm greeting that endeared so many at Castaways.

Connor drifted around for a time, lending a hand here and there, feeling overwhelmed by the number of people and the frenetic activity. An hour after their arrival, he stepped outside to take a call from his Alabama-Russian detective.

"You say check in, so I check," Jones reported. "So far, I find hints but nothing definite."

"But where there's smoke," Connor replied.

"Indeed much smoke. This Hammond fellow, he probably lights many fires. Legal, not legal, I'm thinking this doesn't matter much to him. Only what he can get away with."

Connor felt the renewed sense of electric tension building at gut level. "I need evidence. I need it now."

When Connor returned inside, he found Rick and Carol and Celia and the Castaways kitchen crew had arrived and were busy supervising a new contingent of worker bees in preparing dips and whatever finger food could be left in the refrigerator overnight. Someone set up a portable grill on his back deck. Others began passing around plates of hors d'oeuvres, while the kitchen crew complained bitterly over their food being stuffed down the throats of every lazy Joe who invaded Connor's new home.

A silent auction was basically a reason to hold a giant party, or so it seemed to Connor. Each item would have a bidding sheet attached. People were expected to mill about, eating and drinking and bidding against one another. According to Marcela, the only way to keep a silent auction even barely civil was to assign each person a secret number and to ban all guns.

By the time people started leaving around late afternoon, every flat space in Connor's home was decked out in donated prizes and platters of the goodies that couldn't be crammed into his oversized fridge. His front walk was lined with crates of soda and beer. As Marcela and Rick left for work, they warned him not to drink more than twenty of either. That was not a problem, since he hated both. The wine delivery was late and would now be taken straight to the town hall, along with washtubs of ice. Connor wandered through the rooms, bemused by the absence of people. The air still vibrated slightly from all the noise that had vanished.

Then he spotted Estelle weeping.

She had drawn one of the deck chairs over to the veranda's far corner, beyond a pair of waist-high stone planters that marked his bedroom windows. Connor hesitated over whether he should disturb her. Estelle managed to give sorrow an elegant air. Something about the way she held herself left him fairly certain she knew he was there, so he asked, "Do you need something?"

To her credit, Estelle saw no reason to apologize for her tears. "I am positively overwhelmed with joy."

Connor settled himself on the planter's edge. He was so moved he needed a moment to try and find a response that suited, at least a little. "My life in LA was pretty much defined by solitude. Even when I was surrounded by people, I was alone."

Estelle used both hands to clear her face. "And now?"

Connor sat and watched lights illuminate the streets of his new hometown, and thought of a painting in a restaurant he would probably never visit again. "This is the first housewarming party I've ever had. The fact that it's all been done for someone else makes it even better."

Estelle gave that a moment, then asked, "Will you do something for me?"

"Anything," he replied, and meant it.

"I need to warn you up front, I'll probably bawl my eyes out."

Connor nodded. "I've had some experience at making good women cry. At least this time it'll be because they asked."

Another swipe of the face, then, "When Sylvie was still tiny, her father sang her to sleep almost every night with the same tune. It became the first song she ever sang to me." Estelle took a very hard breath. "I don't think I can even say the name."

"Just tell me the artist," Connor said.

Her chin quivered, but she managed, "Dean Martin."

He knew the one she meant. The song had remained forlorn and forgotten for almost twenty years. Then Dean Martin was fooling around in the studio with the song's author, Ken Lane. They had just one hour of recording time left, and Martin was a song short on his new album, *Dream with Dean.*

Martin had always loved this tune, and suggested they wing it. No arranging, no discussion. Lane was on the piano, with three pals who'd been hanging around the studio on guitar, bass and drums. They finished in one take. They had forty-seven minutes still on the clock, but neither felt like playing it through again.

Listeners loved it so much, Martin took the unheard-of step of recording the same song again on his next album. Only this time, he did so with full orchestration and chorus. His label,

Reprise Records, was so excited by the result, they renamed the album after the song. When released as a single, it knocked the Beatles' *A Hard Day's Night* off the number one position in the Billboard 100. *Everybody Loves Somebody Sometime* remained there for eight weeks and went on to become Dean Martin's defining sound.

Connor rose to his feet and held out his hand. "It will be my pleasure."

CHAPTER 52

Sylvie somehow managed to navigate her way through the busiest Sunday her restaurant had ever known. Almost every table shared the suppressed excitement of people about to burst from holding on to the news of a surprise party. And though she knew about tomorrow's silent auction, Sylvie continued to be surprised. Dumbfounded, in fact.

To outsiders, Californians could seem a superficial, even dismissive people and culture. The reason for this was simple: California was constantly being inundated by newcomers. Its larger cities were filled with people who came from somewhere else. The vast majority still classified that "somewhere else" as home. The only way small-town California remained even partially intact was by being insular. They weren't unfriendly. They weren't closed. It just took time and effort to become accepted as a true member of the local community.

As a result, it was hard to put down roots in this western land, and harder still to be accepted. Nowhere was this more true than along the central coast. The locals nicknamed their region the Middle Kingdom, as in halfway between Los Angeles and San Francisco. It was a world unto itself and beholden to neither.

Sylvie had never felt so bonded to the region or its people than that Sunday. Castaways was jammed with locals. The bar was three deep. Everyone was there, in his or her loudest casual fashion, to show that she was one of Miramar's own.

And there on the wall was her father's painting of Miramar Bay. Right where it belonged . . .

Because of these raucous, pushy, opinionated locals who knew all her secrets and loved her just the same.

And because of a mother who had abandoned her, and had given Sylvie every reason to never forgive or forget. But who now was here, offering support in what would otherwise be a very dark hour indeed.

And because of a man Sylvie had every reason to mistrust.

But Sylvie held it together because that was what a gracious hostess did. To all the people who entered, Sylvie warmly welcomed them to Castaways.

Where they belonged.

CHAPTER 53

On Monday morning, Connor woke just as dawn painted its first strokes upon the sea. He was drawn from slumber by the sound of his own playing. Before he had moved to Los Angeles, such early-morning dreams had been frequent occurrences. As he made his coffee and carried his mug into the parlor, Connor tried to remember the last time he had dreamed about music. Years.

He sat down at the Baldwin baby grand. The handmade instrument was considered by some to be the world's finest for small venues and homes. The sound was warmer and smoother than some professionals cared for. Both the Bösendorfer and Steinways had a cleaner, crisper finish to the keys, but the Baldwin created a more welcoming resonance. As Connor drank his coffee, he fashioned a one-handed melody from the dream's lingering traces. Connor set his mug on the floor by his bench and began to play.

The song that woke him was "Something," written by George Harrison and released on the *Abbey Road* album. It was the only song by Harrison to ever reach number one on the Billboard charts, and Lennon claimed it was the finest song the Beatles ever created. The song was subsequently covered, or rearranged and released, by over a hundred other artists. It reached the top ten another two dozen times. Arranging this song placed Connor in the company of Elvis, Ray Charles, James Brown, Shirley Bassey, Smokey Robinson, and Joe Cocker. Over the next two hours, Connor slowly restructured the song to fit his own voice.

By the time he was satisfied and played it through from beginning to end, he had the sense of taking a giant step toward fashioning his own style. Even so, when Connor rose from the piano a little after eleven, he knew none of this day's accomplishments had really been about the melody.

He made a sandwich and carried it out to the veranda. He stood looking out over the town and the cove and the shimmering Pacific. Connor knew this was why he had come to Miramar. It had never been about the music. It was all about regaining the ability to dream.

As he returned inside, Connor wondered if there was any chance Sylvie would attend the silent auction. If not, Connor hoped that word of this song would get back to her, and she would understand the message behind the words. That Connor was sorry. That he was trying to do as she had said, and hold on to his dreams. That he would never be leaving Miramar. No matter how far his acting career might take him, Connor had found his home.

He was rinsing out the coffeepot when his cell phone rang. "This is Connor."

"Jones here. Remember me?"

"My Alabama Russkie. Sure thing."

"Russkie. Please. Such offensive talk. I am proud to be Ukrainian."

"My sincere apologies. How are tricks?"

"Tricks is an excellent word. I have information. You decide about the tricks."

"So tell."

As he listened to Jones's report, Connor felt the zinging skyrocket explosion of having gotten another something very right.

CHAPTER 54

Estelle found Monday to be an almost impossibly good day.

Even the simplest of acts carried an uncommon sparkle. The air was alive with an excitement no one bothered to hide any longer. She ate breakfast at the diner's largest table, surrounded by eleven of her new best friends. From there, they went straight to the town hall, where they found another dozen people already busy with preparations.

People treated Estelle like a glorified manager. Like she knew what she was doing. Like she *belonged.* Trestle tables were carted in. Red and green felt coverings were tacked into place. Prizes were sorted, bidding sheets were stapled, lists arranged, jobs appointed, bars set up. There were signs, bunting, balloons. . . .

Suddenly, at four, it was all done, or, at least, the core workers had shooed out all the others so they could pretend to work at last-minute details and, in truth, just take a moment to revel in a party that had not yet started. She and Marcela and Rick found a quiet corner by the stage. Marcela asked, "Where's Connor?"

"Handling something with Porter," Rick replied.

Marcela asked, "Does it have anything to do with our party?"

Rick wiggled his hand back and forth. "Yes and no."

"In that case," Marcela said, "it has to wait until tomorrow."

"No way," Rick replied. "This has to happen right now."

"Why is that?"

"I can't tell you."

Marcela said to Estelle, "Does that sound like a man or what?"

But Estelle was busy studying the hall's decoration, the tables lining the room, the prizes, the signs. "Three days ago, this was just some vague idea."

"Nothing brings people together around here better than a party for a good cause," Marcela said.

Rick's phone rang. He excused himself, and then walked away. Estelle said, "If only we could get Sylvie to come."

"Oh, she's coming," Marcela assured her. "She just doesn't know it yet."

"Sylvie might not agree."

"Oh, she may think she has a reason to stay away," Marcela said, "but she's coming anyway."

Estelle resisted the urge to hug the lady. "You're saying Sylvie's feelings about it don't matter?"

"They matter, all right," Marcela replied. "They just don't matter enough."

Rick shut his phone, walked back over, and announced, "Bingo."

"Nice idea, wrong night," Marcela replied. "Whose canary did you swallow?"

"Our boy has come through again," Rick said.

Estelle asked, "You're speaking of Connor?"

"None other." Rick's phone chirped. He checked the read-out. "Perfect. Sol is five minutes out."

Estelle asked, "What's going on?"

"This is Connor's doing," Rick replied. "I'll let him tell you. Right now, we need to find us a very quiet corner."

CHAPTER 55

Rick led Sol Feinnes down the rear corridor and into the mayor's office. Sylvie's attorney was taken aback to find himself confronted by Connor and Porter and Estelle and Marcela. Porter greeted him by saying, "You're late."

"I've spent twenty minutes crawling along the road into town. The traffic was unbelievable. Half the population of the entire central coast must be coming to this silent auction. Am I under arrest?"

Porter demanded, "Did you break any laws getting down here?"

"Not that I'm aware."

"Then you're okay in my book."

Sol surveyed the five faces, all of whom appeared to be holding tightly to a barely suppressed mirth. "Will somebody tell me what's going on?"

Porter used a thumb to direct attention at Connor. "This guy has something to tell you."

"The guy in question being the star whose face is on the front page of my newspaper."

"Right."

"You look better without the scar, by the way."

Porter nodded agreement, and said to Connor, "Tell him."

"I hired a sort of detective," Connor began.

"I'm not sure 'sort of' is a legally recognized term."

"I guess you could call him a researcher," Connor said.

"Slippery word, researcher," Sol observed.

"This is definitely one slippery guy," Connor agreed.

"I'm assuming this means whatever he's uncovered will not be admissible in a court of law."

"You'd be better off presenting the judge with week-old squid," Porter agreed.

Sol said to the chief, "And yet you're here."

"You betcha," Porter said. "Wouldn't miss this for the world."

Rick said, "He's actually responsible for getting your dance partner to show up."

"Excuse me?"

"Phil Hammond," Porter said. "He's the reason we're talking."

"What does that snake have to do with anything?"

"Hammond is minority owner of Castaways," Connor said. "Recently he tried to buy it outright. Sylvie refused. I had this idea, maybe Hammond was somehow connected to everything that's been going on. So I hired this . . ."

"Researcher," Rick chimed in.

"The man has uncovered some serious dirt," Porter said.

When Connor finished laying it out, Sol Feinnes blinked slowly. Then he declared, "This isn't dirt. This is solid gold."

"Told you," Marcela said.

"It's also radioactive," Sol continued. "I couldn't bring this into a courtroom if I was wearing a lead-lined suit."

"But you can use it as a lever," Porter said.

"Oh, my yes." Sol revealed a truly wicked grin. "You say Hammond is coming?"

"He's due any minute," Porter confirmed.

"Then we better plan fast." Sol rubbed his hands together. "This is going to be fun."

CHAPTER 56

Phil Hammond was born to play the prince. He had refined an ability to obtain whatever he wanted without raising his voice. It was a role he had perfected over many episodes, until it became his signature performance. He proceeded down the town hall's back corridor trailed by two nervous young assistants and Harold Rhemus, Phil's bespectacled attorney. Hammond entered the mayor's office with a regal calm. He surveyed the six who waited his arrival with utter disdain. "Could someone please tell me what could not wait until normal business hours? I'm due to speak at an event in Santa Cruz."

Sol was seated in the mayor's chair. Porter stood directly behind him. The other four observers had chairs drawn from the conference room next door. Connor and Rick sat on one side of Sol, Estelle and Marcela were on the other. They faced a lone empty chair on the desk's other side. "Mr. Hammond, I'm Sol Feinnes."

Hammond was dressed in a tailored jacket with a herringbone weave. Striped dress shirt with white collar and cuffs. Massive gold watch. Flash tie. Italian loafers so soft they could probably be rolled up like socks. Phil demanded, "And precisely why is that important to me?"

Hammond's pin-striped attorney said, "Sol is an attorney based in San Luis Obispo."

Hammond flicked an imaginary bit of lint off his sleeve. "Same question."

Sol asked, "Won't you sit down, Mr. Hammond?"

"Thank you, but I won't be staying that long."

Sol said, "Yours is certainly a familiar name to me, sir. I've been at the receiving end of several messes that you initiated."

"Shame you didn't learn to steer clear," Hammond said.

Sol said, "We have a problem and we were hoping you might be able to advise."

"What's your name again?"

"Sol Feinnes, sir."

"I *sell* advice, Feinnes. I give *nothing* away." He turned away. "I think that's more than enough wasted minutes."

"That's actually why I've been asked to speak for these interested parties," Sol said. "We are absolutely willing to pay you the going rate."

That stopped Hammond. "Exactly what rate did you have in mind?"

Porter said, "You get to stay out of jail. Now sit down."

Porter Wright's words were enough to keep Phil Hammond in the room, but he stood behind the chair, arms crossed, fuming.

Sol Feinnes gave no sign he noticed Phil's ire. "We are locked on the horns of a dilemma. You see, our research has turned up the most remarkable set of circumstances. Wouldn't you agree, Porter?"

"Remarkable," Porter agreed. "That's the word."

"The closest casino to Miramar happens to be in Chumash tribal territory. This particular casino, as it happens, has a silent partner. One PH Enterprises, based in Nassau. It's been hard for us to determine who actually owns the company, since that information is carefully guarded. But even the Bahamians can be forced to divulge identities if our federal authorities present evidence of potential illegality—"

Hammond turned around and said to his two young aides, "Out. Now."

When the door clicked shut, Sol continued, "Our research has turned up the most remarkable set of gambling debts."

"Remarkable," Marcela agreed. "I *love* that word."

"We have obtained documentation regarding the casino's outstanding loans to three individuals. A certain judge in the San Luis Obispo regional court. A county prosecutor. And a detective assigned to the sheriff's—"

Harold Rhemus said, "These accusations would never stand up in a court of law."

Estelle said, "Sort of like the accusations you've leveled against my daughter."

"My client has no direct involvement—"

"Stow it," Connor said.

Sol said, "We have dates. We have amounts. We have interest accruing at the astonishing rate of twenty-six percent per annum."

"Astonishing," Marcela said.

"Remarkable," Porter said.

Harold Rhemus said, "No way could this so-called evidence lead to a valid prosecution. You'd be laughed out of court."

"Who said anything about going to court?" Sol held to an almost convivial air. "We're far beyond such an unseemly and time-consuming action. What we intend to do is take what we know to the FBI and the IRS."

"Tomorrow," Porter said.

Hammond dropped heavily into the chair.

"You see, Phil, may I call you Phil? Our Chief Wright, along with the help of several associates, has pieced together a very interesting concept. . . . Explain it to us, Chief, why don't you."

Porter said, "You arranged the coke, the drop, the whole shooting match."

"No attorney on earth could have put it more succinctly," Sol said. "Wouldn't you agree?"

"We know you're behind the Santa Maria development. We know you've hidden your involvement behind the same company that owns the Chumash casino," Porter said, "You needed a front for your projects. A local who would put the town at ease. You needed Sylvie. But she wouldn't play your game, so you decided to buy her out."

Estelle said, "You were going to play carrot and stick with my daughter. Pay her a salary, give her a title, let her keep her restaurant as your little sideline. But only if she did what you said. First you had to get her where you wanted."

Porter said, "It's bothered me since the beginning, how we weren't able to identify even one other company or individual who was receiving drugs by sea. I mean, what's the point of going to all that trouble for just eleven keys? Then it hit me."

Estelle said, "You ran a scam on my daughter. You filth."

"Mere suppositions," the attorney scoffed.

"Oh, it's far more than that," Sol corrected. "Our evidence has uncovered the employment records showing that Carlos, the individual who planted the keys and has subsequently vanished, formerly worked in the casino's security detail."

Estelle said, "You're going down."

"Old Phil," Marcela said, "you've stiffed your last waiter at Castaways."

Sol said, "I'm sure the state investigators would be fascinated with the information regarding the gambling debts of your three friends."

Marcela said, "The best friends money can buy. Right, Phil?"

"No doubt your three friends will be convinced to turn state's evidence against you." Sol offered a cat's smile, all teeth and malice. "Especially when the authorities present them with the alternative of watching their careers ground down to fragments that couldn't be found with an electron microscope."

Phil's attorney clearly knew it was time to ask, "What do you want?"

"We have a few things in mind." Sol glanced over. "Estelle, would you care to lead off?"

CHAPTER 57

Sylvie's Monday crawled by.

There was no longer any pretense of normalcy. Rick or Marcela or Bruno or Carl usually slipped in the back door at some point, ensuring no urgent duty had arisen to cloud their day off. But today Sylvie repeatedly checked downstairs, and no one came.

By four that afternoon, Sylvie had run out of excuses to hide away. She went downstairs and made herself a cappuccino on the machine in the waiters' station. She drank it at the bar, staring at the silent piano in the abalone-shaped alcove. The restaurant was filled with an expectant air, like the energy in a silent room before a big party. Sylvie could almost hear the laughter.

Around five, people started streaming past the windows fronting the street. Sylvie checked her reflection in the washroom mirror; then she let herself out of the restaurant. She was mildly disappointed that neither Rick nor Marcela had thought to come walk with her. After all, it was her party, at least in some respects.

But within ten paces of her front door, Sylvie found herself surrounded by smiling faces and laughter and easy chatter. She could not have named most of those who walked alongside her. Nor did it matter. Not really.

Miramar's town hall stood six blocks farther inland from Castaways. The old-town area, with its raised sidewalks and mock gaslights, gave way to a series of modest buildings that housed the city's offices and one of two supermarkets. The town hall was a fifties-era gray clapboard structure with a broad front veranda of seasoned redwood. The floors and walls and high ceiling of the vast main room formed an echo chamber, such that the crowd's growing din greeted Sylvie as she entered.

That evening, the meeting hall had been cleverly divided into two sections, both of which were packed with people and items waiting to be auctioned. Three tables staffed with volunteers fanned out by the entrance, where each newcomer was handed a number printed on a three-by-five card in exchange for credit card details. It was done in such a friendly and smooth fashion that even the lookie-loos became potential bidders long before they entered the real arena.

Most of the hot-ticket items were placed in the front section, well removed from the exit. The hall's two portions were split by a long cash bar, staffed by a dozen cheerful volunteers and offering a vast selection of donated finger food.

Ringing the walls were balloons and banners urging the growing crowd to help one of their own.

People kept rushing over, laughing and excited in their welcome. They chattered about the prizes, the night, the awful trial. Actually, Sylvie heard very little of what they were saying. Their voices and their embraces formed one great wave of affection that kept surging over her.

When Marcela appeared, she pretended not to notice Sylvie's misty-eyed condition. "Glad you could make it on your own steam. I was about to come up with the six-wheeler and drag you down."

"You're saying I didn't have a choice in the matter?"

"Of course you did. Whether you came on your own steam or mine." Marcela beamed. "You need a drink before we mingle?"

But at that moment, the lights dimmed and Porter Wright stepped to the microphone at the center of the stage. He nervously cleared his throat, then said, "I've been assigned duty tonight, don't ask me why."

The crowd gave him a welcoming cheer. As it subsided, he went on, "We're here to help one of our own. Where's Sylvie? I saw her come in. . . ."

A voice called, "She's back here!"

"Glad you could join us. Folks, give Sylvie a big hand, let her know how much we care for the lady of the hour." He paused for a renewed cheer. "Most of the time when rotten things happen to people for all the wrong reasons, there's not much we can do but stand with them through the dark hour. But in this case, we can really make a difference. So dig deep and buy what you don't need."

Porter was almost off the stage, when his wife called up, "Aren't you forgetting something?"

Shamefaced, he stepped back to the mike and said, "I told Carol they should've gotten somebody up here who knew what he was doing."

"You're doing just fine, honey," Carol said. "Now give them the good news."

"Right. Unless you've been asleep for the past week, you know Connor Larkin. . . ."

Sylvie felt her heart take wings as the crowd applauded. The upsurge of emotions threatened her ability to maintain a calm façade.

"Connor Larkin is fresh from being signed on to play the bad guy in the new James Bond picture. . . ." Porter had to stop a second time.

As he waited, Connor stepped onto the stage. This time, Sylvie felt the applause squeeze her heart with a fierce yearning. She had not expected to feel such a clamor of conflicting emotions. She was the only person in the hall not cheering. Somebody patted her shoulder. Sylvie knew eyes were on her. However, she could not smile, or move, or lift her hands and even pretend to join in.

Porter said, "Connor has agreed to give a private concert for the highest bidder, and here's a sample of what the winner will enjoy."

Sylvie stayed where she was, silent and immobile, desperate to hear him sing one more time.

The lights dimmed a trace more, the audience went still as a sleeping infant, and Connor sang:

> *Something in the way she knows,*
> *And all I have to do is think of her.*

Sylvie knew without a doubt that Connor was singing to her. His music instantly pulled her back to a night of fairyland bliss, when strong arms held her and she had believed in love again. . . .

Connor released a sigh as strong as winter's tempest as Sylvie left the hall. He had handled some tough roles in his acting career, but nothing so difficult as completing his song and smiling his thanks to an audience he could no longer actually see.

Determined to launch the auction on a high note, he shut his eyes to the burn of lost hope and began the final song. He told himself that he had done all he possibly could, and now it was up to Sylvie. All of that helped, at least a little.

Even so, as he rose and accepted their raucous applause, Connor reflected that now he had a gut-level understanding to draw from, when he was next called upon to die beneath the lights.

CHAPTER 58

As far as Sylvie was concerned, the week that followed was one long series of unexpected bright spots.

Early Tuesday morning, she asked Estelle to meet her in the café by the guesthouse. As soon as they were seated, Sylvie declared once more, "I don't want you to go."

"And I don't want to leave. My darling daughter . . ." Estelle lifted three fingers to her trembling lips. She took a long breath, clenched her hands together on the table, and did her best to smile. "There. I said it."

Sylvie asked, "How did it feel?"

"Awesome." Estelle must have seen the conflict in Sylvie's features, for she did not ask how Sylvie felt hearing it. "May I come by the restaurant?"

"Can you . . . Of course."

"There is no 'of course' to anything we're doing here." She smiled then, the joy almost palpable. "You must tell me if I become a nuisance. Otherwise, I might stop by each evening for a glass."

"And a meal."

"I will do no such thing. I will merely sit at the bar and I will watch you." The lips trembled through the smile. "And I will be the happiest and proudest mother on the planet."

On Tuesday afternoon, Sylvie heard from the Castaways linen supplier that Phil Hammond had bought a teacup at the silent auction.

For thirty thousand dollars.

When the delivery van pulled away, and everyone in the kitchen refused to meet her eye, Sylvie demanded, "Did anybody know about this?"

"I might've heard something," Bruno replied. "I bought a vintage T-shirt."

"Rick?"

"I tried to buy half a dozen things," he replied. "But I got outbid every time."

When she turned to Marcela, her friend snapped, "I didn't get a chance to bid, since I spent all night trying to find you. Where did you go, by the way?"

Sylvie had no choice but to reply, "I need to check on tonight's bookings."

"You do that," Marcela huffed. As Sylvie left the kitchen, Marcela said, "She moves almost as fast as my husband did when I asked him to bid on Connor's concert."

It was only later, when the town's deputy mayor and his wife confirmed that Phil's check for thirty grand had already cleared, that Sylvie realized Marcela had succeeded magnificently in changing the subject.

On Wednesday morning, Sol Feinnes woke her at half past six. "Sorry to call so early. But I needed to catch you before you left for San Luis Obispo. The trial has been postponed."

Sylvie had no idea how she felt about a delay. "What does that mean?"

"I try not to deal in rumors. We should know something definite before very long. Two days at the most. You sleeping all right?"

"Surprisingly well, considering."

"Glad to hear it. Hang in there, friend. I'll be back in touch as soon as I know anything for certain."

Most of the other revelations seemed timed to opening hour, when they had the most impact. At least that's what Sylvie told Estelle when she settled at the Castaways bar that evening. Sylvie related how, twenty minutes before she unlocked the front door, Rick announced that an anonymous bidder had paid seventy thousand dollars for Connor's private concert.

Estelle sipped at her glass of white wine and observed, "For seventy thousand dollars, I'm surprised the buyer didn't ask for a teacup to match old Phil's."

"You knew about this," Sylvie realized.

"I might have heard something somewhere."

"You didn't think it might be worth mentioning? Since that one bid covers my entire legal bill?"

Estelle had the remarkable ability to sip her wine without lowering the level in her glass. "Why did you leave the silent auction Monday evening?"

"Why . . . You know full well. I ran away. And don't change the subject."

"I wouldn't dream of doing any such thing." Estelle pointed at the door. "You have customers."

On Thursday afternoon, Phil Hammond's attorney called to say he was stopping by, and that he needed ten minutes of her time. Sylvie was tempted to put him off, but she decided she'd rather hear the bad news now, rather than have another reason to fret through a sleepless night.

Harold Rhemus arrived an hour later, during a tidal wave of early clients. Phil's attorney appeared both nervous and sweaty in his suit and button-down blue shirt and the restaurant's only

tie. She seated him at the long front table, and then was surprised when Estelle and Marcela and Rick shifted over to sur-
round her. At first, Sylvie thought they had come to offer
support, but then she saw smiles being stifled. This only added
to the confusion.

Sylvie asked, "Can I get you something?"

"I'm not staying, thank you." It was only when he adjusted
his spectacles that Sylvie realized Rhemus was trembling. Re-
gardless of how her staff was almost dancing in place, Sylvie
knew Phil and she knew this lawyer. They had no connection to
good news. Whatever had brought him here, it had to be bad.

"Mr. Hammond has elected to withdraw all participation in
food services," Harold said. "As a result, he wishes to divest
himself of his interest in Castaways."

"I-I'm sorry . . . What?"

Rhemus opened his attaché case and drew out a manila
folder. The tremors rose to his voice as he went on, "Mr.
Hammond understands that he has run up quite a large bill.
He is offering you his share in Castaways in exchange for all
outstanding . . ."

The attorney was halted by Estelle and Rick and Marcela,
who were entering into a somewhat clumsy three-way jig. He
cast them a dark glance, then slid the folder in front of Sylvie.
"It's all there in black and white. Sign both copies with a notary
as witness. Return both to me for Mr. Hammond's signature."

Aubrey popped the champagne cork just as the attorney fled
from the restaurant.

CHAPTER 59

Connor took the week at a steady and unhurried pace. The canceled three-week honeymoon left a very convenient hole in his schedule. His new home had not been lived in for almost a year, and he found a multitude of problems that needed urgent attention. Every day was filled with work, sunup to sundown, but he set the pace. He listed the next day's chores over his solitary dinners. He spent his evenings watching all the old Bond films, right back to *Goldfinger.* He also intended to study at least three movies by each of the current stars and the director and the cinematographer. Each night he went to bed early, slept well, and rose ready for more of the same.

Saturday was Porter's day off. He drove Carol and Celia over, selected a deck chair on the rear veranda, and lost himself in one of Lisa Jackson's suspense novels. Estelle arrived a half hour later and joined mother and daughter in a thorough house-cleaning. When Connor offered to help, he got three versions of the same tirade, which he basically translated as, If Connor was any good at cleaning up, they wouldn't be here in the first place.

Connor retreated to the rear patio and asked the police chief, "Why do I get the impression they're not telling me something?"

Porter shook his head without taking his eyes off the page. "Nope. I am not getting volunteered again."

"What are you talking about?"

"You want answers, you go ask the ladies."

"I'm asking you."

Porter glanced over the top of his half-moon reading glasses. "And I am telling you that for once I am not re-upping."

"I have no idea what you just said."

"Watch carefully." Porter turned the page. "This is me enjoying my day off. Now, unless you're going to offer me a fresh cup of coffee, I'd appreciate your not aiming another word in my direction."

Almost half of the patio's flagstones had become dislodged, probably from some tremor the town had slept through. Time and the previous weekend's foot traffic had crumbled some of the corners. Connor refit them with a special cement the Home Depot guy had said was blended for flexibility. He worked through one bucket, long enough to grow completely hot and bothered. Porter ignored him with a cop's stony intent. Finally Connor gave up and walked back to the sliding doors leading to his bedroom. The ladies had already finished up in there, so he showered and dressed in clean shorts and T-shirt.

When he entered the kitchen, he found the trio arrayed against him, all lined up behind the counter.

Estelle said, "We have some news."

"I sorta figured that."

Carol pointed him to one of the stools on the counter's other side. "You're going to want to sit down." When he did, she went on, "Your private concert has been bought for seventy thousand dollars."

Connor looked from one lady to the next. Behind him, he heard the sliding door open. He asked, "Is this a joke?"

Celia asked, "Do we look like we're joking?"

"How long am I supposed to play? A year?"

Carol said, "Sol Feinnes bought it."

"I don't . . . Wait . . . Sylvie's lawyer has refused payment?"

"He didn't refuse anything," Porter said. "He's given it back."

Carol said, "Here's where you ask about Sol's one condition."

Celia said, "We should have a drumroll for this next part."

Carol said, "He bought the concert so you would play for Sylvie."

Celia brought her hands together. "And cymbals."

Carol said, "This was Estelle's idea."

Celia said, "Correction. Her *brilliant* idea."

Estelle said, "You're too kind."

"No she's not," Celia said.

Carol said, "Sol is making the donation on the condition that you play for Sylvie."

Connor replied, "Sylvie won't want that."

Estelle smiled. "You just leave that with me."

CHAPTER 60

The tectonic plates beneath Sylvie's world continued to shift right through the weekend. As she was planning Saturday's specials, Porter entered the kitchen and made a slow circuit, shaking everyone's hands and speaking a few friendly words. Any other season of her life, Sylvie would have found a gentle gratitude in how Miramar's chief of police could be so comfortable around two convicted felons and her other miscreants, including herself. Sylvie Cassick's own record was clean only because her juvie files remained sealed.

However, given the fact that she was just days removed from her delayed felony trial, all Sylvie could manage was to keep her lunch down.

When Porter finally arrived at where she stood frozen to the kitchen's polished concrete floor, he said, "Let's go up front."

Only when he took hold of her arm was she able to move. As she passed through the doors, she glanced back in time to watch Bruno and Carl exchange high fives. Sylvie considered the action almost treacherous.

Porter led her over to the bar and said to Aubrey, "Give us a few minutes."

"No problem." Aubrey added her own disloyal smile to the day's strangeness and departed.

Porter then surprised her by pulling his phone from his shirt pocket and punching in a number. He watched her intently as he waited. Then he said to the phone, "We're good to go." Porter passed over the phone and said, "It's for you."

She needed two hands to lift the phone. "Yes?"

"Sol Feinnes here. I'm happy to inform you that all charges against you have been dropped."

Sol continued to talk for a while about papers and such. She tried hard to listen, but the mist over her eyes had somehow managed to affect her hearing as well. When he went quiet, Sylvie made a total hash of her thanks. Then she handed back the phone, took a few unsteady breaths, and finally managed, "Is this really real?"

"As real as it gets."

"But what if, you know, they come back?" She knew she sounded like a nine-year-old asking about the boogeyman, but she could do nothing about it.

"Actually, that's why I'm here." Porter shifted his lumpish bulk on the stool, leaning closer still. "The sheriff's detective has been reassigned. He's now on guard duty at Lompoc Men's Prison."

"What does that mean?"

"It means there are a lot of others who are very upset about the case against you ever having gone anywhere near a courtroom." Porter was clearly enjoying himself enormously. "The prosecutor has been reassigned to the lovely desert resort of Barstow. And this morning, the judge in question announced he's taking early retirement."

Sylvie gave a very tight sigh, a quick in-and-out breath, like she was recovering from a wound and needed to see how far she could stretch the scar tissue.

Porter liked her silence enough to ease off his stool, lean over, and kiss her on the cheek. He pocketed his phone, patted her on the shoulder, and left without another word.

CHAPTER 61

On Sunday evening, Miramar's mayor and half the town council stopped by Castaways with the auction's official tally. The events had run up a surplus of 104,000 dollars.

"That's not possible," Sylvie told them.

"I absolutely agree." The mayor was a rawboned woman who ran one of Miramar's two veterinary services. It was said she could still a bucking horse with one bark. "But I've gone through the numbers myself. Twice."

They were seated at the long front table. Behind them, the restaurant was filled with the normal weekend clamor. Her staff rushed about, borderline frantic. Sylvie had a dozen things that urgently needed her attention. But just then, all she could accomplish was to sit upright. "What do you want from me?"

"We met with Estelle this afternoon. For all intents and purposes, she's the woman responsible for the whole shooting match. She agrees with us that the money is yours to do with as you please."

"I don't . . . No. Absolutely not. You're not handing me that mess."

"I absolutely am." The mayor's seamed features rearranged themselves into a vast grin. "It's not every day I get to argue with somebody about writing them a check."

"I can't accept that money!"

"Nobody expects you to. You just need to decide which local charities are getting an early Christmas." The mayor rose from her seat. "One thing can't wait. Estelle is still out twenty thousand dollars. She's making noise about how she doesn't want anything paid back. I need you to talk some sense to that lady."

An hour later, Sylvie found a brief quiet moment and phoned Estelle. To Sylvie's surprise, when she insisted that Estelle take back the funds, her mother simply asked, "Are you sure?"

"About this, absolutely."

"All right. I just want you to know that I was glad to be there when you needed me." There was a shaky breath; then she added, "This time."

CHAPTER 62

Late Monday morning Estelle walked along Miramar's central avenue, down past Castaways and on toward the sea. She exchanged greetings with a few people, but she refused to allow anyone to slow her progress. She did not have much time, as she had agreed to volunteer at the animal shelter and there were still a few details to complete regarding the day's main event. But before all that she wanted a few moments in her little seaside haven. And like any good penitent, Estelle felt a need to arrive there on foot.

When she reached the beachfront road she turned left and climbed the gentle slope. She crossed the parking area and took the path through the clifftop park. There was a breathless hush to the air, neither any wind nor the faintest ripple to mar the ocean's surface. The Pacific stretched out in blue-gold majesty to join with the cloudless horizon. The air was a mix of sunlit heat and the water's biting chill. The result was a champagne headiness to her every breath.

Estelle retreated to the open-fronted chapel and was pleased to find it empty. She seated herself and stared at the sunlit vista and silently acknowledged the true significance of the day's events. More was at work, she knew, than her being accepted by the town her daughter called home. More too than helping Sylvie reunite with a man desperately seeking to become someone who deserved her daughter's love.

Miramar had granted Estelle what she could not have brought herself to even ask for. Her past was full of reasons why she should never be granted her silent wish. She remained fully aware of all her many wrongs, including the fractured prayers she had formed while seated right here.

Even so, Estelle had come to discover this town's secret gift. And not just her. Miramar had offered it to three people who yearned for this above all else.

A second chance.

When she was ready, Estelle rose from the bench and whispered the shortest prayer of all.

"Thank you."

On Monday, Sylvie finally reached the decision she had been working toward since the moment Connor had arrived onstage. Only she had needed this long to accept the truth.

She was going to see Connor again.

The question was, how should she make that first huge step?

Her decision only strengthened the whispered refrain of wanting it all to just go away. Simply because she had realized that she needed Connor did not erase the mental arguments. The fears brought up worries for which she only had one answer. She really, really wanted to see him again.

Even so, the internal conflict kept her from taking the desired step. Sylvie went through the motions all through her Monday. Sylvie pretended that she was going to have a normal evening off, eat her usual solitary meal, and join Humphrey Bogart and Ingrid Bergman in their safe black-and-white world. She puttered about the apartment in cutoffs and a raggedy T-shirt. Why shouldn't she? After all, nobody at Rick's Café in Casablanca would care what she wore.

But the lonely hours only clarified the truths she had wrestled with all week. She had fled the auction precisely because she had known even then that she was going to take this step. She was going to invite Connor back into her life.

Nothing about this was safe, or easy. There would be no half step with this man. How could there be? She was already in love with him. Now that she was coming to terms with this undeniable fact, it felt as though she had loved him since the very first moment he had walked into Castaways. And stood there in the doorway, staring blindly about, lost to the song and the chance that they might together actually fly to the moon.

She ran herself a hot bath and spent time on her makeup, though she had no idea what to do with herself once all the preliminaries were out of the way. Thankfully, just as she finished dressing, Estelle phoned and asked, "Are you busy?"

"I have no idea." Sylvie found herself wanting desperately to tell her mother about her growing desire to start anew with Connor, or at least try. If only she knew how. That, of course, meant admitting that Estelle was becoming her friend. Another incredible component of this amazing week. "Is there any chance we could meet?"

"That was actually why I called. I have something I need to talk with you about. I'm volunteering at the animal shelter. The woman who's supposed to be on duty has sprained her hip. Could you come up here?"

"Why don't I just wait until you're finished?"

"Because . . ." Estelle's giggle sounded like an excited young girl's. "Because of a hundred different reasons. Marcela is on her way over to pick you up."

Sylvie started to ask what Marcela had to do with anything, but then she heard a car's horn through her front window. She glanced down and said, "Marcela is already here."

* * *

When Sylvie appeared in the front door of Castaways, Marcela greeted her by saying, "What took you so long?"

"I was down in ten seconds flat." Sylvie watched Marcela do an excited two-step by her car door. "You look like a child at Christmas. What's going on?"

"You'll see. It's a surprise."

Sylvie set the alarm and locked the door and complained, "I hate surprises."

"Don't I know it." Marcela slipped behind the wheel and started the car. "Get in. This one won't wait."

"I need a week off," Sylvie objected. "Calm, no explosions."

"And you're going to get it," Marcela promised. "I have you down for early next year."

They drove a mile farther from the ocean and parked in the lot behind the county buildings. They rose from the car and crossed the street, heading for the town's animal shelter. Sylvie asked, "How did Estelle even hear about this place?"

"This is the mayor's number one project," Marcela replied. "They got to talking about using some of your money for renovations."

"It's not my money," Sylvie countered. But she could see Marcela getting ready to argue the point, and waved it aside. "All right, yes. It's my money until I give it away. So the mayor and my mother know each other now."

"Your mother's become the second most popular person in town, after you." They entered the shelter and asked the volunteer on front-office duty, "Where's Estelle?"

"Seeing to our newest arrivals," the woman cheerfully replied. "Second door on your right. Hi, Sylvie. Prepare to have your heart stolen right out of your chest."

Marcela pushed through the door marked CLINIC, and halted in front of the steel diagnostics table, which held . . .

A basketful of kittens.

Nine of them.

Four were gray fluffballs, soft as smoke and about the size of Sylvie's hand. The other five were calicos, with matching white socks. They mewed and crawled and squirmed. One of the gray furballs lifted its front paws at Sylvie and cried to be picked up.

"Aren't they the most adorable things you've ever seen!" Estelle lifted the gray cat and handed it to her daughter. "Don't you want to take this one home with you?"

Sylvie lifted the kitten to her cheek. "This is the sweetest form of bribery I've ever known."

"Oh, we didn't bring you here for this," Estelle said. "We want to talk with you about Connor."

Sylvie started to put the kitten down, but it chose that moment to purr and nestle beneath her chin. She managed, "Connor?"

"Let's review the situation," Marcela said. "A major hottie has basically been dropped into your life."

"Yes, Connor lied to you," Estelle added. "Yes, you had every reason to respond as you did."

Marcela went on, "So how does he react when you turn him to ashes in public? Does he try to argue his way out? Does he get all defensive and yell at you?"

Estelle said, "Connor does his best to change. He apologizes with his every action."

Sylvie started, "Actually, that's what I wanted—"

"We're talking now," Marcela said. "Your job is to listen."

Estelle said, "My darling daughter, Connor Larkin is head over heels in love with you. It's time you accepted that the feeling is mutual."

Marcela said, "Let's not forget the fact that he's incredibly good-looking and a Hollywood star."

"Not yet," Estelle said. "But he will be once the Bond film is released."

Marcela added, "Did we mention that Connor's moving up?"

Sylvie forced herself to settle the kitten back in the basket, where it looked up at her and mewed plaintively. "Connor Larkin is moving to Miramar."

"He signed a lease on the Kaufmans' place," Estelle said. "He's making this his home."

Sylvie looked from one shining face to the other. Her mother and her best friend were here for one reason. They wanted her to be happy. Sylvie swallowed against the burn and managed, "You are both so precious to me."

Her mother's laugh held a songbird's quick note. She wiped her eyes with the hand not holding a kitten, then said, "This is supposed to be your day for dreams come true. Not mine."

Marcela recommenced her dancing in place. "Now tell her the best part."

CHAPTER 63

When the three ladies arrived back at Castaways, every window in the supposedly closed restaurant gleamed softly. Sylvie thought the place looked like one of her father's paintings. She sat taking tight, little breaths, flooded with an impossible mixture of excitement and fear. As Estelle cut the motor, Sylvie said, "I really don't want to go in there alone."

"If that's what you want, of course we'll stay," Estelle said.

"You expected this?"

"I wouldn't say, 'expect,'" Marcela replied from the rear seat. "More like . . ."

"We thought this might be your response," Estelle replied. "Daughter, do you want to do this? That is the real question."

"Say you do," Marcela pleaded.

Sylvie breathed once again. "More than I know how to say."

Marcela bounced up and down in her seat. "Yippee."

Estelle said, "Carol and Celia have helped with the arrangements. They asked me to tell you that they would like to come join us. But only if you want."

Sylvie saw the front door open and Connor step into view. "I suppose . . . all right. Yes."

Marcela said, "Yippee again."

CHAPTER 64

Connor stood in the doorway and waited. He could see the three ladies were deep in some serious confab. His stomach was too filled with electric butterflies for him to even smile, much less walk over. He knew without the tiniest fraction of doubt that Sylvie was having second thoughts. He personally felt she should receive a medal for making it this far.

He remained where he was, willing to stand there all night if necessary. He had no idea what might make things worse, or even blow this second chance right out of town.

All afternoon, he had become increasingly convinced that this was, in fact, just that, a second chance at making his dreams come true.

That is, if the lady actually did decide to rise from the car and cross the street and enter her restaurant. And let him stay. And listen to him try his best to put his feelings into song.

Connor was alerted to a shift in the evening's currents by the sound of a pickup truck door opening. Until Celia bounded out, Connor had not even been aware that she and her mother had hung around.

She called to him, "Sylvie says we can stay for the party!"

And just like that, Connor knew it was going to be okay.

Sylvie felt as though she floated across the street and through her restaurant's front doorway. She had read about how some women drifted upon clouds as their lovers led them across the ballroom floor. Here she was just coming home. There was no orchestra, no gleaming chandeliers, and certainly no bevy of uniformed waiters ready to leap at her every whim.

Here there were just her friends. Four ladies who only wanted the best for her.

It was already the finest night of her life.

The area behind the bar was mostly dark. Celia and Carol and Connor had positioned a few candles here and there, but the real surprise awaited her as she rounded the bar. The long table was aflame. A gleaming silver bowl was filled with water, and a dozen candles floated in it. The serving platter was surrounded by flowers and ivy. More flowers and candles traced a pattern around the stage's perimeter. Two tall iron stands stood behind the piano, turning the abalone-shaped shell into a varnished rainbow.

Sylvie glanced at her father's painting on the wall. The stage and the painting looked like twin patterns.

For a brief instant, she had the sensation that her father was standing there beside her, inspecting them with her. She allowed herself to be guided forward, grateful for the help just then, because it had become rather hard to see her way.

Connor stood to one side as the ladies seated themselves. His position was that of a formal waiter, silent and attentive and holding to a respectful distance. Once they were comfortable, he went back around the bar and returned with an ice bucket that held two bottles of Dom Pérignon champagne. Another trip and he brought out five glasses, then plate after plate of hot and cold appetizers. He filled their glasses, and then climbed onto the stage.

All without saying a word.

Sylvie's chair was angled slightly, so she could both watch Connor and look out the bay windows, over the rooftop view of her hometown. She observed Connor as he lit the candelabra and set it on a protective cloth atop the keyboard. He seated himself, then started to play.

His first tune was one made famous by Ella Fitzgerald, "Into Each Life Some Rain Must Fall." Her father had played it constantly in the weeks after Estelle's departure. Sylvie had not thought of the song in years. She knew an odd sense of comfort when Estelle leaned forward and cupped her face in her hands. This time, thankfully, the distance between them was not so great. In fact, it seemed natural to reach over and settle her hand upon Estelle's shoulder.

When the song ended, and they all applauded, her mother straightened and turned to Sylvie and whispered, "I had no idea it would be this hard."

Sylvie replied softly, "I'm so glad you're here."

Connor shifted smoothly into Nat King Cole's signature song, "When I Fall in Love." Sylvie found herself carrying on a most intense conversation that rose and fell with the melody. She knew the time would come when she shared her thoughts with Connor. But just then, it was important to discuss this with herself. How the birthday wishes had all come true, even the one of sharing an hour with her father, who drifted just beyond the candle's reach.

More important still, however, was that she had been reminded of how important it was to dream, to ignore all the reasons life offered to give up on hope, and to yearn for the impossible. Believe it was possible to know such things as boundless joy, and the love of a good man.

The moon nudged over the northern coast, and a soft breeze spiced the air with a hint of the Pacific. Sylvie thought the night was gentle as her father's brushstrokes, and loved how her mother kept hold of her hand.

Connor segued into one of Tony Bennett's greatest hits, *The Way You Look Tonight.*

CHAPTER 65

The others were long gone.

Sylvie had joined Connor on the piano bench. He played a little, but mostly they just sat. Connor felt as though they were both getting used to the way they fit together. Communicating at the level of bone and sinew and hearts.

Though he feared the words would get in the way, still he knew he had to say them. He spoke for the first time that night in something other than a melody. "Sylvie, I'm so very, very sorry."

She nestled closer still. "You said that already."

"Did I?"

She touched the keys, though not hard enough to make a sound. "Over and over."

He started to turn, afraid and yet sensing it was time. He was both glad and grateful when she turned to meet him, like two dancers who had practiced the move for years.

They kissed. For Connor, it felt as though the kiss was meant never to end. He leaned back and cupped her face in his hands. Then he let himself fall into her gaze.

Then they kissed again.

He knew if he was ever to write his own lyrics, it would be about this. How a kiss could come and go, and still be part of forever.

MIRAMAR BAY

Davis Bunn

The following discussion questions are included to enhance
your group's reading of *Miramar Bay*.

Discussion Questions

1. Have you ever thought about starting over? Have you ever considered just leaving your life behind and beginning again in another city, or in a small town like Miramar Bay? What would be good and bad about this? What would you miss? What would you be excited about?

2. What do you think about Connor Larkin's decision to hide out in Miramar Bay, using an assumed name? Is this an act of courage or cowardice?

3. Connor has everything that most people think they want—fame, fortune, talent, a bright future. Why is he not happy at the start of this novel?

4. What do you think of Connor's fiancée, Kali? Is Connor being fair or unfair to her?

5. What is it about Miramar Bay that draws Connor? Can you understand the appeal of a place like this?

6. The restaurant that Sylvie owns and runs is called "Castaways". Why do you think that Sylvie and her father chose this name? Do you think it remains an apt name?

7. What is Estelle looking for when she comes to Miramar Bay? Do you think that she knows what she's looking for . . . and does she eventually find it? What do you think of how she handled things in the past with regard to her first husband and her daughter? Does she deserve forgiveness? If you had been her daughter, would you be able to forgive her?

8. Several characters refer to Sylvie as a strong person. Do you agree with this assessment? Where does her strength come from?

9. If you could have your own private concert with Connor, what would you ask him to play for you?

10. Do you have any dreams or talents from earlier in your life that you would love to get back to? What is stopping you?

Don't miss the next warmhearted, wise, and
wonderfully moving novel from the
internationally bestselling Davis Bunn . . .

FIREFLY COVE

Available January 2018

Read on for a preview. . . .

CHAPTER 1

MAY 1, 1969

Most people said Lucius Quarterfield wore a name bigger than he deserved.

As Lucius and his sisters were passed from aunt to grandparent to cousins, family members had often said it to his face. In the forties and fifties, California's central coast was a vibrant farming region with an aggressive go-ahead attitude. Strong men tilled the earth and raised robust families. Lucius Quarterfield was a nice enough boy, quiet and watchful. But the families who took in Lucius and his sisters knew he would never amount to anything. The bullies gradually grew tired of picking on Lucius. Some even slipped into guardian roles, when it suited them. Mostly Lucius grew up being ignored. His quiet nature made that all the more possible. He lost himself in books and schoolwork, though he was careful to hide his passions. He was a cautious fellow by nature, with a zeal for numbers.

The one thing that had come easy to Lucius was success. It did not make up for all the misery and loneliness, but it certainly made it easier to bear.

This particular doctor's office had always struck Lucius as a restful place, which was extremely odd, because most of life's problems had centered on doctors. But Nicolo Barbieri was different from many in the medical fraternity, who assumed a ridiculous superiority and lied to young Lucius with their smiles. Nicolo Barbieri's family was among the original Italian immigrant clans who had moved from Tuscany to till the California earth as tenant farmers. A generation later, they had scraped together enough money to buy land of their own, and planted one of the early central coast vineyards. Nico had fought against the tradition-bound family's wishes and studied medicine. Perhaps as a result, Nico Barbieri was a brusque man without a comforting bone to his body. His patients either adored him or found another doctor. "You're dying, Lucius."

"So what else is new." Lucius buttoned his shirt and pushed himself off the doctor's table. He always perspired when being examined, a leftover effect of all the pain doctors had caused him growing up. "I've been dying for twenty-two years."

"Your heart reminds me of a garbage disposal working on a spoon. I should put you in the hospital and run some tests."

"The tests will tell you what we already know."

Barbieri fished a cigarette from his shirt pocket as he slipped behind his desk. "Are you truly so cavalier about death?"

"You've been telling me I'm dying since I was seven years old," Lucius replied. "And don't light that."

"Sorry. Bad habit." Barbieri stuck the unfiltered Camel cigarette back into the pack. "This is different. Are your affairs in order?"

The room suddenly chilled enough to turn his skin clammy. "You've never asked me that before."

"Never felt the need. Are they?"

"Pretty much. I'm negotiating a new deal. Should be finished next week."

"Lucius, you don't need the stress of another deal. Your

heart can't take it. And I know for a fact you don't need the money." Barbieri opened the patient folder and began making notes. The file was almost three inches thick. "Bad ticker, weak bones, half a lung."

I have this, Lucius thought, knotting his tie and pulling it tight. *I have today.*

As though Barbieri could hear his unspoken reply, he said, "You've made the best you could of a thin life. Now go out and enjoy yourself. While you still have time."

Dr. Barbieri's waiting room always appeared half-full. The patients changed, but the setting remained the same. The adults leafed through old copies of *Life* and *Look* and *National Geographic,* while the children played with toys made sticky from hundreds of little hands. Rooms like this had been one of the few constants in Lucius's early life. He used the phone in the nurses' station to call his banker and cancel the day's meeting. The banker was a longtime acquaintance and Lucius was an important client, so he did not complain when Lucius told him to reschedule the meeting with the seller's lawyers. As he hung up the phone, Lucius caught sight of himself in the mirror behind the weight machine. He was five feet eleven inches tall, when he held himself fully erect, which seldom happened. Lucius was underweight and his posture was awful. His cheeks had become sunken during his early bout of pleurisy and never filled back in. The childhood illness had cost him his sense of taste. Smells were vague entities, like words spoken in some foreign tongue. Eating was a troublesome task. His hair was a mousy brown and limp as old noodles. His eyes . . . Lucius turned away. He rarely bothered with his appearance, even when buying clothes.

Lucius Quarterfield was twenty-eight years old.

The nurse asked, "When does the doctor want to see you again?"

"He didn't say."

Her hand hovered over the appointment book. "Are you sure, Lucius?"

"Not a peep. Maybe he thinks I'm all better."

Her smile carried all the false cheeriness of his childhood. "I'm sure that's it."

Lucius drove his brand-new Chevrolet Impala north from San Luis Obispo. He had not been back to Miramar in almost a year, though for a time he had traveled this road every week. He was not a man given to holidays and easy living. Recently his only days off had been when he was unable to rise from his bed. Otherwise his every waking hour was spent making money. When the doctor said he should take some time off and enjoy himself, this journey was the only thing that came to mind.

Lucius had never much cared for his name, which to him sounded like it was made for a guy with one lung, bad bones, and a poor heart. He had always preferred Luke. He considered Luke to be a hard name, full of the go-ahead spirit that burned with volcanic fury inside him. Three days after his sixteenth birthday, Lucius Quarterfield had taken his meager inheritance, borrowed everything his two older sisters were willing to loan him, and bought a vacant lot a block off Santa Barbara's Fifth Street. Even then his sisters recognized their brother had something most people lacked, a fire his ravaged and weakened body could scarcely contain. Lucius had strung plastic multicolored flags and buntings from the trees, paid a builder to clear the earth and lay down gravel, erected a moth-eaten army surplus tent, and put nine road-weary used cars up for sale. In the twelve years since then, Lucius had built an empire that contained eleven dealerships selling some blend of the GM lines. He also owned another four businesses that combined used cars with farm equipment. His two sisters had long since moved to Florida, as far from their father's memory as they could get, and lived in houses bought with Lucius's earnings. They sent him Christmas cards and phoned when they needed something. Lucius did not blame them for their distance. Their family situation had not been one to forge strong emotional bonds.

His life was embedded in the road. Lucius was free here. He could unleash the Impala's big V8 and let the car be strong for him. Lucius rarely indulged in past regrets. But the doctor's words cast a magnetic force over the morning, drawing in one potent memory after another. His sisters had loathed their father and revered their mother. Their father had been a stonemason and a nasty drunk. Lucius's few memories of his father had been of a burly giant, massive in every way, who had hulked over the dinner table like a bear in a graying T-shirt and suspenders. But he never laid a hand on his own family. The sisters claimed they had all remained shielded by their mother's remarkable grace, so strong it kept peace in the house long after she had died birthing Lucius. The closest he ever came to his father, at least in theory, was when they both went down with pleurisy three days after his sixth birthday. His father had died, while Lucius was delirious with fever. Lucius had spent the next few years being passed around among various relatives, until his sisters had managed to find jobs and get a place of their own. Of course he took care of them now.

The drive from San Luis Obispo to Miramar took just over two hours. The road was fairly awful in places, but Lucius did not mind. The authorities were always talking about building a proper county route, linking Miramar to the new highway. State Route 1, also known as the Pacific Coast Highway, had officially been opened the previous year, but the steep hills surrounding Miramar had forced the coastal thoroughfare inland, isolating this little oceanfront haven. Most of the locals were of two minds over building a better link to the outside world.

Some wanted growth, while others feared all the bad things they remained sheltered from. And in 1969, there was certainly a lot of bad to avoid.

At the top of the hour Lucius turned on the radio to catch the news. It was more out of habit than anything. Virtually none of what he heard had any bearing on his very constricted world. The launch of Apollo 10 was approaching, and this final run before man landed on the moon was the only bright spot in a series of grim tidings. The Basques in Spain had earlier set up a new guerilla army called, of all things, ETA, and their outlaw government were demanding the right to form a nation of their own. British troops arrived in Northern Ireland to reinforce the local constabulary, and the Catholics referred to them as invaders. Harvard's administration building was taken over by Students for a Democratic Society. A ferocious battle had erupted in Vietnam at someplace called Hamburger Hill. The news ended and the announcer introduced a song by Sly and the Family Stone off their new album, *Stand.* Lucius liked the music well enough, though it made him feel more isolated than ever from the sweep of current events and all the good things other people his age were enjoying. He wasn't sorry when the hills closed in and the signal faded.

At the final approach to Miramar, Lucius pulled off the road and parked where a cluster of California pines offered a masking shadow. He peered across the street at the smallest of his dealerships, a Buick-Chevy-Olds he had acquired two years and eleven months ago. Nowadays his banker was pressing him to sell the place and put his money in a region with stronger growth. But Miramar held a special place in his poorly functioning heart.

During Lucius's first visit there, the old man who sold him the dealership had regaled him with legends dating back to the Wild West heyday of abalone fishing and Mexican banditos and the occasional gold prospector. Back then, the rough and frigid waters had earned the town its original name, Castaway Cove.

Around that same period Miramar had latched onto a very odd claim to fame. Stay there for a while, so the tales went, and you might be given a second chance. Second chance at what, Lucius had asked. He had instantly regretted his question, for the old man had taken on the smug look of someone offering a secret of supposedly great worth, but which Lucius already knew was bogus. The old man had then replied, "Whatever it is that you most want to try your hand at again."

Lucius had smiled over the fable, signed the purchase papers, handed the old man his check, and two hours later had fallen head over heels in love.

Whatever else he might think about the town and the lady, Lucius had known it had nothing whatsoever to do with Miramar's fable. For the event was singular. As in, the one time in his short, hard life he had ever known for himself what love actually meant.

Lucius liked to spend a few days loitering around every new acquisition. He called it "kicking the tires." Everyone was on his best behavior, at least at first. But Lucius fit so naturally into quiet corners that gradually the employees relaxed and slipped back into their routines. Lucius learned a great deal in those early days, mostly about money. As in, where the most revenue was generated. Where changes were needed. Where potential profits were being missed. Over his solitary evening meals, Lucius made notes in a script so precise his aging secretary described it as human lithotype. With each new dealership, Lucius brought in the employee he had come to trust the most, named him president of that particular location, and gave him a ten percent share, with an option to purchase another ten percent. Loyalty among his employees was fierce, turnover almost nil. Putting his plans down on paper gave spice to his otherwise tasteless dinner.

One of the first things Lucius noticed about the Miramar dealership was how the salesmen mostly ignored the new vehicles. They clearly made higher commissions pushing used cars. This suggested they were bilking the former owner out of part of his share. On that fateful day Lucius took up station at an empty salesman's desk, blocked from view by a gleaming new Buick Riviera. It was a car he especially liked, with the newly redesigned GM engine and a luxury velvet finish to corners that before had sharp and dangerous edges. As of this year vent windows were a thing of the past, replaced by air-conditioning made standard on all Buicks. It was altogether a beautiful machine, as far as Lucius was concerned. This made the way the salesmen clustered together in the used-car lot all the more irritating. Quiet, silent Lucius Quarterfield was mostly ignored.

Which was when the young woman planted herself directly in front of him and declared, "I hate cars, don't you?"

"Excuse me?"

"Positively despise them." She was far too lovely to be spending time with the likes of him. Tall and willowy, she had a face that was filled with an electric fire that sparked through her wavy auburn hair. Her eyes were alight with a mischievous emerald gleam as she went on. "Great humping metal beasts just looking for an excuse to bellow."

"That bellow is why I'm here," Lucius replied. "I consider it the finest music on earth."

She pulled over a chair and seated herself so close, their knees almost touched. "How positively dreadful."

Normally, he was so shy around women his own age that he could scarcely speak. Today, however, he heard himself reply with ease, "For years I've wanted to own a Jaguar, simply because I love the way their engine sounds."

"Then why on earth don't you buy one?"

Her matter-of-fact tone surprised him. "How do you know I can afford it?"

"Don't be silly. Everybody knows you just bought this business and paid cash."

"Who is everybody?"

"All of Miramar, of course." The way she spoke made it sound like, *All the known universe and beyond.*

"Why do you think I'm talking to you?" she asked.

"I have no idea."

"Because you're fabulously rich and ever so mysterious, of course. I'm Jessica Waverly, by the way."

"Lucius Quarterfield."

"Are you really? I've never met a Lucius before, much less a Quarterfield. You haven't just stepped out of a Charlotte Brontë novel, by any chance."

"I don't know who she is."

"You can't be serious."

"I haven't read a novel since my sixteenth birthday. I left school and went to work. Since then I've hardly had time to read everything I need for my business."

She gave a cheery shrug. "In that case, I shall just have to educate you. Your name should obviously belong to some great strapping stable lad who goes around tossing cows for a living. You don't, I suppose."

"I can state with absolute certainty that I have never tossed a cow in my entire life."

"What a pity. What with owning your own business, and being stinking rich and loving to make these awful motors bellow, if you also tossed cows, I fear my father would marry me off in a flash. That's him over there, by the way, trying to convince my dear mother that he needs a new car more than his next breath."

"Then I'll just have to go out and toss my first cow this very afternoon," Lucius replied. And just like that, his heart was lost to the woman whose fire was as merry as his own was morose.

Lucius relied constantly on his objectivity and his logic. Both of which he lost completely whenever in the company of Miss Jessica Waverly. She referred to their relationship as *Pride and Prejudice,* the title of her favorite novel. Jessica refused to say which aspect referred to him. She remained stubbornly blind to his many frailties. She insisted that her parents positively adored Lucius, when he could see they were growing ever more alarmed by his calls and visits.

Jessica's father was Miramar's only dentist. Jessica had served as his assistant ever since her mother had developed problems with her joints. Her father had pressured Jessica to attend dental school and take over his practice, but Jessica was incredibly stubborn in her capricious manner. She claimed to have no intention of ever working that hard, not in school and certainly not for the rest of her professional life.

Their disapproval of Jessica's lack of ambition and their love of cars were the only two items that Lucius's and Jessica's fathers agreed on.

Jessica confessed in their next time alone that it was neither dentistry nor working alongside her beloved father that made her so passionate about her job. Jessica was, in her own words, born to touch hearts. She saw the fear and discomfort the patients carried as opportunities to share with them her special brand of happy comfort. When she had spoken the words, Lucius had the distinct impression that Jessica expected him to scorn her for aiming too low. She sat there with her chin angled up, defiant and already hurting from what she thought he might say. In truth, Lucius was so moved by her willingness to share the illogicality of her beautiful heart, he needed several minutes to speak at all. When he did, it was to confess the impossible words of love for the very first time.

When her father finally demanded that Jessica address what he called "the Quarterfield situation," Jessica stubbornly insisted to Lucius that it didn't matter, none of it did. Even when Lucius knew full well that Jessica's father had issued an ultimatum to his only child. And in the process had broken her heart.

But when they next met, Jessica did not want to talk about that. She wanted to discuss what color his Jaguar should be. Lucius replied, "I will never buy such a car. But Jessica—"

"Then I just suppose you'll have to sweep me away on your yacht."

"I don't own a rowboat and I can't swim. About your father—"

"Oh, never mind him. I think fifty feet is a nice round number for a boat, don't you?"

"I won't buy a yacht for the same reason I will never own a Jag. I don't like to draw attention to myself."

For a brief instant she sobered. "I understand that."

"Do you really?"

"Actually, I've spent much of my life perfecting the ability to hide in plain sight."

"But why? You're . . ." He started to say "healthy," which sounded like he was sizing up a prize steer. So he said what he really thought, which was "beautiful."

She tilted her head. "Do you really think so?"

"You are quite simply stunning," he replied. "You take what little breath I have completely away."

"See? Why should I let Daddy pester me when a fabulously wealthy man with a lifetime of secrets, and who thinks I'm lovely, is going to buy me a fifty-foot yacht?"

"I will not do any such thing."

"Oh, well, never mind." She waved it aside. "As if beauty ever mattered. All the beautiful ladies in Jane Austen's novels die of the pestilence, alone and ravaged by cruel fate."

Her sudden changes in direction left him dizzy. "Really?"

"Well, no. But they should have."

"Jessica, why do you want to spend time with me?"

She cocked her head and showed him an expression of utter amazement. "Why, because you need me, silly."

It was only later, as he drove back to his lonely house outside Santa Barbara, that he realized she had succeeded in doing precisely what she had intended all along. Which was to tell him about the situation with her father, then avoid talking about it an instant longer than necessary. She was, Lucius decided, the most adroit negotiator he had ever met.

Three days later, Lucius journeyed to Miramar once more. Jessica had made a picnic, her determined method to ignore the fact that he had come with a very definite purpose in mind. He allowed her to take off his socks and shoes and roll up the trouser legs over his pale shins. They set up the picnic by the southern cliffs. The sea was calm, the sunlight fierce for early May. A trio of beachfront eucalyptus offered a perfumed shade. They walked, hand in hand, down the beach, as far as Lucius felt comfortable. Half a mile north, they stopped and watched two young girls and a spaniel race joyfully along the shore, chasing gulls. Jessica released his hand so as to slip her arm around his waist. She settled her head upon his shoulder. Lucius felt the warmth and strength and life in her vibrant form, and was grateful when the breeze tossed her hair into his face and blocked his tears from view.

After the picnic all he wanted was to stretch out beside her and have her rest her face upon his chest. Her every smile almost broke his resolve. But he had to be strong. For her.

"Jessica. Sweetheart."

"You've never called me that before." She rose to a seated position and tucked her knees under her dress and wrapped her arms around her shins. "Is this to be a serious discussion?"

"I fear it must." He shaped the words, very slowly, allowing it to linger on his tongue. And in his heart. "I love you so much."

Her eyes grew huge. "You're saying good-bye." Her breath caught on the last word, like a hook's barb had become lodged in her throat. "Aren't you."

"I love you . . ." He needed a hard breath to dislodge his own barb. "Too much—"

"There's no such thing as 'too much,' " she whispered.

"—to make you my widow."

"Silly you." She tried to laugh. But her tears refused to give her enough air. "We're all dying. Every day is just one more step toward the final end."

"Not this soon," Lucius replied. "You have years left to live."

"You don't know that."

"I have weeks. A few months. Perhaps only days."

"You don't know that, either," she said, but the words were mangled now. She refused to stop talking, not even when her every word was forced around sobs that convulsed her entire frame. "Shall I tell you why I love you, Lucius? Because you are the loneliest man on God's green earth."

It was true. The truest thing he had ever heard. So true he was silenced. His reasons for doing as he did vanished in the flood of her sorrow. But not his resolve. All he could do was sit there, the distance between them impossibly wide. Even when she pleaded desperately for him to reach over and offer the comfort that only his arms could give.

When he did not speak, Jessica went on talking. "You need me to give you what you will never have without me. And that, my dearest beloved, is joy."

That is true as well, he wanted to tell her. He could not even have named the flavor of ecstasy until their first conversation. Even now, when he was filled with bitter regret, he knew he was saying not just farewell to her, but to any shred of happiness. Any hope of bliss.

His silence defeated her. She started crying too hard to help him gather up their belongings. When the car was packed, he came back to where she sat, staring blindly at the Pacific, helped her to stand, and supported her weight back to the parking lot. One cripple helping another.

The first comforting sign that he had done the right thing came when he pulled up in front of her parents' home. Jessica had recently taken an apartment in town. But Lucius did not want to take her back there, both because he did not want her to be alone just then, and because he did not want to test his broken resolve. As he rounded the final corner, he saw Jessica's mother standing on the front walk, waiting for them. There was no way the older woman could have known what had just taken place, yet there she was, watching worriedly as Lucius pulled up. When he cut the motor, Jessica fumbled blindly for the latch. Finally her mother opened the door and enfolded Jessica in a comforting embrace.

Lucius watched the two women climb the steps and enter the house and seal him out. Only then did he rise from the car and open the trunk and lift the remnants of their last day together. He started up the drive, carrying the blanket and the hamper and her shoes. The garage door opened, and Jessica's father emerged. Jessica's father set the burdens on a shelf by the door leading into the house. Then he unbent enough to take Lucius in a strong embrace. Lucius was so shocked he did not know how to react. He stood there, frozen in place. He had only shaken the man's hand twice, and one of those was the day he had sold the man his new Buick. Then Jessica's father released him and stepped back and shut the garage door. All without saying a word.

That had taken place eleven months ago. Today was the first time since then that Lucius had returned to Miramar.

Connect with

Visit us online at
KensingtonBooks.com
to read more from your favorite authors, see books
by series, view reading group guides, and more.

Join us on social media
for sneak peeks, chances to win books and prize packs,
and to share your thoughts with other readers.

facebook.com/kensingtonpublishing
twitter.com/kensingtonbooks

Tell us what you think!
To share your thoughts, submit a review,
or sign up for our eNewsletters, please visit:
KensingtonBooks.com/TellUs.